Everything Else is Hearsay

by
Rebecca Black

Everything Else is Hearsay

The Hearsay Series, Volume 1

Rebecca Black

Published by Rebecca Black, 2023.

This is a work of fiction. Similarities to real people, places, or events are entirely coincidental.

EVERYTHING ELSE IS HEARSAY

First edition. March 3, 2023.

Written by Rebecca Black.

For my Hubit

*

Author's Note

*This book is intended for an adult audience as there
are scenes of a sexual nature.*

Chapter 1

I stepped out of my treatment room into the kitchen to make a coffee and do a quick tidy-up. It had been a busy week, and I was thankful I only had one client left. The coffee machine was low, so I grabbed another bag of beans from the walk-in cupboard, turned, and nearly launched the beans across the room when I saw a man standing in the hallway.

'Hey, sorry. I didn't mean to make you jump,' he said.

I flushed and mumbled my unnecessary apology, and I realised he must be the American guest who had checked in earlier that day. He moved into the light of the kitchen. He was tall and had the most amazing, intense green eyes, which forced me to look at the floor at his bashed-up black Allstars.

'Where did you get that?' he asked, pointing to the coffee bag.

Dragging my gaze back up to his face, I noticed he was wearing a washed-out Mudhoney t-shirt, a band I'd seen back in the day.

'Um, in here,' I replied, gesturing with my thumb over my shoulder. 'Or you might find an open bag in the fridge,' I added.

He gave me a cheeky half-smile from behind his long dark fringe, which he tucked behind his ear and said, 'I'm Will, by the way.' He put his hand out.

Remembering my manners and trying not to stare, I shot my hand out to shake his and introduce myself. His hands felt a little rough, but his grip was firm and confident. 'I'm Lucy... did you want a coffee?' I asked.

'Yes, please, I'm not sure I can be trusted to use that machine. It looks complicated,' he said in his soft New York accent, nodding toward it.

The mood relaxed a little as I turned, and I went about making the coffee, although I could feel him looking at me, and it was almost as if the hairs on my neck were standing to attention.

'Do you work here?' he asked.

'Yes.' I replied, waving towards my room. 'I'm a physiotherapist. I run this place actually, it's my home too.'

'Ahh, so Frankie must be your son. He showed me to my room earlier,' he said, figuring the family set-up out.

'Yes, that's one of them. Sorry, I must have been with a client when you arrived. Do you have everything you need?' I asked.

'Yeah, thanks, just what I was looking for,' he said, nodding with a strange look in his eyes, like he had been waiting for something.

I had started up the B&B to make ends meet when my husband and I separated eight years ago. With that and the physio business, the boys and I did okay, and it wouldn't be long before Paddy left sixth form and could get a job to contribute a little. Mike, my ex, and I had been childhood sweethearts and had pretty much grown up together, but we had both changed so much, and the realisation that we had been coexisting for a few years had hit us just before our fifteenth wedding anniversary. Frankie and Paddy were ten and eight at the time. Breaking up our family was the most challenging decision we had ever made. Just so sad and unbelievably emotional.

Mike moved in with his mum until he got himself sorted. He now lived in Exeter. We have a fairly good relationship, considering. He pays the mortgage, which is more than his fair share, but we've never actually divorced.

I turned and passed the mug of steaming coffee over to him. 'The milk and sugar are over there,' I gestured, but he clearly took it black or was desperate, as he sipped it immediately without breaking his gaze and then nodded gratefully.

'Boy, I've been looking forward to this. The coffee on the flight was pretty crappy,' he admitted.

'So, what brings you to Clevedon?' I asked, intrigued by why a guy from New York was visiting our little town. I guessed he must have family here.

'I flew into Bristol and found this place when I searched up places to stay. I was tempted with Weston-Super-Mare, but I got the vibe it was a bit... tacky?' he suggested, and I laughed, nodding in agreement. 'Clevedon is more... quaint. I thought it would be more inspiring, and we Americans love the whole Victorian thing.'

'Well, I'm not sure it's quaint, but it's certainly Victorian. Are you on holiday then?' I pressed.

'Kinda,' he said, dragging a hand through his long fringe and messing his shorter hair up at the back while he stretched, revealing a slice of pale skin above his skinny black jeans. I had asked too many questions. I didn't mean to pry and had to prepare for my next client.

'Well, it's been nice to meet you. I'd better get on. Breakfast is at eight thirty if you'd like cooked. Otherwise, you'll find some cereals, fruit, etcetera, in your room.'

'Sure, err, I'll probably skip breakfast. I'm not really a morning person, but thanks.'

I was relieved, as I had an early start the next day and needed to walk the dogs first thing.

'Well, if you need anything, just let me know,' I said as I picked up my coffee, and walked towards my treatment room.

He moved over to the counter where I had been standing, watching me with a slight frown, and before I had the chance to close my door, he said, 'I would normally give you my number around about now, but I guess you already have it.'

I looked straight at him, catching my breath and not really knowing what to say. It had been so long. Was he actually hitting on me? He was blowing on his coffee, covering his mouth so I couldn't see his full expression, but his eyes were shining with a hint of a smile and looking straight at me. My cheeks flushed, and I had no idea what to say. I was more than rusty, and I could feel my face burning.

He pushed himself off the counter, heading back towards the hallway. 'I need someone to show me the not-so-quaint hotspots of Clevedon.' And he disappeared out of sight. I closed my door and quickly turned, leaning my back against it. Oh, my God! How embarrassing. What am I supposed to say to him the next time I see him? Before I could think about it any longer, the buzzer went, alerting me to my next appointment, and I quickly peeled myself off the door and brushed myself down before greeting my client.

Once my last customer had paid and left, I did my banking, collected the towels, and locked up. After walking the dogs and making dinner, I rushed out to pick Frankie up from football. I wouldn't say I liked football, but Frankie loved it, and it was a good way for him to keep fit, so I supported him but believe me, I could not wait for him to pass his driving test so that he could bring himself back. At least I shared the driving with Zara, one of the other mums.

'All right, Mrs D?' George said, Frankie's best friend, as they both piled into the back.

'Can you take us to the clubhouse, Mum?' Frankie asked, undoing his top knot and then redoing it.

'What, now? You haven't even showered!' I said as I pulled away.

'I know, but the game is on....' I was a bit annoyed, and I couldn't help but feel that George had put him up to this, and I felt a bit like a taxi service.

'Fine, but you're gonna have to make your own way home, and don't forget we have a guest in for the next couple of weeks, so you'll have to be quiet when you get back.'

'Aww, thanks, Mum. Yeah, I met him earlier, the American writer. He's cool.' I looked in the rear-view mirror, and Frankie looked straight back with a twinkle in his eye. I ignored him. A writer, eh? Maybe that's what he needed inspiration for.

I finally sat down in the lounge to watch TV before heading to bed. There was nothing on. While scrolling through my phone, I plumped for an old episode of Gavin

& Stacey. Zara had texted to ask if I wanted to go to the new bar on the High Street on Saturday night, just girls. I cringed slightly at the 'just girls' reference, as if I still needed to be warned eight years on that there might be husbands/boyfriends there and not to feel like a gooseberry, but she meant well. I figured it would be the usual gang, including Steph, who was my absolute bestie, so I quickly tapped back to get the details.

I hadn't been out since Christmas, and as I brushed my teeth, I looked at myself in the mirror for the first time in what felt like ages. My brown bob had grown out and flicked up and out to the side of my shoulders. I wasn't one for make-up unless I was going out-out, and I knew it was bedtime, but jeez, I looked tired - major dark circles. And looking at the rest of me, I didn't like what I saw, and I wasn't sure if my size twelve 'going out' dress would actually fit. If only I could just find the time to do some exercise. I can't even find the time to do ten minutes of yoga, let alone an entire exercise class. Balls. I didn't need to lose weight, but I could certainly do with toning up a bit. My five-foot-six-inch, big-busted silhouette was looking a bit squidgy.

Are you going on Saturday? I quickly messaged Steph.

Yes, you?

Yes, but I have nothing to wear, and my hair looks like shit.

Well, book yourself a hair appointment, and we'll find you something to wear.

I could probably afford to get my hair done, but a dress, too? That was a push. How did everyone else do it? Once the usual bills, the boy's activities, and the bloody vet bills had been paid, it didn't leave much. My little business paid okay, but the B&B was a bonus, really, as I couldn't rely on year-round bookings, so it was our holiday fund. I needed to find another form of income.

I can't afford both... So I can get a nice dress and come out with shit hair or the other way round!

Claire will do your hair, and we'll go dress shopping tomorrow morning.

Of course, Claire! She was a trained hairdresser but didn't practice as one. She had a full-time job in marketing, and before the kids came along, we would all get ready together, and she was always on hair duty. I loved her. She was naturally beautiful, had the perfect teeth and lovely flowing strawberry blonde hair. She loved hanging out in sweatpants, but when it was time to go out, it was as if she employed a rock-chick persona, and after a few drinks, she became feisty but ultimately loyal. Before I could reply, Steph messaged back.

Claire can do it tomorrow before we go out.

Really? That would be amazing!

And then a text from Claire arrived.

See you here at 7 pm on Saturday, Mrs D xoxox.

Daniels, that's what the D stood for. Mike Daniels. I hadn't bothered changing my name because we hadn't divorced, and the paperwork would have been a nightmare. I was still standing in front of the mirror when I heard the front door go. Shit. I quickly pegged it across the landing to my bedroom. I'd forgotten about our American visitor and didn't want to get caught on the landing after his parting comment. I hadn't had a moment to think about what he had said or time to construct a reply to his suggestion.

Chapter 2

I looked at my clock for the fourth time. It was nearly two in the morning, and I had been tossing and turning since I got into bed. I had just nodded off when Frankie came home, and I woke up with a start and then couldn't get back to sleep. So many things were swirling around in my mind. How I would earn more money, what sort of dress to look for, what hairstyle, and what I would say to the American when I inevitably saw him the next day... today.

'Mum, where's my rucksack?' Paddy shouted.

Shit, what's the time? Three minutes to eight, shit shit shit. I had overslept.

'Mum?'

'Erm, I don't know? In the cupboard under the stairs?'

I leapt out of bed, pulled my dressing gown on, and charged towards the bathroom, doing it up as I went and ran straight into Will.

'Shit!' I said out loud this time, as he grabbed my shoulders to steady me, my hands awkwardly bashing into his belly while I was still struggling with the knot of my gown.

'I'm so sorry. I'm in such a rush.' I barrelled past him and made it into the bathroom without looking back.

So that's what I was going to say to him. *Shit*. Just perfect. I quickly showered, pulled my crappy old dog-walking jeans on and a sweatshirt, blast-dried my hair, and made it downstairs in record time.

'Hey,' Will said, standing in the kitchen with a coffee. He'd either worked out how to use the machine, or one of the boys had made him one.

'I thought you weren't a morning person,' I replied, a bit off hand. There was no way I'd have time to make him breakfast if he'd changed his mind.

'I'm not normally. It must be jet lag. I'm gonna take a walk along the coast. Do you want me to take the dogs? You seem pretty flat out.'

Now I felt terrible about being off hand, and his offer would make my life much easier. Fridays were always my catch-up day, and somehow, I had to fit in dress shopping. I hesitated, and he could tell I was unsure. 'I'd really like to. I sometimes walk my Mom's dog back home. I'm not a complete novice.'

'Are you sure? I would be really grateful. This is Grayson, and this is Luna.' They both sat by the side door, looking at us expectantly with their beautiful grey eyes and shiny grey coats. They were Pointers, Weimaraners, to be precise, and they were both very regal, lean dogs.

<hr />

It was so weird being in the house without the kids and the dogs, and somehow so much easier to get things done. I had tidied, hoovered, cleaned the bathrooms, and sorted the washing while listening to Royal Blood blaring out of the stereo, loud enough for me to hear it over the vacuum. Finally, I popped into Will's room to open the curtains, collect the mugs and glasses he'd acquired, and empty the bin.

I loved this room. I had designed it from scratch. It was simple but had everything one might need when staying overnight. A double bed stood on a wooden floor with simple white linen, facing the window which overlooked the garden. A low Scandinavian-style bedside table on either side and a little mini-fridge in the corner below the window. I had even found a small piece of furniture which doubled as some hanging space on one side and a petite dressing table on the other, which kind of leant against the wall. I spotted a guitar resting up against it. He must have brought that over on the flight. That's dedication to a hobby.

Steph texted to say she'd pick me up at eleven, only half an hour away, but Will hadn't returned with the dogs. I quickly changed and made myself a drink. Will hadn't mentioned anything about our conversation yesterday. Maybe he'd changed his mind? Hopefully, he'd changed his mind, as I clearly wasn't ready. If I were, I wouldn't be overthinking it. Although, it was nice to know that someone had thought about taking me out.

The side door flung open, and the dogs bound in, leaving wet paw prints all over the freshly mopped floor. Last I looked, it hadn't been raining. I turned to see Will in the doorway, dripping wet. 'So, Luna can't swim, but thankfully I can.'

'Oh, my God, I'm so sorry, you must be freezing!' I said, aghast, as I rushed down the hall to grab some towels out of the airing cupboard.

By the time I got back, Will had taken his t-shirt off and was wringing it out in the sink. The muscles in his back rippled as he twisted it. He had broad shoulders and surprisingly toned arms.

'Are you checking me out?' he asked, glancing over his shoulder with a glimmer of a smile.

'No!' I said, snapping out of my trance and using a shrill voice. 'Here.' I handed him the towels, and as I did, I couldn't help but stifle a smile. I tried to hold my lips together with my teeth, but a little snorty giggle escaped.

'Well, that's nice,' he said sarcastically while drying his hair.

'Sorry, I should have warned you she couldn't swim,' I apologised.

'No, I meant your smile,' he clarified.

Oh. I forgot Americans didn't do sarcasm.

'I think Luna thinks she's a duck, but putting it into practice is another thing entirely,' he said. We laughed, and it looked as though Will was about to say something when I heard Steph.

'Cooee.' She appeared in the doorway. 'Oh! I'm not interrupting, am I?' she asked, hovering in the doorway, looking from me to Will. She was wearing her running leggings and trainers with a slouchy sweatshirt. She loved running and consequently had a physique to aspire to, very toned and tall, but her smooth, wavy brown curls always softened her look.

'No. Hi Steph. Sorry, I won't be a sec. This is Will, by the way. Will, Steph.' It all came out in a rush while I gathered my keys and bag, and quickly checked the dogs were okay. The sofa was now also soaked, typical.

'Great to meet you, Steph, err, I'm gonna take a shower.' Will held up his hand in a wave to make his excuses, taking his sopping shoes off before heading up the stairs.

'Looks like you've already had one,' Steph said, winking at me while he walked away.

We sat in her car driving along the M5 towards the out-of-town shopping centre. She looked at me, then the road, and then at me again.

'Well!?' she asked.

'What?' I knew she was awaiting an explanation, but I made her work for it.

'Are you going to tell me what was happening back there?'

'There's not much to explain,' I said.

I told her that Will was a guest and that he'd taken the dogs out and had to rescue Luna, omitting the checking me out comment and the awkward tension and the squiffy feeling I had in my stomach.

'And that's all?' she asked, giving me a sideways glance.

'Yes,' I clarified.

'Because he's tight. I mean really tight, and he looks oddly familiar. Did you see his pecs?'

I changed the subject and hoped Luna was okay after her ordeal. Thank God Will had been with her because there would have been no way I would have jumped in after her.

The problem with shopping with Steph was that she had no budget. I would have been happy with cheaper brands, but we were straight into the department store, looking through high end lines. Steph didn't have a budget, because she didn't need one. She had a great job in recruitment.

Moreover, her husband (also called Steph, which was funny and yet confusing at times - The Stephs) had a great career in banking. She wasn't flash with her money, though. You wouldn't know she was wealthy if you met her on the street.

We had met at a National Childbirth Trust get-together about fifteen years ago when the kids were young, both re-alising that NCT get-togethers were not our thing and had been firm friends ever since. We'd had family holidays to-gether, girly trips, and ultimately been there for each other when things got tough. She had girls, I had boys, and we al-ways joked that it would be hilarious if they married each other one day.

'What about this?' She held up a short dress with a high ruffle neck and ruffly shoulders.

'Babe, these are 34Gs,' I said, pointing at my boobs. 'I need a low neckline.'

Steph had been holding up all sorts of outfits for the past forty-five minutes, and I had come up with a reason not to try every single one. She was getting frustrated, and I was getting bored.

'Right!' she said, spinning around, grabbing a random selection of dresses from various rails. 'Come on.' She took my hand and headed toward the changing rooms. After sev-eral false starts, I walked out of the cubicle with an air of con-fidence. 'Yes,' she said, whistled, and moved my shoulders in opposite directions, turning me. 'Bingo! It's long enough not to be slutty. It's low enough to show a glimpse of cleavage, and smart enough not to be too girly.'

I think she meant it was the right style for my age, but I felt good in it either way. It was more than I'd typically spend on a dress, but it would go perfectly with my trusty black ankle boots, so there was no need to buy shoes.

I arrived home to find the boys plugged into their Xbox, two sleeping dogs, and no sign of our guest. My shoulders dropped with relief. I loved having the occasional guest but keeping the house tidy and always being prepared to help with a smile was sometimes exhausting. I cherished our beautiful Victorian home with many original features—fireplaces in the lounge and bedrooms and a lovely Aga in the kitchen-diner. Mike and I had bought it when the boys were little, and it needed everything done to it. Over the years, we had done it up, and despite it probably needing a fresh lick of paint, it was a perfect family home.

'Do you fancy pizza?' I called upstairs. I don't know why I bothered asking. It wasn't as if they would say no! Before I knew it, I was full of pizza and nodding off on the sofa, so I went up to bed. I hadn't heard Will come in, and I couldn't see his light on, so I figured he was still out, but he knew the key code and could let himself in.

Chapter 3

I loved Saturday mornings. The boys always slept in, and other than the food shopping, having my hair cut, and getting ready for tonight, I had nothing to do. I made a coffee, crept back upstairs, flung the curtains back, and slipped back into bed. It was just dawn. I watched the birds flying around and the leaves on the trees bristling in the breeze. It was so peaceful.

And then I heard a massive bang on the door, some whispering, and the key in the lock. I lay in bed, frozen. There was more whispering on the way up the stairs. Oh God, Will had brought someone back. I lay there, unable to do anything but listen. Thankfully, they were extremely quiet, or they had passed out. I looked up at the ceiling. Why was I angry? It's not as if he had actually asked me out, not that I would go anyway, but he thought my smile was nice. He thought my smile was nice? As if that was grounds for a potential romance. I was such an idiot. I got out of bed, dressed, crept back downstairs, and took the dogs out.

When I returned, the boys were still in bed, and there was no sign of Will or his plus one. So, I dumped the dogs, grabbed the shopping bags, and headed off to the supermarket. As I walked back into the kitchen, two bags in each hand, I could hear a guitar in the lounge. Great, I thought, he's serenading her, and now I'm going to have to do the awkward "meet and greet the one-night stand".

Will had heard me and came out to the kitchen, and as I was putting the bags on the floor, he said, 'Hey Lucy, can I introduce you to Paul?' Jesus Christ, I did not see that coming. He's gay? I stood and stared for a moment as Paul appeared in the kitchen. 'Err, we... we write together.' He elaborated. Is that what you call it these days? I held out my hand to shake Paul's while he shot a perplexed glance at Will.

'Good to meet you. Will has told me all about you and this place. It's awesome,' he said genuinely. Paul was a bit shorter than Will and had amiable eyes with symmetrical crow's feet. He obviously laughed a lot. Paul framed his eyes with thick-rimmed glasses and a very 'normal' mousey brown, short back and sides hairstyle. He was American too. Maybe that's what had drawn them to each other. He would certainly not have been coming up on my gaydar if I had met him elsewhere, but maybe I was out of touch.

'I'm sorry we got back late, well, early,' Will stammered. Was he embarrassed? 'That was totally unacceptable. We were in Bristol and didn't realise how late it was, so we had to call a car and... we were pretty drunk.'

I couldn't help but laugh. They looked like a pair of schoolboys in front of their teacher, explaining why they hadn't done their homework.

'It's fine. That's why we have the key press.' I didn't want them to think I was a prude or disapproving. Paul returned to the lounge and started gathering his things while I put the shopping away. Will began talking to Paul about where they would meet next, so I switched the radio on to give them some privacy.

Later, I lowered myself into the free-standing bath. It was almost too hot, but I liked it that way. I loved our bath. When Mike and I had done the bathroom up, the tub was non-negotiable, so we had to save for that and a walk-in shower. I had a proper pamper, cucumber slices over my eyes, a face pack, and lots of bubbles. I hoped the cucumber would help with the dark circles under my eyes. I was blessed with my mum's skin and hardly suffered with spots or blemishes and consequently rarely used make-up, but tonight I would make an effort, so if the cucumber didn't work, it would be concealer all the way. I had even poured myself a glass of wine to get myself in the mood. I had to time everything perfectly to be nearly ready, but still with wet hair, before heading to Claire's place.

'Is that this year's look?' Will nodded toward my towel turban as I made it downstairs at quarter to seven.

'Yes.' I said, giving him a twirl. I felt so much more relaxed around him, knowing he was gay. He laughed.

'Nice dress.' He gave me a wolf whistle, looking straight into my eyes. They were so striking, and I allowed myself to hold his stare for a moment. 'Where are you going?' he asked as he turned the coffee machine on. Coffee at this time? I'd be awake all night.

'A new place on the High Street. It's only about ten minutes away, but first I'm getting my hair cut. Are you going out this evening?'

'Nah, I'm pretty tired after last night, but if you're not up to much tomorrow, I would love to take you out to lunch to apologise for my behaviour last night, well, this morning. I don't make a habit of doing shit like that. Just to be clear.'

'I would love that!' I surprised myself with the ease of my response. I made a note not to get too wasted tonight. 'Right boys, I'm off,' I called.

Nothing.

Will laughed again.

'I'll tell them. Have a good night.'

———— ◉ ————

Steph and Zara were already at Claire's place when I arrived. The fizz was on ice, and Claire had put out some little canapés for us to share on the island in the kitchen.

'Are we celebrating?' I asked Claire.

'No, I just thought I'd make it a bit spesh. You haven't been out for bloody ages, and we haven't been together in such a long time. So, sit down. Your new do awaits!'

Claire gestured towards the stool she'd placed in the middle of the room. Zara handed me a glass, and we all clinked.

Zara looked a bit pale. I noticed while she talked to Steph. Had she lost weight? She didn't seem like her usual smiley self. Claire removed my towel and placed it around my shoulders. Zara was George's mum. We met at the school gates, our eldest boys starting school on the same day. She was pregnant with her third at that point and then had two more. She was like a baby machine. Claire combed my hair. Her youngest was still at primary. Consequently, she was always busy, ferrying them all around to their after-school activities, and one of them always seemed to be off sick.

Zara didn't really 'do' fashion, she was always in jeans and swapped her tops from casual fitted t-shirts during the day to sparkly, slightly smarter tops for going out. She had always worn her long, straight blonde hair loose with a side parting. I can't recall her ever even putting it in a ponytail.

'So, what are we doing today?' Claire asked, pulling me back from my thoughts.

'Erm, I guess a bob... again?' Claire rolled her eyes with a smile on her face.

'Okay, well, why don't we go for a French bob? It's like a normal bob but with a fringe and is a bit more flicky at the bottom. A tiny bit shorter than a classic bob.'

Claire scrolled through her phone to get some examples, and I peered at the pictures. I wasn't sure, but what the hell?

'Let's do it,' I said.

Half an hour later, and she was blowing it out, there was an awful lot of hair on the floor, and I hadn't seen myself in a mirror, but I'd had a couple of glasses of Prosecco by then, so I was assuring myself it would be fine. She switched off the dryer, scooped the tiniest blob of putty stuff out of a tin, rubbed it between her hands, and told me to put my head between my knees. She went to work massaging it right into the roots, lifted my shoulders back to a sitting position, swished it this way and that, tucked some behind my ear, styled some towards my chin, and then grabbed the mirror and handed it to me.

'Wow! I never knew my hair had so much volume!' I beamed. 'Thank you so much.'

'So, when you're going out like tonight, you can add volume and style it like this, but if you can't be arsed and you just want to wash and go, you can,' she said, pulling the towel off me and brushing off the stray hairs from my dress.

'It's wonderful - thank you.' I gave her a big hug.

'Get those tits away from me. You're making mine feel inadequate.'

Everyone laughed and cooed at the new do.

'Right then, ladies, let's go,' Steph said, gathering everyone's coats. 'I've reserved us a table because I am not queueing in these shoes.' I looked down and was only slightly jealous when I saw her high-heels with red soles. I rolled my eyes at her, and she winked.

Several cocktails later, and we were all well oiled, sat at a high round polished table on four deep blue leather studded bar stools. The bar was packed, and I was glad Steph had booked a table. I was having such a laugh. I couldn't believe we had worked out that it had been five months since we had been together.

Steph held court for the main, and she was on top form. 'Anyway, Lucy has a new guest, and he is hot! I caught them together in the kitchen, and he was half-naked!'

They all turned in unison to see my reaction.

Claire pushed my shoulder and said, 'I wondered why you wanted a new do.'

My cheeks flashed with heat. 'He was half-naked because he jumped into the sea to rescue Luna and was wringing his t-shirt out in the sink. And anyway, I have since discovered he's gay, so button it, Steph.'

'That guy is not gay!' Steph stated.

'Well, he brought a man back with him last night who I met this morning, so I think you'll find he is!' I replied, looking at Steph with my eyebrows high as if to say, *so there.*

'I think Andy's having an affair!' Zara suddenly blurted out.

All three of us looked at her, mouths open. Andy was a well-respected local businessman, and although I didn't actually know what he did, it involved a lot of travelling, which meant Zara was left with the kids for long periods.

'What makes you think that?' Claire asked and Zara held up her phone showing the 'Find My' app, the little blue dot pulsing over a road somewhere in Cornwall.

'He told me he was in London...' she said, welling up. 'And this isn't the first time. It's the fifth.' We all looked at her sorrowfully as she burst into tears, covering her face with her hands and leaning over the table. I glanced at Steph. She rolled her eyes unsympathetically, and I frowned. Had I missed something?

'Right, come on ladies, let's get out of here.' Steph announced, and I couldn't help but think that Steph was annoyed that our night had clearly come to an abrupt end. Claire helped Zara gather her things as we all made our way outside.

'Do you want me to call you a taxi, babe?' Zara looked up at me, her nose and eyes red and blotchy, and nodded. Thankfully, I managed to get her a cab, and soon we were each hugging her with our goodbyes while she promised to confront Andy when he returned. I was ready for bed.

'One for the road?' Steph suggested eagerly. She had it about her this evening and was not ready for the night to end.

'I'm pretty tired, but you're welcome back to mine if you fancy a night cap,' I bartered.

Claire made her excuses, but Steph was keen, so we headed back, walking Claire to her door before going back to mine. Steph poured us both a gin and tonic and we flopped on the sofa.

'She's got a lot to think about, eh? I can't believe Andy could do that to her,' I pondered.

'Happens all the time, babe. I've been suspicious of Steph in the past.'

'Really?' I was shocked.

'Yep, I booked us a dirty weekend in Paris a few years back and showed him what he was missing.' I vaguely remembered her going to Paris, but she had never mentioned anything.

'And you didn't quiz him on it?' I asked.

I suddenly had a different outlook on their marriage. If someone had done that to me, I couldn't continue. She was a dark horse sometimes.

'I didn't need to. I found a text on Steph's phone from her, so I called her and told her I'd make sure she'd never work again if she ever contacted him again. You've gotta keep on top of these things. The kids were small, I was preoccupied, and he started looking elsewhere. So, I had to up my game, which is exactly what's happened to Zara. She's too occupied with the kids. Zara has taken her eye off the ball.'

I couldn't believe it. Was she on Andy's side?

'She's too occupied with the kids because he's never there to help out,' I replied defensively on Zara 's behalf. 'He is totally out of order leaving her to look after them while he goes off and gets his end away. She needs to tell him to move out....' My voice was getting louder by the second, and I was getting cross with Steph's attitude. 'Contact a Solicitor and show them the evidence. She needs to tell the kids that he's a, a....'

'Man, that needs a shag?' Steph interjected.

'What! And that's an excuse?' I said, standing up.

'No, I'm just stating the facts. Zara 's always been... a bit plain Jane, to be honest, I thought you were heading down the same road, but there's still life in you yet, girl.' She winked.

I could not believe what I was hearing. How dare she?

'You need to find yourself a new man before....'

'Evening ladies, is everything okay?' Will was standing in the doorway. 'Cos, it seems to be getting a little heated.' He put his hands in his jeans' back pockets to signify a neutral stance.

'I think it's time you went home,' I said to Steph, not wanting to continue the argument with Will there.

How long had he been standing there?

'Oh, come on, Lu, we were just having a discussion. I know you can take a few home truths.' She stood up, aiming the last comment towards Will, and said, 'I'd better be going, anyway. It's late.' She put her coat on and kissed me on the cheek, which I didn't return. I was still a bit shell-shocked.

'Do you want me to walk you home?' Will asked politely and then looked at me for reassurance that he'd said the right thing. I looked away, still unable to find the right words because I was too angry.

'No, I'll be fine, it's only round the corner.'

She picked up her clutch and left.

'Are you okay?' He took one hand out of his pocket and gently placed it on my shoulder, trying to catch my eye.

'Yes, sorry, that was... unprofessional,' I said for want of a better word.

'Unprofessional?' he laughed. 'I don't think sticking up for your friend is unprofessional, and for the record, I do not agree with Steph.' It was good to know that I wasn't being irrational, but Steph and I had never argued, and I had to blink away the sting of tears. He had clearly heard most of the discussion, as she called it. I looked up, his eyes were searching mine, and I felt my heart lurch from my stomach to my throat.

'I had better go to bed,' I said finally.

Will dropped his hand and shook his head a little.

'Yes, you need to be fully rested before tomorrow's lunch date. Do you think I need to book somewhere?' he wondered aloud as he pulled his phone out of his back pocket.

'Date?' It was my turn to laugh. He looked up, about to say something else, but I beat him to it. 'Sunday might be tricky, so it's probably best to book. No.6 is good or The Olive Branch, if it's a traditional English Sunday roast you're looking for.' I started to head up the stairs. 'Good night, Will.'

Chapter 4

I woke up with a bit of a fuzzy head—bloody cocktails. I reached into my bedside drawer and rummaged around until a blister pack of pain killers appeared. I heard one of the dogs bark. They needed to go out, and they were not used to me sleeping in. So, I necked the tablets and got dressed. A good walk would blow the cobwebs away.

It was a beautiful fresh summer morning, a bit nippy and blustery but dry and sunny. I always headed to the beach when my head needed clearing. It gave me a bit of perspective on life. I was still feeling cross about Steph. She had no right to say that about Zara or me. I wasn't particularly close to Zara, but I knew what it was like to break up with someone. And just because I hadn't had a relationship since Mike, didn't mean that I was plain.

Did it?

That had been my choice. Having been in Mike's shadow for so many years while his career blossomed, I had found a new kind of confidence since we had split. I had retrained and set up my own business, which worked around the kids. I didn't dread driving to new places alone because I just had to get on with it. And I had done a week's charity walk with a group of people I didn't know, which I would never have done before. Because I grew up with Mike, we had assumed our roles and stuck with them, and it had become effortless and safe, so safe it began to get boring.

After throwing the float into the sea for the millionth time for Grayson, I realised it was later than I had thought. So, I walked home quickly and managed to get back by midday, but Will was nowhere to be seen. So, I hopped in the shower and quickly dressed in my smart jeans and animal print blouse, paired with a long cardigan to cover up my slight muffin-top. Thankfully Claire was right, my new do looked okay after a quick blast, and I just popped some mascara on my top eyelashes to bring out my eyes.

I got downstairs, but Will was still nowhere to be seen. Maybe he had changed his mind.

'Hi, Mum,' Frankie said. 'Will said to meet him at The Olive Branch at one for your date.'

'What? Oh, for God's sake, I'm going to be late, and it's not a date.'

Frankie lifted his hands in defence.

'I'm just passing on what he said. Why don't you drive?'

Now that was a good idea, and I grabbed the keys.

'Enjoy your date!'

'It's not a date,' I said as I ran out of the door.

'Whatever, Mum,' I heard him say as I left.

I managed to find a parking space and pegged it up the road. Thank God I was wearing flats. At first, I couldn't see Will, and then spotted him peering over a menu in the corner. It was almost as if he was using it to shield his face. The waitress came over to take my jacket, and Will hopped up to pull my chair out for me. As I walked across the small restaurant, it felt like all eyes were on me, so I quickly sat down.

'Hey, you look lovely,' he said as he sat opposite me. He glanced from left to right and said, 'I feel kinda dressed down.' He wore his usual attire, a leather jacket on the chair behind him.

'Well, don't. They don't have a dress code here, so anything goes. I'm sorry I'm a bit late. I lost track of time walking the dogs. I needed to clear my head.'

'It's cool. It sounded like a pretty intense night... I'm assuming there was no swimming involved during your walk,' he said with a smile.

'I'm really very sorry about that.'

'It's something to write home about, I suppose.'

'And where is home exactly?' I asked while scanning the menu.

'Brooklyn.' He hesitated and then reaffirmed, 'Brooklyn born and bred, but my mom lives in Staten Island now.'

'And your Dad?'

'He's... not a part of our lives, left when my brother and I were little. I don't really remember him, and Mom doesn't like to talk about him, so it was just us. How about your folks?'

Before I could answer, the waitress came back to ask if we were ready to order. Will went for the roast beef, and I went for the lamb. I never cooked lamb at home, so it was always a treat. We ordered a bottle of the house red and some tap water too.

'They live here, in Clevedon. I'm pretty lucky to have them so close. They practically took charge of the boys when Mike and I split up.'

'Mike being your ex?' Will asked, putting his elbows on the table and cradling his chin in his hands to bring his gaze in line with mine.

'Yes, Frankie and Paddy's Dad. We'd been together since we were at school, but we... grew apart. So, it's just been the three of us and the dogs for the last eight years.'

'Well, that's the shortest life story I've ever heard,' he said, leaning back on his chair and smiling.

How much information did he want? I mean, it would be weird to go into the ins and outs of why our marriage broke down and the emotional roller coaster that ensued, wouldn't it?

Deflection.

'Well, what about you? I know you live in Brooklyn, and you're a writer,' I replied to even things out.

He leaned forward again and fiddled with the edge of the menu.

'I guess I'm not just a writer. I may have misled you there.'

The waitress returned with our wine and water and proceeded to pour.

'I'm not really supposed to ask you this, but would it be possible to have your autograph? My sister is a massive fan.' The waitress held out her notepad and pen and bit her bottom lip.

I was suddenly aware that everyone was looking at us, and I could hear hushed whispering. Well, this was awkward, she'd clearly got the wrong person, or Will was more of an accomplished writer than I realised.

'Sure, what's her name?' Will asked quickly.

'Kate.'

Will promptly signed his name, put the pen on the pad a little too abruptly, and slid both back towards her. He glanced up at her without moving his head, and she quickly thanked him and scurried away.

What the hell? Will did not have a smile on his face, and he looked positively pissed off.

'Are you ok?' I asked quietly.

'As I was saying... not just a writer. I'm in a band. The 'king Band.'

I'd heard of them, I didn't think I could hum any of their tunes on-demand, but I had heard of them. I was rubbish with celebrities. I had to ask Claire once who Meghan Markle was, for goodness' sake.

'Paul, who you met the other day, he's our bass player, and then there's Jake—he's on drums.'

I bet he feels like a gooseberry, I thought.

'Sorry I didn't mention it before, I was trying to lie low, and do a bit of writing before our gig in Bristol next week, and I was kinda... enjoying the fact you didn't know. It felt... It felt normal.'

'It's fine,' I said, waving my hand as if I was physically brushing the situation away, but at the same time, I suddenly felt glued to my seat, the centre of attention.

Will leant in.

'Do you wanna get out of here?' Will asked.

Yes, I really wanted to tap my heels and wake up at home. But instead, it felt like someone had turned out the lights and put a spotlight on our table.

'No, it's fine,' I said, shaking my head in true British style.

'Because we could totally make a run for it,' he half-whispered while taking my hand above the table, looking into my eyes intensely.

I simultaneously pushed my chair back as I stood up, not breaking his line of sight and not quite believing what my legs were doing. He chucked some cash on the table, grabbed his jacket with his other hand, and we half-ran across the restaurant and out the door. We didn't stop running until we were at the top of the hill. Completely out of breath, panting, and laughing. My heart was beating wildly. I felt like a child getting back to base without getting tagged, and I had a massive grin on my face.

'I left my coat in there,' I said when I got my breath back. He slipped his jacket off and placed it over my shoulders, draping his arm over the top to secure it as we headed up the road. We walked along in silence for a bit. I directed Will through Victoria Gardens. He wanted Victorian, and you couldn't get more Victorian than that. There was a stand selling ice creams.

'Do you want one? It's not quite Sunday roast, but I'm not sure they'll serve us if we go back,' he mused.

'I'd love one.'

We stopped by the menu, there was too much choice, and my tummy was rumbling, so I plumped for vanilla. Will ordered a raspberry ripple which made me smile.

'Do you want to walk along the pier?' I asked.

'Sure, are you taking me on a school history trip?'

I smiled up at him. 'Well, at least you'll have some local hotspots under your belt, ready to show Paul on your next date.'

A few moments later I realised I was walking alone. I looked back up the road and realised Will had stopped in his tracks.

'What?' I said, looking up towards him, using my spare hand to shield my eyes from the sun.

'You think I'm gay?' he asked, astonished.

My jaw dropped a little, and my mind was reeling. He had brought Paul back to stay the night. I had not imagined that, and I heard them arranging their next date. But then, he had joked about leaving his number, and there was the whole eye thing. Had I totally misread this? I looked down at the pavement, and my cheeks started to heat. I didn't know what to say.

Suddenly Will took two long strides toward me, closing the gap between us and discarding his remaining ice cream in a bin on the way. He lifted my face with both hands and kissed me without hesitation. It was firm and I could taste a hint of raspberry on his lips, but it was brief, too brief. I couldn't believe he had just done that.

I looked up at him in shock, and he said, 'I can assure you, I am definitely not gay...' He let go of my face, pulled his jacket back over my shoulders, and said, 'but if I have just blown two pounds and fifty-five pence on the wrong person...' he shook his head, and I laughed. 'Are you gonna take me to this pier, or do I need to take you home because you haven't actually said anything in a real long time?'

'I... I thought... Christ! I don't know what I thought. It's just that when you brought Paul back the other night, I just assumed... It's not that I didn't feel... but I don't....'

'Don't like constructing full sentences?' He smiled.

My ice cream was dripping onto the pavement. He took it from me and plopped it in the bin while I licked the ice cream off the back of my hand. He turned and grabbed my hand and said, 'To the pier, then?'

I nodded and smiled. So, this was a date? Damn it, Frankie was right.

'You might have to blow another couple of quid to get us in,' I said.

'I think I can afford that.' He paused and then added, 'I can't wait to tell Paul about this.'

Chapter 5

It was windy on the pier. We strolled along while I held his jacket around my shoulders, and he had one arm loosely around my waist. I don't know why I didn't just put the coat on. I didn't quite feel I could change positions, it felt so weird having someone's arm around me, and I was terrified of bumping into someone I knew. Not because I was embarrassed, Will was good-looking and a gentleman, but it's the small-town thing. Gossip spread like wildfire. People kept staring, people I didn't know or recognise. They were not staring at me, they were staring at Will, but he seemed oblivious or was very good at ignoring them.

We were both quite rosy-cheeked from the wind by the time we reached the end. We walked up the external metal staircase to grab a hot drink from the little café. Suddenly I was boiling. The glass café was like a greenhouse. It was old school, and there wasn't a coffee machine, just a big hot water urn, so the options were tea or coffee, and all the cakes were homemade tray bakes. Thankfully they'd done away with the polystyrene cups they used to serve their drinks in and replaced them with eco-friendly ones. But, gosh, when was the last time I walked along the pier? Years.

'Two Americanos, please, one with a double shot.'

The elderly lady looked at Will, perplexed, and I chuckled.

'Just two coffees, please.' I smiled. She nodded and poured them out.

'Did you wannna grab something to eat?' Will asked.

I was starving but having just had some ice cream, the cake was not what I fancied.

'No, but you go ahead.'

He ordered a big slice of sponge with a marbled ice topping. We headed back downstairs and sat on one of the benches on the sheltered side. Wales was clear across the water. You could even see the smoke churning out of the big chimney in Port Talbot.

'You mentioned you have a gig in Bristol next week.'

'Yeah, it kicks off the start of our European tour,' he said, leaning his elbows on his knees and looking down between the planks at the water below.

'So, you're pretty big then, the band, I mean.' I said, suddenly colouring up.

Thankfully he didn't notice.

'Yeah, we have a good fan base. We've been together since we were kids, hanging out in my Mom's garage with my brother. That's kinda where it all started. We've got three dates over here, Bristol, Manchester, and London. Then we have a couple in France and Spain, one in Portugal and Germany, and then we're back here for a festival before heading back to the States.'

'Wow! That's quite a schedule.'

I'd been abroad a few times, Paris on the school trip, Greece, Spain for a wedding, and Sweden, but we were campers. We spent our holidays in Devon and Cornwall. I always wanted to travel but never had the opportunity. Loads of my friends had gap years and went off to weird and wonderful places, but by that time, I was already a mum, doing tours of the toddler groups and soft play areas. Not very rock and roll.

'This is a delicious cake,' he said with half a mouthful. 'Do you want some?'

'No, I'm good, thanks. I'm getting a bit chilly, though. You must be freezing. Shall we wander back? There's a pub along the promenade that might still be doing food.'

He shovelled the last bit of cake in his mouth, hopped up, and held his hand out to pull me up. 'Sounds like a plan!'

We meandered along the prom. He told me about how he'd dropped out of school to pursue music, much to his mum's dismay at the time. He'd lived with the band and their tour manager, half in a tour bus, half in crappy rentals, until they got their first big break. He then bought an apartment in Brooklyn. I told him about my life, leaving school with semi-okay grades but no actual plans. I worked in a few bars and had an admin job for a while but never really found what I wanted to do career-wise and then fell pregnant with Frankie. Mike and I had been together throughout until we went our separate ways. Summarising it like that made me realise how boring my life was.

'And then you retrained? After Mike had left?' he asked.

'Yes, I came into some money from a loan that had been incorrectly sold, so I paid for the training and set the treatment room up. Then, I had our spare room redecorated and kitted out as a B&B.'

'Sounds like you've done more with your life since you parted with Mike. I mean, being a single mom and running two businesses, that's no mean feat.'

'Well, when you put it like that... but I'm hardly a single mum. Mike is still around. He has the boys every other weekend, takes them on holidays, and contributes financially. He's a good dad. I just... his career was more important I suppose.'

We arrived at the pub to discover that they had stopped making Sunday lunch, but the bar menu was still available. So, we ordered some chips, a surf and turf sharing platter, and two pints of lager. The pub had recently built some covered outside seating pods with heaters, so we slid into one of the pods opposite each other and sipped on our pints.

'I like a girl with a beer,' he said with a smile.

'Is that how you choose your women?' I asked, raising an eyebrow, hoping it would lead to his past girlfriends or wife, but instead, he asked what my future plans were.

'Future plans?' When would I have had the time to think about that? My life was busy enough as it was. All I knew was that I needed to earn enough money to get by. 'Um, it sounds really lame, but I don't really have any. The last eight years have been survival, I suppose. I'm just committed to supporting the boys until they finish their education, and then... I don't know?'

He frowned a little and said, 'okay, let me rephrase that. What would you do if you could do anything, the boys and money aside?'

'Anything?' I asked.

'Anything at all.'

I twisted my body around so that I could look out to sea. 'I would move somewhere warmer, maybe run a small B&B by the sea,' I said wistfully.

I imagined myself walking along the shallows of a sandy beach at sunset wearing a white maxi dress, sandals, the skirt in one hand, and picking up shells with the other.

Our food arrived, and I quickly twisted back around, realising I had my feet on the bench.

Will ordered two more pints.

'Anyway, enough about me, how about you? What are your future plans?'

We shared the platter, dipping breaded whitebait into tartar sauce and trying not to get too messy eating the mini sticky ribs. It was delicious, and I was very thankful that it was soaking up the pint I had consumed on an empty stomach.

Just then, a couple approached us, and the guy said, 'Sorry to disturb you, but my girlfriend was wondering if there was any chance she could have a selfie with you?' I looked at the couple in their late twenties. She was almost hiding behind him, looking coy and embarrassed.

'Sure,' Will said.

He hopped up as if it was completely normal, and I sipped my drink. Was I the only person that didn't know who Will was? I was beginning to feel a bit stupid. I would be having an appointment with the world wide web when I got home. I was the complete opposite of the boys, a total technophobe. I half-watched as she practically melted when he put his arm around her and smiled for the camera. Her boyfriend was watching with a weird expression on his face. I couldn't determine if he was happy or jealous.

They thanked him repeatedly and then headed out of the pub garden. Will sat back down and picked up where he left off and told me that the band wanted to concentrate on writing some new material after the tour. They hadn't toured for a couple of years because he'd been in what he called a 'dark place' for a while, but he was excited about the future.

I took a long sip of my beer while trying to compute what had just happened. Was this something that would occur frequently—the asking for autographs and selfies? I felt really out of the loop and once again in the spotlight as the whole selfie thing had caused practically everyone in the pub to stare. I managed to drag myself back to the conversation and avoid appearing rude.

'So, what brought on this tour?'

'Paul. He's getting married next month, and we hadn't toured the previous album for one reason or another, so he wanted to get it done this summer.'

'Get it done? It sounds like you had to force yourselves.'

'Kinda, if you don't tour an album straight away, it goes a bit stale. We're all getting on a bit, and touring is exhausting, so it is a drag, but I felt like I owed him.'

'Owed him for what?'

Will looked thoughtful and then leaned across to wipe some stray bbq sauce from my chin with his thumb. He then brushed some of my hair out of my face, which sent tingles down my left arm. I couldn't believe how his touch made me feel. Was it the way he looked into my eyes while he did it, or was it the fact that no one had touched me in that way for so long? It was caring and intimate. Once again, I felt that all eyes were on me.

He glanced around the garden briefly as if checking out the other patrons for the first time and said, 'shall we catch the sunset?'

'Yes! I know just the spot. We need to walk up there, though,' I said, pointing at the headland and immediately gathered my belongings, thankful for the opportunity to extricate ourselves from the heavy weight of watchful eyes.

'Do you think they do take-outs?' he said, looking back at the bar.

***

The wind had dropped, the sun was low, and I was feeling the effects of the beer. We walked up around the coast path to the top of the hill, there were several benches we could have sat on, but I took Will up onto the grass on the very top of the hill. We had a full panoramic view of Clevedon. You could see right across the Severn to Penarth and the next headland along the west coast.

Will put his coat down on the grass for us to sit on and took his keys out of his pocket. He used one to flip the lids off a couple of the beers he'd bought from the bar and gestured for me to sit while handing me one of the bottles. So, I sat, but I was so hot from the hike up the hill that I took my cardigan off to extend our little makeshift picnic blanket, and he lay beside me, propping himself up on his elbows to get the best vantage point. We sipped our beers in comfortable silence while the sun dipped and finally blipped behind the mountains leaving bright orange clouds in its wake.

'That was amazing,' he said, breaking the silence while still looking towards where the sun had been moments before. He turned on his side toward me, and I shivered.

'Come closer,' he said, beckoning.

I carefully put my empty beer bottle down so it didn't roll away, and slid down to mirror him, bending my left arm to support myself and resting my head on my hand. I looked at him, hesitant about his intentions. He shuffled closer still and put his arm lazily over my waist.

'Is this okay?' he asked, but before I had time to answer, his lips were on mine, and he pulled me in further. I couldn't quite believe it. I felt like cardboard, not wanting to move an inch because I felt nervous, excited, and apprehensive. I mean, I barely knew the guy, but at the same time, I felt I could trust him. It had been so long, and I was massively out of practice.

I forced myself to move my left hand up to his neck and into his hair. He deepened the kiss, and I was torn between being super aware that we were making out in public and letting go. He gently pushed me onto my back and placed his knee between mine. I held my hands out in front of me, almost holding him back, and reading my body language, he pulled away for a split second and said, 'are you nervous?'

But I didn't answer, and slowly moved my hands around him. He swooped back in, kissing my neck all the way until he reached my lips again. I slipped my right hand under his t-shirt and delicately danced my fingers up his back towards his shoulder blades. He made a low humming sound and pushed his hips against my thigh.

It was all happening at once, far too quickly, but at the same time, I didn't want it to stop. He started pulling my blouse out of my jeans, but we heard voices just then. Someone was walking along the path below us, and we were both suddenly pulled back into reality.

'Woah,' he whispered with a huge grin on his face, his fringe hanging around our faces, tickling my cheeks as he hovered above me. I tried to stifle a laugh, and he quickly placed a hand over my mouth to help smother any noise escaping. The talking and footsteps faded, and he moved his hand away from my mouth and tucked his fringe behind his ear.

'Sorry, that got a little out of hand. I always forget the beer over here is way stronger than I'm used to. Are you okay?' He said, rolling back onto his side and trying to adjust his jeans to make himself more comfortable.

'Well, I guess this proves you're definitely not gay,' I said.

He laughed and jumped up, leaning down and holding out both hands to pull me back to standing. He kissed me gently and then bent down to pick up our things.

'Do you want another beer?' he asked as I came back around from our dalliance, reality suddenly slapping me in the face.

I wanted to rewind a few moments and feel him against me again. One minute we were kissing, and the next, we were standing. I had just kissed someone for the first time in eight years, and it wasn't Mike, it was someone famous! I realised he was looking at me, waiting for me to answer with a slight smile on his face.

'I have work tomorrow. Believe me, seeing clients with a hangover is not a great experience. So, I guess we had better walk home. I'll have to pick the car and my coat up tomorrow.'

We walked all the way back, hand in hand. I didn't want the night to end. I had a warm feeling inside me. I didn't think I had felt this way since I was sixteen. We talked all the way back. He was easy to chat with. Will seemed genuinely interested in Frankie and Paddy and wanted to know what they wanted to do when they left school. I asked him more about the band. He was the singer and guitarist and wrote most of their stuff. He loved that I didn't really know who they were, and admitted he struggled to meet new people who genuinely wanted to get to know him. Before we knew it, we were home.

'I really enjoyed today,' he said as we approached the front door.

'Me too,' I replied.

Will kissed me again while we lingered under the storm porch, but I knew the date was over as soon as the key unlocked the door.

After checking in on the boys and preparing my treatment room for the week ahead, I sat in the lounge, flicking through the channels on the TV, trying to calm the buzz I had in my stomach, constantly being distracted by thoughts of Will hovering over me. He had headed up to his room when we got in, and I couldn't help but smile to myself every time I remembered feeling him against me. It was a thrill to know I could still do that to someone.

I checked over my shoulder that the boys weren't lurking and couldn't resist any longer. I searched up Will Reynolds. Oh boy, there was so much. Pages and pages of pictures. Snaps of him on stage, mug shots, photos with the rest of the band, holding a guitar, standing with famous people, and ones of him at award ceremonies with glamorous women and a backdrop of whichever sponsor was supporting the event. Articles about anything and everything, from the latest tour information, gig reviews, and random stuff like taking his mom out for lunch. I could have sat there all night staring at his face like a love-struck teenager, but eventually, I flipped the lights out and headed up.

I had kissed a rockstar!

Chapter 6

Once again, it had taken me ages to get off to sleep, and consequently, I woke up late. I shot across the landing and couldn't help but notice that Will's door was open, bed made, and daylight was flooding through his window. Had he already left for the day? I thought he wasn't a morning person. Unfortunately, I didn't have time to ponder. I needed a shower.

The kitchen was a bomb site, a trail of destruction that only two teenagers could leave. I just about had time to clear everything away and make myself a coffee before my first client arrived. The funny buzzy feeling was still evident in my tummy, and I kept having to draw my focus while I was working. My second client, a regular with whom I got on well, was his usual chatty self.

'Hey, did you hear that the lead singer of The 'king Band is staying in Clevedon?'

'Really?' I said, feigning ignorance.

'Yeah, it's all over social media. He was spotted in The Olive Branch.' Shit. It must have been that waitress. 'I love that band, I tried to get tickets, but it's a complete sell-out.'

'Shame...' I kneaded my elbow into his glutes, and he took a sharp intake of breath.

I didn't have long for lunch, but I was drawn back to Will's room. It was empty, with no bag, no guitar, nothing. A sinking feeling overcame me, and I suddenly felt a bit used. I

44

thought we'd connected, but maybe he did this with women in every town he visited. I couldn't believe I'd fallen for it. 'He lives in Brooklyn.' I whispered to myself, and it was never going to last. Why on earth would he be interested in me, anyway? Lucy Daniels, thirty-eight, mother of two and a physiotherapist.

As the day went on, I became angrier. After I finished work, I went for a walk to try to settle my anger. It was drizzling, so I put my jacket hood up and marched along. I felt so stupid, and I was cross with myself that I had fallen for his charms. I was too old to be dealing with feelings like this. I consoled myself by concluding that it would never have worked, anyway.

When I returned, I set about making dinner, spaghetti Bolognese, the kid's fave. Dinner time was the only time me and the boys tried to ensure we were together. It was an opportunity for me to find out what they were up to, and ensure they had some nutrients each day. They were such good lads. Don't get me wrong, they had done some bloody foolish things over the years, but thankfully I could only count the number of drunken rescues on one hand.

'So, is Dad picking you up on Friday?'

'Yep.' Paddy said. 'Actually, he said he would come a bit earlier because he wanted to talk to you about something.'

'Oh, okay.'

So why hadn't he texted me that? Surely we were passed the point of sending messages through the kids.

'Can you wash my football kit tonight, Mum?' Frankie asked. 'I would do it myself, but my shift starts at eight o'clock.'

The week Frankie turned eighteen, he'd taken a job at one of the local pubs. He loved it, and I had a feeling he was seeing one of the girls that worked there.

'Yes, I suppose so. Leave it at the bottom of the stairs before you go,' I said with an air of annoyance.

As I was packing everything into the dishwasher, there was a knock at the side door. I opened it, and a big bunch of flowers was thrust into my face. I took them to find a very pained-looking Steph behind them.

'Sorry.' She pursed her lips and closed her eyes, anticipating a slap she did not receive.

'Oh, come in, you stupid twat. Cuppa? I bet you had a sore head yesterday.' I made a brew and found a vase for the gorgeous flowers.

'Yes, I did, I didn't get out of bed till ten and then felt rubbish all day, and I know it serves me right before you say it. So, what did you get up to?'

I wasn't prepared for this question. Should I tell her? Would he want me to? I don't think I would be breaking any confidentiality rules in a business sense. Will had clearly been lying low here because he didn't want anyone to know he was in town, but the news was out now. And he'd left. I'd probably never see him again.

'I went out to lunch with Will.' There, that was the truth, just not the whole truth.

'Gay Will?'

I rolled my eyes.

'I knew it, I bloody knew it! So, he's not gay, is he?'

'No, he's very much straight. I guess I got the wrong end of the stick. And you know you said you recognised him...'

she looked up, searching my face, 'well, he's Will Reynolds from The 'king Band.' Her face lit up.

'Oh, my God!' She smacked her hand over her mouth. 'Did something happen? Lucy Daniels, look at me!' I looked up. 'Ahhhhh, it did!! Tell me everything.' She picked up both mugs of tea in one hand, linked our arms with her other, and pulled me into the lounge.

I kept to the basics, skipping the snogging after sundown, and didn't divulge anything I thought might be classed as personal information. I told her we kissed under the storm porch to appease her excitement. I didn't want her to think I'd fallen so quickly. I was embarrassed with myself.

'Well, you've still got it, Sister. This is brilliant!' she said, clapping her hands. 'Are you seeing him again?'

'No, he's checked out, actually. So, no.' My heart felt incredibly heavy, considering the short time I had spent with him.

'I thought he was staying for a couple of weeks? But anyway, this is the start of it, babe, you are back in the game!!' She was so pleased for me, I couldn't bear to tell her I was feeling so low and just a little bit slutty.

Chapter 7

Groundhog Day had returned. I couldn't shake my sinking feeling every time I thought of him, but life went on. The only thing I was thankful for was that I was busy, because every spare moment I had to myself, I thought about what a boring life I had. Will had given me the chance to reflect, to dream, and the more I thought about those things, the more depressed I became.

On Wednesday, I finished at three-thirty, and my mum was popping by to drop something round for the boys. I loved my mum and dad. They were fantastic. We were more like mates than parents and daughter. They had been such tremendous support over the last few years, forever, actually.

'Hello?' My mum walked in carrying a big Pyrex dish and a carrier bag. 'I made you a fish pie.' She placed it carefully on the counter. 'It will need reheating, or you can put it in the fridge for tomorrow if you have something lined up for tonight, and I bought the boys some socks. They have feet like your father, always putting their big toe through. What's wrong?'

I was crying.

'Oh, sorry, Mum, it's been one of those days, weeks actually.'

She folded me up in a great big hug as I sobbed onto her shoulder.

'Oh, love, do you want to talk about it?' No, I did not! I mean, we were mates, and I could talk to her about most things, but this was not one of them.

'It's nothing really, just everything getting on top of me.' Quite literally, in fact. She tactfully changed the subject and put the kettle on. It was nice to catch up with her. As she was getting ready to go, she picked up her keys, and I suddenly remembered that I hadn't picked the car up. 'Mum, do you mind if I hop in, I need to pick the car up from The High Street, and could you do me a favour?' I grabbed the keys and locked up.

<hr />

I waited in the car and watched as mum returned from The Olive Branch with my coat. 'Thanks, Mum,' I said as she reached the car. 'You're a star.'

'No problem, and if you need to talk, I'm just a phone call away.'

Bless her, and she gave me a knowing look. Mums always know, don't they? When I got home, it was dark, and the house was quiet. Paddy had athletics after school, and there was no sign of Frankie. I hung the keys up and pulled the blinds in the kitchen. I never usually drank during the week, but sod it, I was going to have a gin and tonic. I may as well drown my sorrows. I wandered through to the lounge, hoping there was still some gin left in the cabinet, flicked the light on, and stopped dead.

'Jesus Christ!' I almost shouted. The dogs started barking, sensing my fear. There was a man asleep on the sofa. It was Will. He was fully dressed, with his guitar and bag on the floor, and began to stir.

'Hey,' he said sleepily, using his arm to shield his eyes from the light, lifting his t-shirt as he did so, and I averted my gaze.

'What are you doing here?' I asked, trying to stay professional and not sound too angry.

'Err, well, I'm staying here, remember?' He slowly sat up and rubbed his eyes. 'But the bed wasn't made up, so I thought I'd wait for you to return, and I must have nodded off. We've been in rehearsals for the last few days, and we've had some pretty late nights. Did you get my text?'

'No... no, I didn't get a text.'

I stood there, half-struck one o'clock. So, he hadn't left? He just had a three-day rehearsal? Where had he stayed? Why hadn't he called?

'I'm sorry I didn't call. We had more work to do in the rehearsals than we'd realised, so they went on a bit. I ended up crashing at Paul's hotel,' he answered, reading my mind.

He looked at me. I was still standing there, nailed to the spot. Not really knowing what to say or do. He stood up. 'Did you think I had left?' he asked, frowning.

'I... I didn't get a text,' I said again, shell-shocked and not wanting to catch his eye.

'Shit, Lucy, I'm sorry I didn't call,' he said as he moved towards me. 'Because I've been thinking about you a lot.'

He had? I still couldn't move. He was standing in front of me. He lifted my chin, forcing me to look at him.

'You must have been thinking I was a complete asshole.'

I stared into his eyes as he searched mine. All the emotion from the last couple of days bubbled up inside me, the anger, the buzzy feeling, the heartache. I put my hands around his neck, pushed onto my toes slightly, and kissed him firmly.

I think he was a bit taken aback but quickly recovered and returned my kiss, wrapping his arms around my waist, pulling me in, and then walking me backwards until I came up against the wall. He shook his leather jacket off, and it thudded on the floor as he pushed my chin up, almost banging the back of my head and kissing my neck. I lowered my hands and pulled his hips towards me as he breathed heavily into my ear. His hand disappeared up my work polo, and he traced the profile of my nipple with his thumb. Oh God, I can't do this, not in my lounge. The boys could turn up any minute, and where was this going exactly? Will was here on tour.

'I'm sorry, I can't.'

I dropped my arms, and he stopped immediately, pulling my top back down as he went and tracing the hem around with his finger and thumb.

'No, it's fine. I'm sorry. Things keep moving a little quick when I'm with you.'

Dragging his hand through his hair, he smiled. I really wanted him, but I needed to cool off. I hadn't had time to think. Where were we taking this? Were we going to end up having sex, and then I'd never see him again after his gig in Bristol? I didn't want to feel used, and I certainly didn't want to shag someone for the first time in over eight years for the sake of it. I wasn't a teenager.

'What are you thinking?' He stood in front of me, his hand above me on the wall.

Oh crap, I couldn't tell him all of that. He'd think I was crazy.

'That I need to make the dinner.'

He shook his head and let his arm drop by his side. 'Okay, I'll take my things upstairs... if it's still okay to stay?'

'Of course, I'm just going to put the dinner in the oven, and I'll bring up some sheets.'

I took some fresh bedding out of the airing cupboard and went upstairs. I could hear the shower running, so I went into Will's room and made the bed. As I came out, he came out of the bathroom with a towel around his waist, water dripping off his long fringe and down his torso. It was an awkward moment. I had kissed this man, felt him hard against me, but I felt like I wasn't allowed to look, and he was looking at me with a strange expression on his face, almost like he was waiting for a reaction.

'Do you want to join us for dinner? It's fish pie,' I asked brightly.

The question had come out of my mouth before I'd had the chance to think about it, and I was purposefully looking straight into his eyes, and not allowing them to lower to his bare pecs and lean stomach. He smiled, shaking a little laugh off.

'I'd love to, as long as you're sure?'

When I got back downstairs, I looked at my phone. Will said he'd text me. But, come to think of it, I hadn't received a text for ages. So, I switched it off, checked on the pie, and switched it back on again, and sure enough, when it lit back up, I had several text messages.

Steph: *I'm sorry about Saturday night. I'm a bellend. I had no right to say what I said. I blame it on the booze, and you can blame it on my massive arse.*

Unrecognised number: *Missing those lips x*

That must be from Will. Swoon. How did he get my number? Maybe from my business website? I created a new contact.

Mike: *We need to talk when I pick the boys up on Friday. Are you around?*

Frankie: *Won't be back for dinner, save me some, F x*

FFS, bloody phones.

Missing those lips.

So, he had texted, and if I had received it, I could have contacted him to find out where he was. And what on earth did Mike want? It sounded serious—bloody hell.

'You know...' I startled upon hearing Will's voice. 'When I didn't hear back from you, I was worried about coming back. I wasn't sure if you wanted to see me again,' Will said as he entered the kitchen, still towelling his hair, grinning wickedly at my jumpiness. The side door opened before I could respond, and Paddy walked in.

'Hey, Pads, was athletics good?' I asked.

'Yep, what's for dinner? Hi,' he said, lifting a hand to Will, Will air high-fived him back.

'It's fish pie. You've got just enough time to have a quick shower.'

I made up a salad, and we sat eating in silence for a while. My mum's fish pie was so good. I kept meaning to get the recipe from her but never remembered.

'Will, are you the man from that band?' Paddy asked suddenly.

I was about to tell him not to be rude, but Will replied, 'Yeah, but don't tell anyone, okay? I'm trying to lie low.'

'Knew it,' he said as he stood up, grabbing his plate and cutlery.

'Where are you going?' I asked, frowning at him.

'I told Fred I'd be online at seven.'

Paddy dashed up to his room—bloody Xbox. Will had finished too.

'Do you want some more? There's plenty.'

'It's delicious, yes, please.'

I scooped some more out of the serving dish and explained that I couldn't take credit for it.

After polishing off his second helping, he looked up. 'Can we talk?'

I looked down at my plate and started playing with one of the salad leaves with my fork.

'Because I don't know where this is going,' he said, moving his fork from me to him. 'But I really like you, and I guess I need to know what you're thinking.'

I bit my lip. I wasn't used to men being so direct, nor was I used to putting my feelings into words. Years of zero communication between Mike and me meant I had little practice.

'Not here...' I said, 'but we could go for a walk?'

We headed out towards the river, and we ambled along the river's edge once we got there. We didn't hold hands, we just walked. I knew it would be quiet, and it was a lovely evening.

'Talk to me,' Will said, eventually.

I still hadn't really formulated what I would say, but I took a deep breath.

'Okay, here goes. I really like you too, but you're here on tour, and soon you'll be going home, and home is a long way away. I don't want anything to happen between us that I'm going to regret, because,' once it started to come, I couldn't stop, 'there's no... future for us.' I shot him a glance. Talking about our future seemed a little forward, but he was looking at the floor. 'I haven't been with anyone for such a long time, and I guess I'm trying to protect myself because when I'm close to you, things happen that are out of my control, and feelings are there that I haven't felt for such a long time.' I took a long breath in. 'I'm scared.' I announced. There, that's what it boiled down to. I was scared.

Will caught my hand to stop me from walking on, and he turned toward me, placing his forehead on mine.

'I'm scared too, you know, but I figure if we both want the same thing, we can make it work, right? I know this conversation feels a bit premature, but I needed to know what was going through your head,' he said, and I could feel his breath on my face.

'It's premature because we're on a time limit, don't you see that?'

He pulled his head away to see my face, and I looked him straight in the eye.

'But it doesn't need to be, I'm pretty flexible over the next week or so,' he began.

'A week!'

I pulled away. It was my turn to shake my head. He took my hands back.

'And then we can work it out. I'll still be in the UK for another week before heading to France, and France isn't that far or Spain or Portugal. So, I can fly back, or you can fly to me.'

'I can't afford that, and I have to work,' I reminded him.

He couldn't see how ridiculous this was.

'Lucy, you're searching for excuses when you should be searching for solutions.'

I looked at his feet, the ground was muddy, and he had specs of mud splashed up his jeans. 'Maybe I am, but I'm being realistic.' I looked back up at him, tears stinging the backs of my eyes. How had we got here so quickly? It was like speed dating on... speed.

'Just give it a chance,' he implored, scooping my face up and kissing me, not urgently or particularly firm, but it was sensual. Like he was trying to convey in a kiss that we didn't need to move fast, we could take it slow.

I couldn't get my head around it. Why did he like me? What did I have to offer a rockstar? And how would his fame affect us? 'Can I think about it?' I asked when our kiss eventually came to an end.

'Sure,' he agreed, looking defeated.

Chapter 8

And think I did. Another sleepless night ensued. It felt like I had a nest of mice in my tummy. I tossed and turned. Earlier in the week, I thought he'd left, and I felt bereft. Now that he's back, it was all so complicated, and this time last week, I hadn't even met him.

This was crazy!

At two-thirty, I got up and went downstairs, made myself a cup of herbal tea, and crept into the lounge. I sat there in the dark, sipping my tea, wishing I could rewind a week and for my life to have taken a different path.

'Are you okay?'

Shit! I slopped my tea all down my night vest and shorts. I shot up.

'Will, could you stop doing that?' I whisper-shouted at him.

I put my tea on the side and rushed past him back to the kitchen to dab the spillage with kitchen roll. Will followed. He clearly found this far funnier than I did. My hair was all over the place, and the tea stain had quickly gone cold, making my nipples impossible to hide.

'Can I help with that?' he asked, taking the kitchen roll from me and gently dabbing it over my chest. Christ, this was embarrassing. 'Can't sleep?' he asked, or was he admitting he couldn't either? I could see he was wearing yet another t-shirt and his boxers in the half-light. How many t-shirts did he have? I held his wrist to stop him from dabbing me. It was ruined anyway. I had never been able to get a tea stain out of a white piece of clothing before. I stepped back and stumbled backwards over one of the boy's shoes, but Will somehow caught me just in time. He pulled me up, I'm not sure whether it was accidental, but he pulled me right up against him and then righted me.

The feel of him against me made my insides flip, my skin went all goose-bumpy, and there was a weird electricity between us. We stood there, staring at each other, frozen for a second. His eyes were shining, pouring into mine like he was looking for some sort of confirmation that he could touch me. I licked a dry corner of my mouth. He took a sharp intake of breath and then kissed me, almost pushing me over again. But his hands were around me before I could fall, almost lifting me off the floor as I steadied myself by clinging onto his shoulders. He was surprisingly strong. Will was carnal, ravishing me. Things were moving way too fast again, but the mice nest began dissipating, and I felt warm, really warm. But then, like a dark cloud, thoughts of feeling used and bereft crept in. No, I shouldn't be doing this. It will never last, no.

'No,' I said out loud, pushing myself away from him.

'No?' He sort of stated and asked.

'I'm sorry, Will, I can't do this. Things are moving too fast. I need more time.'

'Okay, okay,' he said, holding his hands up. 'I'm sorry.' He smoothed his hands over his face and then pushed his fingers up into his hair like he was trying to brush away his natural instincts and think of what to say. 'Let's take it slower.'

'What do you mean?' We really didn't have the time.

'You like me, and I like you....'

'Why?' I interjected.

'What?' he asked, confused.

'Why do you like me?' I asked. 'Why does Will Reynolds of The 'king Band like me?'

He paused then, understanding the weight of my question. He lifted his hand to hold his chin and looked at me with a hard stare. Had he guessed that I'd looked him up online? Was he trying to think of a plausible explanation?

'I like you because you like me for who I am, not what I am. You're caring, considerate, loyal, and well, hot.'

My cheeks flushed as I breathed out. Will sounded so sincere, even if I didn't believe him. I was not *hot*. Mike used to tell me he loved me, but I had never asked him to clarify his feelings, and here was Will, laying his cards on the table after a week.

'So, can we just see where this takes us? It doesn't have to get heavy,' he said.

Gosh, this was difficult, I really didn't want to get hurt, but at the same time, I really liked him. And there was this pull between us. He was good-looking, kind, a gentleman, and... he was a bloody rockstar. He could obviously tell I was hesitating.

'Please, Lucy.' He put his hands on my shoulders, and there was that electricity again.

Oh, for Christ's sake. 'Okay.' I said, shaking my head, wondering what an earth I was getting myself into, and looking at the floor to avoid his intense gaze.

He smiled, gently taking my cheek in his hand and kissing me softly. 'I'll see you tomorrow.' And then he slowly took a step back, turned, and disappeared through the kitchen and up the stairs.

I smiled at myself, shaking my head again and touching my lips where Will's mouth had just been. What the hell was I doing? I didn't know, but I couldn't deny it felt good and exciting, and the knot in my stomach made itself comfortable as I headed up to bed myself.

Chapter 9

What was that bloody noise? Oh. It was my alarm. How was it morning already? I looked down, and I was still wearing my tea-stained vest. I smiled, took it off, and lay back down. I had a vision of my nipples looking like two teddy bears' noses while I stood in the kitchen. I then grabbed a pillow to cover my blushes even though I was alone. I made it downstairs with plenty of time to have a coffee before work. I only had a couple of clients that morning.

Will was obviously enjoying a lie-in as he still hadn't come down when my first client had left. I did, however, have a text from him just saying, *Good Morning xx*. I imagined him lying upstairs and then quickly forced the thought from my mind. Thinking about him was not conducive to doing my job properly. I finished up for the morning, I was so hasty to get my client out that I forgot to rebook the next appointment. I quickly cleared down and locked the files away before heading upstairs. Will had showered and packed, and I found him sitting on the edge of the bed.

My heart sank.

'You're leaving?'

'No, this is just my backpack. It just happens to have sixteen pairs of rolled-up boxers, eight t-shirts, and a spare pair of jeans stuffed into the bottom of it.'

I giggled.

'What are you doing now?' he asked.

'I've got a few errands to run,' I replied.

'Okay, what are you doing later?'

'I don't think I have any plans.'

'Good, do you wanna come to the gig?'

'I thought the gig was on Saturday?' I replied.

'The main gig is on Saturday, but we have to do a small, secret gig tonight for the mega-fans and a few people from the record company. It will be an acoustic set and probably seated.'

'I would love to,' I said, immediately shitting myself.

'Awesome. I can introduce you to everyone.' That didn't make me feel any better. 'If you get there at six, I should be able to come out and meet you, but I'll make sure your name is on the door. So, you won't have to queue.' He handed me a piece of paper. 'That's the venue. You promise you'll come?'

'Mmm hmmm,' I said, nodding. Will stood and put his hand on my shoulder. I looked up, and he was looking at me, still waiting for a reply.

'Yes, yes, I promise.'

Even though I was currently working through my entire wardrobe in my head, throwing clothes over my shoulder that wouldn't be suitable for a gig, a gig whose lead singer I was seeing. Then he kissed me, breaking my train of thought, and I kissed him back and curled his hair between my fingers. My other hand made its way over his abdomen, up and over his pecs, but he gently pulled away, smiling.

'I've got to get to a meeting, and we're taking things slow, right?'

He lifted his eyebrows as if to confirm his reason for pulling away and bent down to pick up his bag and guitar.

'Meeting?' I frowned, feeling a little singed.

'Yeah, a meeting with our tour manager. I need to organise some additional transport for the tour. I met someone you see, and I kinda like her.'

Oh. That was me.

I stupidly decided to have a disco nap, and in true Lucy style, the twenty minutes it was supposed to be, turned into an hour.

Shit.

Thank god I showered that morning. A quick refresh would have to do.

What to wear? What to wear... damn you wardrobe, tell me!

I mean, if it was small and personal, wouldn't it be a more formal affair? I pulled out my NYE dress. It was basically a gold, sequin, long stretchy vest that just about covered enough of my thighs. With my knee-highs, I could then dress it down with my leather jacket.

Plan.

I found an old red clutch that was just big enough to fit my phone, keys, and cards, so I paired it with red lipstick to tie everything in.

There was already a queue starting to form when I reached the venue. I texted Will, but he didn't reply, so I called him, and it went straight to voicemail. Bugger, I would have to speak to the big burly man on the door.

'Hi, my name should be on the list?'

He looked up and smiled.

'And what is your name, Miss?'

'Oh yes, Lucy Daniels.'

'Lovely.' He picked up a fabric sticker and came around the counter to lift the rope for me. 'This way, Miss.'

I followed him in, leaving a hush of whispers from the crowd behind me. Steph was going to be so jealous. I had texted her before I left to tell her that Will had checked back in, and I was going out on another date with him. She was obviously busy as she'd responded with a clapping emoji and a row of hearts.

He showed me through to the main room, passing me my sticker. 'There you are.'

Before I could ask where Will was, he was gone. I stood there holding my clutch with white knuckles. Maybe this is what they were named after? There was a bar to my right and round tables and chairs in front of me, all facing the stage on the other side of the room. The ceiling was relatively low, a bit like a 1930s American comedy theatre. A couple of people with lanyards and clipboards stood by the stage. The stage itself wasn't very high, but it had a single stool, a mic set-up, a mic to the left, a stripped-down drum kit, and a row of monitors.

'Lucy? It is you! What on earth are you doing here?'

The voice I heard was not Will's, and I turned to see a familiar face. It was Dave Bennett, the husband of one of the Mums I had met at one of the many toddler groups back in the day. I hadn't seen him for ages.

'Hi!' I said brightly and gave him a little hug. 'Um, I'm here with a friend. What are you doing here?'

He was wearing some scruffy old jeans, an oversized t-shirt, and trainers. 'I'm doing the lighting.'

Of course, I vaguely remembered him telling me once he did the lighting for shows. The walkie-talkie hanging from his jeans pocket sprang into life. 'I'd better go. Enjoy the show, Lu.'

He strode down toward the stage.

'A friend,' Will whispered in my ear. I spun around, and he put his hand on my hip. 'You look stunning,' he said, eyes travelling down to my boots.

'Thanks,' I said with too big a smile.

The coffee I had before I came out made me a bit jittery.

Will glanced around the room.

'Come out back. There are some people I want you to meet.'

He took my hand and led me through a door to the side of the room. It was dark, and the person who stood at the door shone a very bright torch at my waist to check my sticker. He took me along the corridor and opened another door. Inside were a couple of bashed-up sofas, a makeshift black ash dressing table with a stool that had a rip in it. A mirror was stuck to the wall, not quite straight. A couple of bowls of crisps were untouched on a coffee table between the sofas, and there was a distinct smell of sick.

'Classy, huh,' Will said, chuckling.

Admittedly it wasn't quite the green room I had in mind. I was thinking more *Jonathan Ross*.

'I don't know where everyone's gone. Stay here. I'll be back in a minute.'

Will left, and a few moments later, a woman walked in, super skinny with skin-tight black leather trousers and a skimpy black vest top. Her dark brown hair was unbelievably straight and so shiny it made the mirror look sorry for itself. Her eyes had perfectly painted bat wings which enhanced her pointy face, and she had *all* the tattoos on her arms.

'Oh! Hello. Who are you with?' she asked, glancing down at her list, completely uninterested.

'Will,' I said. She slowly looked back up at me, taking every inch of me in, and making me feel really awkward. A half-smile appeared on her face that didn't reach her eyes. 'You must be Lucy. Nice to meet you.' She put her hand out to shake mine, but it was so brief I didn't have time to shake back. 'Left you already, has he?' she said, and I couldn't help but detect a hint of bitterness in her remark.

'He's gone to find some people.' As if on cue, Will came barreling back in laughing with two other men, one of which I recognised. He looked at the woman, and she pursed her lips and then left.

'Lucy, you've met Paul,' he said, pointing to Paul. 'This is Jake, our drummer.'

'Lovely to meet you, Jake.' I shook his hand. 'And Paul, again.' I nodded, shaking his hand for good measure.

'Just for the record, Jake is not my boyfriend,' Paul said as I closed my eyes while he and Will shared the joke.

'I'm never going to live that down, am I?' I smiled.

Will put his arm around me to make me feel more comfortable.

'Who was that woman?' I asked.

'That's Alysa. She's our tour manager,' Will replied.

Paul and Jake looked at the floor. Paul even kicked an imaginary stone.

'It won't be long until they let everyone in. Do you wanna grab a table?'

He didn't wait for me to answer and held the door open. As we walked back along the dark corridor, Will pulled me to one side and slid his arm around my waist.

'You look hot in this dress,' he whispered, kissing me. Slow and firm, but as soon as he heard someone coming, he pulled away and grabbed my hand, leading me out to where the tables were.

Will pulled out a chair next to one of the tables at the front, gesturing for me to sit, and then crouched down beside me, leaning on my thigh. 'So, once everyone is in and they've got a drink and sat down, we'll do a half-hour set. Then, I normally chat to the crowd a bit to make them feel included and then play a couple more. I'm hoping we'll be done within an hour, but they'll be the usual signing and chatting to a few people. But you'll stay, right?'

'Sure, if you want me to?'

'I want you to,' he said, leaning in and lowering his voice just enough to send a shiver down my spine. He looked around as if checking who was watching, and then kissed me briefly and disappeared backstage again.

'Good luck,' I called after him.

The show was amazing. Will made everyone feel like they were listening to them in their own living rooms. He responded to the odd funny heckle and generally worked the crowd like putty in his hand, making jokes and giving away little tidbits of information about the songs. Occasionally while he was singing, he'd lazily look over to me, not to cause attention but just long enough for me to know, and every time he did it, the hairs on the back of my neck would stand to attention. Then, as they finished, the applause was electric. Everyone gave a standing ovation, whistled, and whooped. The three of them left the stage, but only momentarily. They were back in the bar, bottles of beer already in their hands, towels around their necks, and the music was switched on in the bar.

I watched Will from a distance, laughing and chatting. Scribbling the odd autograph on record sleeves, CDs, and random bits of paper, posing for selfies, and generally making all the women swoon. He was so confident, standing tall with his legs parted to bring his eye level down to the person he was talking to, making sure he gave each person his undivided attention, however brief.

I noticed Alysa was holding court, ensuring Will was moving on to the next group of people eager to speak to him. Now and again, he would look over to make sure I was still there. At one point, he mouthed, *I'm sorry,* while no one was looking.

Paul appeared at my side a few moments later, holding a beer bottle out for me. 'Will asked if I'd come and keep you company for a bit.'

I smiled and thanked him for the beer, in turn, thanking him for his company.

'He always gets caught up after these sorts of gigs. It's all for the super fans, and the hotshots at the record company.' He explained.

I smiled again, a little embarrassed around him, especially as he knew I had thought he was gay.

'So... when did you meet Will?' I asked for want of a better question.

'At Kindergarten,' he responded with a little laugh. 'We were always getting up to mischief. He was a pretty messed up kid.'

I looked at Paul with a puzzled expression.

'Probably because he didn't have a father figure, his mom did her best, but Will's brother was always getting into trouble, so he was kind of left to his own devices.'

Knowing what it was like having two boys of my own, I immediately felt for his mum. At such a young age, too, that must have been tough.

'And when did you start the band?'

'I guess we must have been about eight or nine. Will, Jake, Alysa, Will's brother, and I were hanging out in the parking lot one day, and we found an old guitar in a trash can, and Will took it home. He pretty much taught himself to play. I had bass lessons at school, and Jake drums, so we just kind of mucked about in his garage, trying stuff out. Will's brother sang sometimes, but because he was older, he'd go off with his mates and get himself caught up in all sorts of shit, so Will started singing instead.'

'It's quite sweet that you're all still together,' I smiled, and he laughed.

'Yeah, I guess so. It's not always been easy.'

I wanted to ask more questions, particularly about Alysa, as they had obviously known each other for a long time, but Dave appeared between us.

'Hey man, thanks for tonight. You got the atmosphere just right.'

'No worries,' Dave replied, and then he turned to me and said, 'what did you think?'

Paul nodded his goodbye as he slipped back into the crowd, satisfied that I wasn't being left alone.

'Truly amazing, so so good,' I said, leaning towards his ear for him to hear.

'So, I've gotta ask, how do you know Will?' he said, still looking straight ahead.

'He's a guest at the B&B.'

It was the best I could come up with on the spot.

'Oh, so that's where Will has been hiding from Alysa.'

His walkie-talkie crackled again, and he shrugged a sorry and left. I didn't know what to make of his comment. Had they been seeing each other at some stage? Did I want to know? I looked back up, but Will had gone. So, I sat down, resting my chin on my arms on the back of the chair to watch the crowd as it slowly dispersed.

'Lucy, Lucy.'

Will stroked my arm and pushed my hair out of my eyes. Oh, my God, had I nodded off? Will was crouched down in front of me. I had red lipstick all over my arm. The room was pretty much empty, and a staff member was sweeping the floor.

'Someone keep you awake last night?' He smiled devilishly. 'We're all done. Let's go.'

'Where are we going?' I asked, trying to hide my yawn as I stood up, rubbing my arm to try to remove the lipstick.

'I don't know, but I. Am. Hungry,' he said with far too much excitement in his voice for this end of the day.

We caught up with Paul and Jake. Jake held a girl's hand to whom I hadn't been introduced. Had he picked her up tonight? A member of security was leading the way. We stepped out into the fresh air, a people carrier had been backed up the side ally, out of sight, but a small huddle of girls stood in the road, blocking our escape. Will gently pushed me towards the security man, who ushered me into the car along with Paul, Jake, and the mystery girl, and slid the door shut.

Will was left outside with the guard to deal with the girls. I didn't quite know what to do with myself, so I applied some lip balm while trying not to stare. Paul leaned over from the back and put his hand on my shoulder, 'He won't be long. Bill won't let them linger.' I thought he was referring to Will as Bill for a moment, but then I realised he was talking about the security guard. Bill was *their* security guard, not the venue's man. I could hear Will laughing and chatting, he was all smiles for the selfies and charming too, but sure enough, Bill tapped him on the shoulder and opened the sliding door. I heard Will say *goodnight, ladies*, before he slipped inside, Bill locking us in before jumping in the front with the driver.

'Sorry about that,' Will said as he swooped in for a kiss.

'What do you fancy, lads?' the driver said.

'I could kill a burger,' Will replied, and the others agreed. Will put his hand on my knee, and I tensed up. I wasn't sure I was ready to show affection in front of other people. I thought the driver would take them to a restaurant, but instead, he pulled up at a drive-through. I couldn't quite believe how much food they all ordered. Everyone started unwrapping their burgers as the driver pulled away, and the general chat returned.

Will asked, 'so, you enjoyed the show?'

'I loved it, Will, I really did. I've never been to a gig like it. You're very good with the crowd.'

'I didn't use to be.' He wiped some ketchup off his lips with the back of his hand. 'It's just experience, I guess.' He took one more sip from his drink and then put everything back in the paper bag, wedging it into the footwell. 'Do you wanna get back? I've got the post-gig buzz, but you look pretty tired.'

I really was, and as much as I wanted to spend more time with him, I had to work the next day. So, after dropping everyone off at their hotel, we headed back home. Will held my hand as I dozed, leaning my head on his shoulder.

The house was quiet, and we headed upstairs. The boy's doors were shut, so I figured they were asleep. I wasn't about to check. I'd made that mistake before. We hovered outside his bedroom door, kissing lazily. 'I should get to bed. I have work in the morning,' I whispered.

'Mmm hmm,' he responded, still kissing me, but I eventually broke it off and looked at him.

He smiled and then whispered, 'Thanks for coming tonight. Will you come on Saturday? I mean, it will be a totally different vibe, but you could bring a friend?'

'I'd love to. I'll see if Steph is free.'

'You made up then?'

I'd forgotten he'd walked in on our disagreement.

'Yeah, she's tough to stay cross with,' I said quietly.

'And how about your other friend?'

'Zara, I don't know. I haven't heard. I'm not particularly close to her.'

The poor woman must be going through hell.

I kissed him again to wish him goodnight, but it became slower and deeper. It would have been so easy to take it further, but that was not what we had agreed. Finally, I pulled back, and he looked at me, his eyes dark and longing.

I smiled, 'I'm going to go to bed now.'

He accepted my decision with a half-smile and looked at the floor. As I stepped away, he caught my fingers, and I looked back.

'Good night,' he whispered.

I lay in bed, wide awake, thinking about him lying in his bed. Every time I closed my eyes, I could see him, and my stomach was so knotted that I swore it felt more toned. I desperately tried to go to sleep, but it wouldn't take me, despite being tired. His eyes, toned back and arms, fringe, and lips. I was still lying there an hour later, and I needed the bathroom.

I washed my hands quickly, half drying them, and crept back onto the landing. I jumped as I spotted Will leaning against his door frame, looking at me in my night shirt and shorts. I stopped, staring straight back in the half-light, not sure if he was waiting to use the bathroom or whether he was waiting for me.

He put his hand out. I still wasn't sure of his intentions, but I automatically took it. Pulling me into his bedroom, into him while he shut the door and then kissed me so forcefully, I was pushed back against it. Something in me switched. Suddenly, I wanted him, and the tension I held in my belly radiated outwards as I responded in kind.

His hands were everywhere, and I could feel my legs going between the kissing and the touching and the kneading. He pulled away for a moment, took my hand, and led me to the edge of the bed, gently pushing me back, allowing me to hold his hands so I didn't fall, and then took the opportunity to remove his top. He was joining me seconds later, pushing himself against my pelvis while I wrapped my legs around him. He groaned quietly while kissing me as I explored his back with my hands.

We didn't talk. We didn't need to. We were silently reading each other, enjoying each other. He pulled back and began lifting my nightshirt, but I took over and wriggled out of it. He stopped for a second, drinking me in, looking at my tits, and then suddenly took my nipple in his mouth, taking my breath away. His tongue explored as my hand found his waistband, and he moved back slightly, giving my hand room to touch him. He was so hard that I could feel the velvety veins pulsing under my touch. I took him in my hand. It felt big. He pushed and then found a rhythm. I was looking into his eyes. The power I had over him was so arousing.

He sat back on his knees suddenly, forcing me to lose grip. He pulled my shorts down and off without ceremony. Then, holding my hips still, my legs were practically shaking. He leaned down and kissed my waist. His hand moved between my legs, brushing his thumb over my clit, my hips jolting reflexively. I was so wet, it was almost embarrassing. His kisses moved down until he kissed me right on target. I moaned. I could have let myself go right there and then, but

I wanted more. He was using his thumb to explore, coating himself in my arousal before slowly pushing it inside me. We found a rhythm again until I couldn't take any more.

'Will!' I whispered with urgency, and he stopped, slowly removing his thumb and trailing his kisses back up towards my mouth.

'Do you want me to see if I can find a condom?' he whispered back.

'Yes!' I said without hesitation.

I couldn't believe I had let it get this far without thinking about it. And I couldn't work out if he asked me to clarify if I wanted it to go that far or whether he was checking if I was protected by another means. Then, standing up, he pulled his shorts off completely and rummaged around in his bag. I hadn't used a condom since I was about fifteen. I had gone on the pill, and later Mike had had the snip after having the boys, so there had been no need. Thinking about it, I felt like a teenager. I couldn't help but grin. Will held up the shiny foil in his hand like a trophy, but I could see he needed some work before it would be worth opening it.

I sat up as he reached the bed and tucked my knees underneath me, licking my lips. I gently held onto his hips and kissed his abdomen. He was getting harder by the second with anticipation. I looked up at him, and he gazed straight back, his fringe hanging loose as I took him in my mouth. I worked my tongue around the tip and occasionally took him in deeper, teasing him until he took hold of the back of my head with both hands and thrust himself right to the back of my throat, practically choking me. He growled and quickly withdrew, ripping the packet open and smoothing the condom down himself. He looked at me so intently I thought he would smack me for a split second, but he roughly pushed me back onto the bed and held himself over me. I looked straight at him, wondering why he was stalling. His lips brushed over mine, and then he kissed me softly.

'Will, what are you doing?' I whispered.

'Savouring the moment,' he said as he took hold of himself, brushing his tip over me before slowly sliding inside.

'Ahhh,' I said as my pelvis arched up to meet him.

He was big, and I wasn't sure if I could take it. He stayed still for a moment, clearly having had to do this on many occasions, and then dipped his thumb into my mouth before circling it around my clit again, helping me relax. Wow, he knew what he was doing.

Gradually, he started to move, rotating his hips at first, and then the pace began to change. His thrusts became stronger and more insistent. My legs parted even further, taking him in. Suddenly everything intensified. My skin began to tingle all over, radiating towards the source of the pleasure. Every fold, every follicle responded to the slightest movement or touch. 'Are you close? because I seriously can't hold on for much longer,' he admitted.

'Yes, so close,' I pined.

He picked up speed and pinched one of my nipples, which was enough to tip me over, my orgasm rippling through me as he thrust into me for his own release. My insides were still contracting as our breathing slowed.

I lay there speechless as he gently pulled out of me and removed the condom, tying it in a knot and tossing it on top of his t-shirt. I moved on to my side to give him some room to lie on his side beside me. He cradled his head in his hand, brushed my hair away from my face, and kissed me softly.

'I'm not sure that was classed as taking it slow,' he said, smiling.

'I told you that things get out of control when I'm close to you,' I replied, smiling back.

'Are you seriously trying to tell me that you haven't been with anyone since Mike?' he asked, raising his eyebrows questionably.

'Not even a kiss.'

We lay in comfortable silence for a while. I wished this moment would last forever. It felt so easy when I was actually with him. Why did he have to live in bloody Brooklyn? Damn you stars, and your crappy aligning. Will was starting to nod off, but I did not want the boys to know I was in here in the morning. I couldn't quite believe what I had done. It had been so risky with the boys across the landing, but so exciting.

'Will, I need to go back to bed,' I whispered.

'Hmmm,' he said sleepily.

I shook him gently, and he opened his eyes.

'I'm going to bed,' I started to move.

'What, again?' he said, confused.

'No! I need to go to bed before I fall asleep, and the boys realise I'm in here in the morning.'

A big grin spread across his face. Was he drunk? I climbed over him, picked up my things, and slipped out of the room.

Chapter 10

The following morning, I struggled to get up, finally dragging myself out of bed when the boys were about to leave for the day. After saying goodbye, I switched the coffee machine on to warm up and sent the dogs out into the garden. My body ached in places that it hadn't ached in such a long time, and I felt sore but in a good way. When I returned to the kitchen, Will was standing in the doorway, and my stomach flipped.

'Good morning, beautiful,' he said, his eyes following me as I walked to the fridge to get the milk.

'Good morning... did you sleep well?'

'The first half of the night, not so, but the second half of the night was good,' he said, still watching me as I poured the milk into the jug.

'Oh?' I said, frowning. 'What was the turning point?' I smiled, biting my thumbnail coquettishly, looking straight at him. He moved toward me, and I turned before he reached me to put the milk jug under the frothing nozzle. Will stood behind me, and just as he took a breath in to say something in my ear, I turned on the steamer. I was biting my lip, trying not to laugh as he whipped me around to face him, laughing, then cupped my face in his hands and kissed me.

As the steamer came to an end, he said, 'so, you're okay about last night? The tempo has kind of stepped up a gear.'

I put my hands around his waist. 'I'm not okay about the fact we had sex across the hall from the boys, but I'm good with the tempo.'

He nodded, smiling, and then kissed me again.

'Coffee?'

'Yes, please,' he replied.

Once we had finished our coffees, Will and I took the dogs for a walk in the woods. It was a bright but fresh morning. Will looked out of place amongst the dog walkers with their elbow-patched jackets and mock riding boots, and people kept staring, but he didn't seem to care.

'I think I've managed to sort my schedule to maximise our time together. I'm waiting for Alysa's confirmation that the additional flights have been booked.'

'And who is Alysa exactly?' Hoping Will would elaborate.

'I told you, she's our TM.' Troublemaker? I looked at him, confused. 'Sorry, our Tour Manager, she grew up with us, lived on the same street as us when we were kids. Speaking of flights, do you have a valid passport?'

'Yes... I think.'

'Well, check. I think she needs your passport number.'

'Will, I do have to work, you know.'

'Don't stress. It's all cool.' He lobbed the ball, and the dogs pegged it off, chasing it down the hill. Completely unaware that I was desperately trying to remember where the passports were.

It was nearly time for the boys to be collected. Will was in his room making calls, and the boys were changing and packing their bags. Then, the doorbell went, and I flung the door open, fully expecting it to be Mike but instead, it was a delivery. A large square box, what on earth could that be? 'Will Reynolds?' the delivery guy asked.

'Erm, yes, I can take that for him.' The driver handed me the box, which was incredibly light for such a large item, and he lifted what I thought would be his phone to take a picture as proof of delivery but instead, he said, 'Smile.' He lifted a giant camera and snapped a picture of me. I stood there for a second, stunned, while he took about twenty more shots quickly before I had the where with all to put the box down and shut the door.

Shit!

I rushed upstairs.

'Will!' I called, knocking on his door. 'There was a man at the door. With... with a camera,' I said, out of breath.

I didn't know which piece of information to get out first.

'Fuck. I've gotta go.' He ended his call and came to the door. 'Are you okay?'

'Yes, I'm fine, but they took a picture of me. I thought it was a delivery. He had a box. I'm sorry.'

'Mum, what's going on?' Frankie and Paddy had come out onto the landing.

'It's fine, but I think there's a reporter outside.'

'Wicked!' Paddy said, rushing over to his bedroom window. 'There's not just one, Mum. There's a few out here.'

'Err, Paddy, it's probably best you step away from the window,' Will suggested.

'Yes, Paddy, come here,' I added.

'So, you are *Will Reynolds*?' Frankie asked.

'I told you he was. I knew you wouldn't believe me,' Paddy said. Everyone looked at Paddy. 'What?' He asked, looking back at us all.

'How many people have you told Paddy?' I asked.

'No one! Well, I told Jason, but I swore him to secrecy.'

'Paddy,' I said in the most disappointed-mum voice I could muster.

'Let's not start placing blame here,' Will said tactfully. 'It could have been anyone, the girl from the restaurant? Someone may have even followed us.'

'Us?' Frankie said, looking at me, then to Will, and then back to me. 'I knew it was a bloody date.'

This wasn't quite how I'd imagined this conversation going.

'You're seeing each other?' Paddy asked.

'Who's seeing who?' I heard as Mike came striding up the stairs. Or that one, I thought. 'And why is there a load of people outside? Are they doing some sort of *History of Clevedon* film? There are cameramen out there.'

After an awkward introduction and explanation, Will returned to his room to finish his calls and inform Alysa that the paparazzi were there. The boys returned to their rooms to finish packing while Mike and I headed downstairs. My mind was reeling, wondering what the press would do with that picture of me. I must have looked so startled. How did they find me?

'So, you wanted to talk,' I said as Mike sat down, looking pensive.

'I've been made redundant,' he stated. I looked straight at him.

'Oh God, I'm so sorry.'

This *was* serious. Mike worked as a civil servant and had done since he left school. He'd worked his way up and was on a fairly decent salary.

'Yeah, it's a bit of a kick in the balls. I found out last week. I get a bit of a payout because I've been there for so long, but it's hardly a retirement fund.'

'Oh no, what are you going to do?'

'Well, I've done some figures, but ultimately, I think we'll have to sell the house unless I get another job.'

'What?' I almost shouted. 'The house?'

'Worst-case scenario, yes. Unless you can buy me out or I find another job in the next couple of weeks.'

He knew I couldn't afford to buy him out unless I won the bloody lottery and finding another job in a week was highly unlikely.

'Anyway, I know it's a bit of a shock, but we'll work it out. The house would have gone up in value since we bought it, and if we both have to find something smaller, maybe I could have one of the boys live with me?'

This was all too much. I really didn't want to cry in front of Mike, but a tear escaped and rolled down my cheek, splashing on the floor and then another until I was actually blubbing. Mike went off to find a tissue, and he gently patted my back which felt utterly strange, as I blew my nose and tried to recover myself. Mike called for the boys, and they hugged me while Mike promised to explain what was happening to them in the car. I waved them off, blotchy-faced and holding back the tears.

I walked back into the kitchen, and my tears retraced their tracks down my cheeks. I leaned against the counter and slid down the cupboard door, hugging my knees in. My thoughts scattered in a million different directions.

'Hey, hey, what's wrong?' Will was crouching beside me.

I didn't know how long I'd been there, ten minutes, an hour. Will held out a tissue for me.

'Is it the press?' he asked, concern in his voice.

'Mike has lost his job and wants to sell the house,' I explained, and Will took a sharp intake of breath through his teeth and winced. He sat down beside me, assuming the same position. 'He thinks we'll have to find smaller places and split the boys up. I haven't even thought about what will happen to my business. I'll have to rent somewhere, which will cost a fortune.'

He put his arm around me. 'I know it's a shock, but these things have a way of working themselves out. Don't stress.'

'That's easy for you to say,' I sniffed.

'This probably isn't going to help matters, but the media are all over those pictures, just to warn you.'

Oh no, I looked up at him. I must have looked a state. He kissed me on the forehead and pushed himself up. Then, holding out his hands for me to take, he said, 'Come on, I've booked us into a hotel for the night. We can get some room service.'

'Is that necessary?' I said, taking his hands.

'It's probably for the best in case fans start turning up... I can run you a bath?' he suggested, trying to think of something appealing.

'With bubbles?' I asked pathetically.

'With all the bubbles.' He smiled.

'What about the dogs?' I remembered suddenly.

After realising I could bribe Steph with a ticket for the gig on Saturday in exchange for an overnight dog sit, we escaped through the back gate. Bill and Terry picked us up, leaving the paparazzi behind, and we headed to the hotel. It was super swanky. The bed alone was bigger than my bedroom at home. Twin basins, a roll-top bath, and a walk-in shower in the bathroom. I couldn't see the view because it was dark, but the driveway's length and the building's size suggested it would be beautiful. I put my bag on the luggage rack, and Will looked in the minibar.

'What do you fancy?' he asked.

You! I thought as he bent over, peering inside the fridge. 'Umm?'

'Or I could order something up? Let's do that,' he said, answering his own question.

So, I sat in the bath with a glass of fizz in hand, and sloshed the bubbles around, occasionally putting my foot up to see my toes peep through the bubbles. I was desperately trying to enjoy myself and forget about everything, but it wasn't working. Someone had followed us or recognised me and contacted the press. I didn't quite feel safe, and I was worried about what the press would say about me. That coupled with the whole redundancy thing and potentially having to split the boys up.

What a day.

I could see Will sitting on the bed through the door, doing something on his laptop. He shook his head and then picked up his phone. 'Have you seen the latest? It's totally out of order.' He glanced over at me and caught my eye. 'I'll call you back.' He hung up.

'Everything ok?' I asked tentatively.

'You might need to phone the boys, maybe your parents... possibly a few friends?' I sat up, causing a wave of water to slosh over the end of the bath.

'Why, what's happened?' Will took a towel and put it on the floor to soak up the water and crouched by the side of the bath.

'They've fabricated a story about you leaving Mike for me.'

That didn't make sense. Mike and I weren't together.

'They have a picture of me coming into the house with the dogs.' The dogs... that was before our lunch date. Someone must have spotted Will when he arrived in Clevedon. 'A picture of you answering the door, and a picture of you waving to the boys as they got in the car with Mike.' Oh, my God. The boys? 'Alysa has contacted our Publicist to take them down, but it's unlikely, if I'm honest. I'm sorry.'

'It's not your fault,' I said automatically, simultaneously wondering who I was going to call first.

'It kinda is.' Will took another towel and put his hand out for me to step out of the bath, but instead of wrapping the towel around me, he drew me in, feeding his long arms around me and getting completely soaked in the process. We kissed, my hair dripping all over our faces. He discarded the towel and then stepped back to take his jacket off. That jacket was like a second skin, and he always wore it.

He took the opportunity to stare at me, and I immediately tried to cover myself with my arms as I went all goosebumpy.

'You're beautiful,' he said as he took my hands and placed them by my sides, his eyes moving from my face to my shoulders and then to my breasts. There it was again, the electricity coursing between us, and despite feeling utterly unveiled, I was under some kind of spell in his presence.

He delicately lifted my boob to his mouth and covered my nipple, my insides bloomed, and I wanted him, needed him, like a drug. I pulled his t-shirt off, and he kissed me again while I undid his jeans. I didn't want to be the only one naked any longer. He was fully erect, happily springing free as I pulled his boxers down. It was a sight to behold, and I still couldn't quite believe how it fit.

Will took my hand and led me over to the bed. 'Lie down,' he said.

'I'm wet,' I stated.

He smiled salaciously, and I realised what I had said. 'I meant... the sheets... the bath.'

He moved forward, forcing me back, and climbed on top of me.

'So, we ask for more bedding,' he said, kissing me behind my ear.

'And the lights?' I said, and he looked at me quizzically before realising my unease and reached over to lower them but not switch them off.

Damn.

He began a slow, thorough descent. Surveying every scar, blemish, and feature as he kissed, licked, and traced. I was so wet by the time he reached his destination that additional bedding would be required.

He pushed my thighs further apart, continuing his survey with a leisurely pace as if he was trying to identify exactly what it was that would make me gasp or arch my back. Eventually, I had to hold my breath, bite my lip and look at the ceiling. If he so much as moved his tongue or his fingers once more, it would set me off. As if he sensed my impending orgasm, he moved back up, kissing me as he did so until he was level with me. He looked into my eyes like he was cataloguing every shade and fleck of colour in my irises, and then he murmured, 'can I fuck you now?'

The breath I was holding escaped as a '*yes*' fell from my lips, and before I knew it, he was rolling a condom down his length. He lifted my leg as he moved back into position, staring into my eyes once more. I looked directly back at him. Losing myself in his arresting emerald eyes, framed with dark lashes, he began to inch his way inside me. I tried to hold his gaze, but as my insides adjusted, I had to close my eyes for a moment while suppressing a moan. I sensed he was trying to keep control over his own breathing pattern or maybe his body, as he appeared to be clenching his jaw when I looked back.

The second my body relaxed around him, he let go, driving a steady fast pace, kissing me. Devouring me in every sense. It was punishingly delicious, and the kissing... the kissing was hedonistic. He was so God damn good at this. I was trying hard to push my thoughts of the reasons behind his expertise aside, and I began to imagine all the sexy women he had slept with.

Will broke away from our kiss, 'stay with me.' he said breathlessly, catching my gaze.

He kissed my neck, just below my ear and whispered, 'you take me to a sentient place, Lucy.'

I didn't quite know how to respond, it was as if he could read me and wanted to put me at ease, but instead, I felt unmasked. He was back on my lips in less than a second.

Without breaking our kiss, Will pushed my leg up higher, his thrusts becoming deeper, and I half sighed, half whimpered into his mouth as I began to climb. Will's momentum sped up, taking me higher and higher and just as I was on the brink, Will pulled away from our kiss. He pressed his forehead against mine, studying my eyes as I fell apart, and he pounded his release into me. He didn't stop staring at me until our breathing had plateaued.

'Amazing,' he murmured.

I was still basking in the warmth of our post-coital bubble when I heard my phone. I tried to ignore it, but that would not be possible.

'I knew we wouldn't have long,' Will said.

'What shall I say?' I asked, suddenly hesitant.

'What do you want to say?'

That wasn't fair. He was indirectly asking me to confirm whether we were an item or not, and I didn't feel that decision was up to me.

'What you say to your friends and family is what matters. Everything else is hearsay,' he said as if to clarify, but that didn't make it any easier.

I called Frankie and Paddy first. Paddy thought it was *sick* and was clearly excited. Frankie was more reserved and asked if I was okay. 'I'm fine. I'm staying in a hotel.'

'With Will?' Frankie asked.

Hmmm, confirming that would clarify that we were sleeping together. He was an adult. Why would I lie to him?

'Yes, with Will.'

Will splashed shaving foam off his face in the bathroom and turned to look at me. I looked at him, and he smiled before getting in the shower.

I rang Mum next.

'Yes, I know that's what it says, Mum, but they've made it up.' I rolled my eyes, knowing she couldn't see me. 'Yes, I know it's a terrible picture.'

Will laughed, and I threw a cushion at him as he stepped out of the shower. For Christ's sake, why didn't I wait to see if they'd actually seen the bloody news rather than telling them where to find it. In the end, I wrote a text reply to one person and then copied it to whoever contacted me that I cared about. It was surprising how many people got in touch that I hadn't spoken to for years.

We lay on the bed in our bathrobes watching TV, phones off, laptops away, and two vast trays of leftover room service on the floor. Will didn't think it was a good idea to go down to the bar, so I felt a little restless, imprisoned in our room.

'Do you have to deal with this a lot?' I asked.

'What? Entertaining women in hotel rooms?'

I gave his arm a shove and then thought, actually, I'd really like to know the answer to that.

'I don't normally deal with it. I was only concerned because, this time, it affected you. It kind of comes with the territory, and I've learnt to ignore it. Alysa deals with it. That's what she's paid for. But, I've gotta warn you, it could get pretty shitty. It depends on how the media hype it up and what spin they decide to take on it, but you need to remember that what we say and do when we're together is... all that's true.'

I reflected for a moment, wondering if I'd done something in the past that the media could pick me up on, but I drew a blank. 'And women in hotel rooms?'

He laughed. 'I don't think it's affecting any other women in hotel rooms.'

'Will, you know what I'm getting at,' I said as I sat up. 'I have been quite open with you about my past, but you have been... allusive.'

'Does it really matter? It's in the past.'

No, but I want to know. I'm a girl, I thought. I pursed my lips to show my annoyance. Will sat up too.

'I've been with... a lot of women,' he begrudgingly admitted, and despite my suspicions, it still stung. 'One who I thought was the one, but she cheated on me. The end.'

Oh.

He lay back down and stared back at the TV. Well, that didn't go quite according to plan.

'I'm sorry. I just... wanted to know.'

He didn't say anything, just staring at the TV, and I felt really awkward. I sat there for a bit, contemplating my options. I could go down to the bar. I could go home. I could go to my mum and dad's. I mean, all this shit and none of it had anything to do with me. I could go home, and it would just all blow over, and I could go back to my everyday life, and Will could get on with his.

I started getting dressed.

'What are you doing?' Will asked.

'Packing,' I said as I walked into the bathroom to get my sponge bag. Will was in there like a shot.

'You can't just go,' he stated, spinning me around and looking at me, stricken. I looked back at him, not sure of what to say. After a moment, he took an enormous breath. 'I don't wanna look back at the past. I just wanna concentrate on the future. Is that okay?'

He took my face in his hands, searching my eyes as if he was trying to take control of my actions. 'Come to bed with me.'

I closed my eyes with a thousand thoughts flying through my brain. I couldn't help but think we were hurtling towards brick wall. Was I going to divert and take the easy route, or would we crash into it head-on? My mum always used to say, *sleep on it*. Will kissed me, it was his weapon, and I was completely helpless, the electricity sparking between us again.

━━━◉━━━

I woke to an empty bed, light shooting through the gaps in the curtains, and I was entangled in the sheets. I had slept but not well. Having the sense, I had been dreaming... or were they nightmares? I did not feel easy, something had shifted, and I felt a strange anxiety.

I was in the shower when Will came into the bathroom. He closed the door and leaned against one of the oversized basins, crossing his arms and pushing his sunglasses onto his head. He did not look happy. I rinsed the shampoo out of my hair, grabbed a towel, wrapped it around me, and took another towel to dry it. Will watched me the entire time. When I turned the shower off, I could hear voices I didn't recognise coming from the bedroom. What the hell? The anxious feeling I had when I woke enveloped me.

'Will, what is going on?'

'We need to talk,' he said, and I could feel the colour draining from my face. Was he going to end it? Instead, he pulled me into him. Ok, maybe not.

'Who is that in the bedroom?' I asked.

Will bit his lip and looked at the floor.

'I need you to hear me out.' I reached up and made a half-arsed attempt at drying my hair before throwing the towel into the empty bath and turning back to him. 'The press have gone a bit crazy over the story.' He had my full attention. 'Alysa has arranged for a couple of guys from the media team to give you a briefing.' A what? 'They just want to tell you what to say to your family and friends and give you some advice on dealing with the media.'

'Tell me?' I repeated. He closed his eyes.

'Advise you.' He corrected himself. I looked at him then, and he looked tired. What time did he get up?

'What does a bit crazy mean exactly?'

He looked me straight in the eye and then lifted his hand to cradle the side of my neck. I leaned into his hand, afraid of what he was going to say.

'They've done their research. The latest headline is, *Serving the King, not his Wife*, and they mentioned the boy's school.'

Will let that sink in for a moment. As in Civil Servant... as in me? The school? What. The. Fuck? Tears pricked my eyes, and I closed them tight, hoping I was still dreaming.

'I'm sorry. I was really hoping they wouldn't snap.' He closed his eyes and shook his head. 'Don't run.'

I wanted to run, run until I couldn't run anymore. I wanted to shout. I wanted to turn back time. Mike would be livid. The boys... I didn't actually know what the boy's reaction would be. But everyone that knew me, and everyone I cared about would surely know this was a complete load of bullshit because they all knew I wasn't with Mike. And Will... here was Will holding me, hoping I wouldn't run. A single tear rolled down my cheek, and Will stopped it in its tracks with his thumb.

'What you say to your friends and family is what matters. Everything else is hearsay,' he whispered, repeating what he had said yesterday, but it held so much more gravity today. He kissed me and then placed his forehead against mine. 'They know what they're talking about. They're professionals.'

I took a deep breath. 'I'm not talking to them in my towel,' I said.

Will smiled, realising I was accepting the situation, enveloping me in the biggest, most secure hug I could imagine. He held me there for the longest time, our hearts beating together.

'I'll get your things,' he said eventually.

An hour later, I'd received a crash course in all things media-related. They had switched all my social media accounts to private, not that I used them much, but I had already racked up several hundred follower requests overnight. I wasn't to talk to these reporters; I was to comment to those reporters; if I was unsure, I had to contact them. My security would be monitored and reviewed regularly. Still, they didn't feel I needed any at the moment. However, it was recommended that cameras should be installed around the house. Could I take a sabbatical? Seriously? Be aware that reporters might pose as clients.

Christ.

I should drive the kids to school. I shouldn't walk the dogs in secluded places. I should be careful when opening post. The list went on, and my tiny brain was utterly fried when they left the hotel room.

Will showed them out. I was speechless, had nothing left, and was scared. Like a rabbit in the headlights.

'I'm sorry, I know it's a lot to take on,' Will said as I nodded vacantly.

'A lot to take on,' I repeated as I was clearly unable to think up my own sentences. He scooped me up, lay me on the bed, and came to lie down beside me. How had it come to this so damn quickly? I was really conscious that my phone was still off, and this time we had, was the calm before the storm. I was just staring at the ceiling, and Will stroked my hair, his leg over mine.

'What are you thinking?' he asked, eventually.

'I have so many *thinks* going around in my head, I can't actually pick one to concentrate on. They're all kind of mushed together in this massive swirling clump,' I replied honestly.

'Thinks?' he said, smiling and kissing my nose. 'I know what you need to do,' he said, getting up. 'You need to drink coffee and make a plan.'

I pushed myself up onto my elbows as he picked up the phone to order the coffees and started pulling drawers open in the desk until he found a pad and pen. He pulled the chair out and walked back over to me, offering his hand for me to take. He pulled me up, guided me over to the chair, and sat me down.

'Write a list, make a plan, get everything down. Then I'll get Terry to take you home.'

I looked up at him, my anxiety blooming.

'Take me home?' I asked as my words were caught in a slight gasp. I really didn't want to go back to those reporters on my own.

'Terry will take you in, make sure you're okay. I've gotta meet up with the others. We've got a whole bunch of pre-gig shit to do.' He lifted my chin and kissed me. 'Do your plan. You'll feel better.'

I began scrawling on the hotel-branded notepaper. I had to call Mike, then the boys. Call my parents again. Then Steph and check how the dogs were. Call the school and then set up an autoreply for work.

And then I needed to go on a bloody long walk.

Chapter 11

Once Terry had safely delivered me home via the back gate. I switched on my phone. I had to wait for it to stop pinging before calling Mike. I had so many text messages, not just from people I knew but from random mobile numbers. I didn't have time to look.

It rang once, 'Lu!! What the hell?'

He was mad. I knew he would be. He did not like being in the limelight. 'Where have you been?' He breathed heavily. He was walking at a pace. 'With him?' He said it with such venom. 'Lu... are you there?'

I didn't want to fight with him, so I kept calm as I always did. He already knew I was with Will because the boys would have told him.

'Yes, I'm here. I switched my phone off for a bit. I'm sorry. We needed to come up with a plan.'

'We? So, it's official, you're a *we* now? So, you're with Will Reynolds? This is insane.'

I wanted to say yes, isn't it exciting? Are you happy for me? I wanted him to rejoice in this moment with me like we used to when something exciting happened in our family, a promotion or booking a holiday, but that was clearly not going to happen.

'We are dating. It's early days,' I said, trying to play it down. 'I'm sorry about the article.'

'It's not cool, Lucy. I've got colleagues contacting me. I had to call my mother,' he said, but the anger in his words had dissipated.

I'm sure his mother, Mary Jeannette QC, would have been delighted, having to use her precious time to speak to her son.

'I'm sorry. I'm sure it will all blow over soon. It's mainly local press,' I said, not believing my own words.

'I think the boys should stay at mine,' he said decisively.

'What? How is that going to work with Frankie's job, and after school activities?' I asked.

There was a pause, and I could tell he was thinking about how that would impact his social life, so I used it to my advantage.

'Maybe we should ask the boys what they would like to do,' I suggested, knowing full well they'd want to stay here.

'Fine,' he said with annoyance. 'I've got to go,' he said, and hung up before giving me the opportunity to say goodbye.

I rolled my eyes and proceeded to sift through some of my text messages to try to find Steph's.

Are you ok? This was from Cara, who I'd sat next to in year nine science class. She hadn't thought about me since school, but now she thought it was a good time to drop me a line. *Saw the article. Sending best wishes to you and your family.* Who she'd never met and wouldn't ever meet.

Then there were messages from people I didn't know. They were scarier. Some asked if I could arrange a meeting with Will. Could I get tickets to their next show? Some were insulting messages. I had a feeling I was going to have to change my phone number if this carried on. All I wanted to do was find Steph's text. Instead, I called her.

'Here she is! Girlfriend of biggest rockstar known to man,' she said excitedly. 'Bet Mike was mightily impressed with that article.'

'He was livid, and I wouldn't say girlfriend. We're seeing each other,' I corrected her, and she guffawed dismissively.

'What are you wearing tonight for the gig? And how are we getting there?' she asked.

'Do you think we should still go? I'm feeling a bit... anxious.'

'Of course, we should still go! You need to have a drink and let your hair down,' she replied, and I wondered whether she was being slightly selfish as I expected that's what she wanted to do.

'Okay... Jeans?' I suggested. It was a gig after all. 'Will is sending a car at seven.'

'Yay! See you at six, you little minx.'

Then she hung up! It was nice to know she was excited. I was too, but I couldn't help but feel anxious. What if someone recognised me? What if there were some people there that had sent those text messages?

Steph brought a bottle of fizz round for us to drink before we went, but the car pulled up outside before finishing the first glass. I wore my skinny jeans, red Allstars, and a fitted black top that twisted at the front, creating a V neck at the top, revealing possibly a bit too much cleavage and a slight lift at the bottom, showing a small triangle of my waist. Big hoop earrings, smokey eyes, and no bag. Pockets would have to do this evening. Bags meant you couldn't hold two drinks, three if you included your mouth.

On the back seat of the car was a big white envelope. Inside were two AAA passes for Steph and I and a note from Will, *Can't wait to see you x*. Steph put hers around her neck straight away for a selfie of her looking like a maniac, then she turned the phone to include me, and I held my middle finger up.

'What does AAA stand for?' Steph asked.

'I dunno, something to do with batteries?' I guessed.

'No, it stands for something,' she said, turning the pass to see if there was an explanation.

'Anyone and anything,' I suggested as she searched it up on her phone. 'Arses and anal,' I added for good measure.

'Hmmm, America Automobile Association, maybe they're a sponsor?'

'Maybe,' I mused.

'You are so loved up, Lu! It's radiating from you.' I smiled, my cheeks pinching. 'Is he...' she raised her eyebrows, '*you know*,' gesturing with her hands to gauge the appropriate length.

'I couldn't possibly discuss that with you,' I said in my most hoity-toity accent and then gauged with my hands. We both laughed, really laughed. The car pulled up at the venue, and before we got out, Terry informed us that he would escort us in. Steph shot me a glance as if to say, *you've been told*.

It made me feel uneasy. There was a long line of people outside, three deep, and right near the front was Big Jeff, a true Bristol legend who attended all the gigs. He didn't know me, but everyone knew him. Above was a great big sign lit up with, 'The 'king Band plus special guests.' There were three lines with ticket booths, and as we walked up to them, a bouncer unhooked the little gate. 'Ladies,' he said, gesturing with his arm for us to walk through. The woman in the booth scanned our QR codes on the passes and simply pointed for us to go through.

It was weird standing in an empty venue. Makes you realise it's the people that make the atmosphere and also how sticky the floor is. Terry disappeared, and Steph and I went upstairs to the bar. My phone vibrated in my pocket.

You're here! X

It was Will. I looked around, but I couldn't see him.

Steph ordered two double vodka and cokes.

'This should get us in the mood,' she said, handing me the plastic cup with far too little coke in it.

'Lucy, over here,' Will called from a side door, waving us over. We went to meet him and headed backstage. Will put his arm around me and squeezed my arse.

'Aww, you two better not start being inappropriate,' Steph chided. 'Otherwise, I'm going home.'

'Hi, Steph,' Will said.

'Whatever,' she said in jest, waving her hand dismissively.

Will took us into a room bustling with people and showed us where the free drinks were. There were a few coffee tables and chairs, but no one was sitting at them. They all wore similar clothes to Will, like it was their uniform, milling about in twos and threes. There was a weird electricity in the room, a mix of nerves and excitement.

An hour later, the number of people had thinned slightly, and I could hear the support band starting up. Steph was engrossed in a debate with some random guy about whether Michael Jackson's music should be allowed airtime on the radio or not, when Will suddenly pulled me into what I can only describe as a cleaning cupboard. Well, it had a mop in it, but I couldn't see much else.

'I'm sorry about last night,' he said. I thought he meant all the media coverage. 'It's not a time of my life I like to remember.' Oh, he meant about his past. 'She, my ex, pretty much managed to screw my whole life over, not just our relationship. It's taken a while to get back on track. If it wasn't for Paul and Jake, I'm not sure where I'd be.'

'I won't mention it again. My lips are sealed.'

I silently pretended to do my lips up like a zip. He gently took hold of my hand and then unexpectedly pushed me against the wall and kissed me insistently. A bolt of energy surged through me as our kiss became more passionate, but I was not about to take it any further with a mop staring at us. I pulled back and tugged my top back into place, wiping my mouth to pick up any smudged lip gloss. Will smiled, respecting my decision.

'How did your plan go?' he asked.

'I spoke to Mike. He's not happy,' I admitted.

'I'm not sure I would be if I were in his position,' he said thoughtfully.

'The boys are okay, their friends have been messaging them, but I think they're quite enjoying the drama.' I rolled my eyes, and Will smiled. 'I think I might need to change my mobile number, though.' Will knitted his eyebrows together. 'I've had a few... unsavoury messages.'

'Have you got your mobile number on social media?' he asked.

'I don't think so...' I wasn't the most tech-savvy person.

'What about your business website?' he enquired.

'Well, yes—it's how my clients get in touch.' I said plainly.

'Take it off,' he said bluntly.

'Will, it's for my business. I can't just take it off,' I replied, sounding a little defensive.

He paused, realising he'd been a bit flippant. 'I'll speak to the team. I'm sure they'll be able to suggest some alternative options.'

I looked down at the floor. I was starting to feel like my life was being managed. Will lifted my chin immediately, searching my eyes.

'I know it's a lot to take on. I'm sorry. Just try to ignore them. The team is there to help, I promise.'

He tried to assure me, and I nodded. He gently kissed me again and cradled my head, trying to soothe my worries. We slipped back into the room, both a little flushed hoping no one would notice. I think we got away with it.

'Will?' I said, pulling on his hand to bring his ear in line with my mouth. 'What does AAA stand for?'

A small smile appeared on his face as he turned, giving me a filthy look, and then leaned in, his lips brushing over my ear.

'Access... *all*... areas,' he said in a low, sexy voice.

Goosebumps scattered across my neck and chest as his hand smoothed down the side of my waist, and round to the front of my hip. His thumb momentarily slipping into the crease at the top of my inner thigh, before pulling back. Quietly chuckling to himself at the shocked expression on my face.

'As in, you can get back here without me escorting you.' He confirmed.

'Oh,' I said, smiling shyly at the double entendre.

'It won't be long until we go on. Do you wanna go out front or watch from the side?'

I looked over at Steph, gesticulating wildly with her arms, chatting and laughing with the same guy. She was clearly taking advantage of the free bar.

'Probably best if we go out front,' I confirmed.

'Okay, well, meet me back here afterwards, yeah?'

He scanned the room quickly, kissed me briefly, and then nodded to Paul and Jake, who, at the same time, made their excuses, and they all disappeared through another door. I spotted Alysa in the corner looking at me, and she immediately looked away. I took a bottle of beer from the bar and moved toward Steph.

'This is Frank. He's part of the crew for *Springs*, the support band.'

'Great to meet you. Shall we get out there? I don't think it will be long before they start.'

We arrived at the main auditorium. It was heaving, and the air-con was struggling against all the hot, sweaty bodies. Steph grabbed my hand and dragged me into the throng of the crowd, following Frank. We found a little space, relatively central and a few metres back from the front.

The lights suddenly dipped low, the chattering petered out, and the crowd turned in unison to face the front. A few people whooped and whistled in the calm before the show. The excitement in the room from the expectant crowd was almost palpable. A spotlight shot down straight onto Will as he strummed the first chord, and all the lights then came up, highlighting the rest of the stage. Will and Paul stepped towards their mics at the same time as the tune started, and the crowd went crazy, surging forward. Steph and I grabbed each other for fear of being pulled in different directions. There was a bit of jostling, but once everyone had found their space, we all fell into the song's beat, dancing, and singing.

I looked up, and Will was jumping around the stage in between choruses, occasionally stopping to put his foot on a monitor to vigorously strum out the chords or turning to face Jake for the heavier sections, swooping back to the mic just in time for the verses. He was in his element.

Steph yanked my arm, 'Stop gawping, you loser,' she shouted right in my ear.

I pushed her back as we grinned at each other and danced, jumping around. The next song took a slower pace, and as we stood swaying, thoughts of Mike, the house, the media, and the kids crept in. Why now? We couldn't split the boys up. It wasn't fair. How would we choose? I hoped it wouldn't come to that.

Steph signalled with the universal sign for sipping a drink. I nodded and followed her out of the crowd and up the stairs toward the bar.

There was a different vibe at the bar. More chilled out, and we could talk at a relatively normal level. Groups of people stood about chatting, and actually, there was a great view of the stage. As we stood watching, I told Steph about the situation.

'He'll find a job, babe,' she said with utter certainty. 'I can keep a look out if you like. Is he on one of the professional networking sites?'

I had no idea, but it would be fantastic if she could help in any way.

'And this stuff with the press will die down. I expect the press in the UK are particularly interested at the moment because they're touring, and everyone's talking about them.'

Maybe she was right. I really hoped so.

'Hold that. I've gotta go for a piss,' Steph said.

She was all style, that girl. I turned back towards the band, leaning over the railings.

It wasn't long before I realised someone was leaning over the railings to my right. I glanced across. A tall man with short dark hair and a rather messy goaty beard had joined me, too close for comfort. He didn't look at me, but after a while, he said, 'You should steer clear of him.' He nodded towards the stage. 'He's bad news.'

Who was this guy, and how did he know me?

'I'm sorry, do I know you?'

'Lucy, right?'

He looked over. His eyes were just like Will's. He had a similar accent and the same 'uniform', it was uncanny, but his face was thinner, and pock-marked. His hair was quite greasy, and his hands were dirty on closer inspection.

'He'll screw you over and then dump your ass.'

I glanced over my left shoulder towards the toilets, willing Steph to come back because I didn't want to spend a second longer with this man. He was repulsive. When I turned back, he'd gone. I looked around, but he had disappeared entirely.

What the hell?

I told Steph all about it when she got back. She didn't even seem fazed. In fact, she brushed it off, saying that he was likely to be a deluded fan. She gulped the remains of her drink down and put her arm around me. 'You're gonna have to get used to this, Daniels. Come on, let's get back down there.'

We rejoined the crowd. We couldn't find Frank, so we snuck down the side and found a pretty good position. The sea of people moved to the beat with such enthusiasm. I thought seeing your fans like this must be an amazing reward. As the show went on, during a guitar swap, Will swiped a bottle of water from one of the girls at the front of the stage and, after taking a gulp, dowsed himself with the rest, causing a ripple of shrieks. He unhooked the mic from the stand, and Jake took a lighter approach on the drums while Paul found a moment to swig his own drink.

'Good evening Bristol,' he shouted, a little out of breath. The crowd clapped and roared. 'Sorry, it's taken us a while to get here.' More applause, and someone shouted a song request as Will stood there addressing the crowd. 'Shit happens,' he added, and they launched into another song that everyone knew. The whole room sang along. It was like karaoke on drugs. Steph took hold of my hand and lifted it in the air swaying from side to side, singing her heart out.

I told Steph to wait while I nipped off to the loo, using my pass to access the one's backstage. As I washed my hands, Alysa came out of one of the cubicles.

'Hello again,' she said in a monotone way.

'Hi,' I said, smiling brightly, almost to make up for her tone. As I reapplied my lipstick, she took what looked like a tiny metal version of a smoothie straw out of her pocket and used it to scoop up some white powder from a small plastic bag. She snorted it up her nose right in front of me. I didn't say anything and peered into the mirror, pretending I had something in my eye. She walked towards the door, but just before she left, she said, 'Enjoy it while it lasts.' And she turned and walked out. What a bitch! I didn't know what her problem was, but she clearly had it in for me.

Thankfully I found Steph almost straight away. The band was nowhere to be seen. Shit, I had missed the end, but someone next to me shouted, 'encore,' and it was like a domino effect until the whole room was chanting. 'Encore, encore...' Eventually, the lights came back up on the stage, and the band hurried back to their places. They ended the show with two more banging tunes, and before the last few notes were played, Will reared up towards the mic again and shouted, 'Thanks for having us.' And they left, leaving our ears ringing.

'That was amazing,' Steph said.

'It was fantastic,' I agreed. 'I promised Will I'd meet him backstage afterwards. You coming?'

Steph looked at her watch. 'You know I love you, but the last thing I wanna do is watch you and Will dry hump each other all night, so I'm gonna go.'

I was slightly disappointed, but it was her call, and she had already fired up the taxi app. We hugged each other, and she squeezed me hard and said, 'look after yourself, okay?' As if she didn't quite believe I could.

I watched her go until I couldn't see her and then turned to make my way backstage.

After scanning my laminate several times, I made it back to the room with the free bar. It was packed. I couldn't see Will, so I squeezed in, weaved my way back to where the cupboard was, and then spotted him sitting on one of the chairs, feet up on the coffee table and a beer in hand. It seemed that everyone in the room wanted to talk to him, and he was only too happy to oblige, thanking everyone for their compliments and clinking bottles with people as they moved around the room. I felt a bit out of place. I saw Alysa stalk up behind Will and whisper something in his ear. He frowned and brushed her away like an annoying fly. I could see from her face that she was not impressed. I turned to see what was left to drink. The bar had been demolished, but a couple of beers were left, so I took one and took a long swig. As I turned back, Will spotted me and signalled for me to come over.

I couldn't quite get through, what with all the people standing around wanting to be the next person to speak to him, so Will stood up, and everyone parted, a little like he was some kind of God. He reached forward and took my hand, pulling me towards him. Wrapping his long arms around me, he kissed me deeply right there in front of everyone. I was a bit taken aback by his public display of affection, he seemed to have been conscious of an audience before now, and I was more than a little embarrassed. I could feel my cheeks burning. He pulled away a little, his wet fringe creating a curtain to hide our faces, and he smiled cheekily. Was he embarrassing me on purpose? 'Hey, beautiful. Did you enjoy the show?' Unable to speak with embarrassment taking hold, I just nodded before he kissed me again. He was so wet with sweat, but I didn't care. He smelt so good. When we finally broke away, everyone did their very best to mind their own business. I hoped my cheeks weren't too red.

Will pulled another seat next to him, and I quickly sat down, thankful not to be the centre of attention. Paul, sitting opposite, leaned in, 'Lucy, this is Hannah, my fiancé.' Gesturing to the woman next to him.

'Hi, lovely to meet you,' I said, offering my hand to shake hers, and she took it with both hands.

'And it is so lovely to meet you!' she said, beaming with enthusiasm. 'I love your earrings. They're so hip.'

They were a pair of hoops that one of the boys had bought me a few Christmases ago. Hannah was beautiful. She had long blonde hair, extraordinarily straight teeth, and blue eyes. She wore a red mini dress with pretty gold heels, which I was sure were feeling very sorry for themselves being subjected to the state of this floor.

'Thanks!'

Before I could return a compliment, she was in there like swimwear. 'So, how did you two meet?'

I looked over at Will, unsure how much information I should divulge, but since he'd just kissed me in public, I guess it didn't matter. He had turned his attention to one of the guys who I think was in the other band and was in deep conversation. So, I just explained that we had met at the B&B. Apparently, that was *so sweet*, and *it was meant to be*. She was lovely, just on the right side of annoying. She had travelled over to the UK to see Paul and go shopping in London. She'd not been before and was obviously excited about it.

'I just wanted to come over before the big day, see Buckingham Palace, and eat a scone,' she said. 'Are there any palaces in Bristol?'

I think I was looking at her like I was stupefied. 'Um, no, no palaces but plenty of places to get a scone. You could go all out and have a cream tea, although they are more traditional in Devon & Cornwall.'

'Aww, would you listen to her, Paul? She's so British.'

Okay, maybe on the wrong side of annoying. Steph would hate her. Will looked over and smiled a knowing smile and squeezed my knee. I took the break in our conversation to politely make my excuses and go to the loo. I checked my phone. I was still getting messages from people who had seen the press. Claire kindly sent me a snap of the front page of the local rag with the headline, STAR BREAKS UP LOCAL FAMILY.

Christ, they could at least get their facts straight.

The sick thing was that I had received unheard-of levels of inquiries for treatment requests. The comment from the media team about the possibility of reporters trying to book was weighing heavy on my mind. They could wait until Monday, I thought, pushing my phone back into my pocket.

As I wandered back along the corridor, struggling with the back of my earring that had caught up in my hair, I heard raised voices. I thought it was Alysa, but I couldn't hear the other voice.

'Yes, I've cancelled it,' she hissed. 'Now give me the bag, you asshole.'

I didn't want to get involved, so I quickly ducked back into the room. There were fewer people, and the staff was trying to clear up around everyone, silently signalling that it was closing time to the remaining stragglers.

I wandered back over to Will, who excused himself from the person he was talking to and got up. 'Shall we go?' he asked.

'Is that okay? I need to get back and let the dogs out.'

So rock and roll.

Will said his goodbyes while I waited by the door, and then he threw his backpack over his arm and took my hand, leading me along the corridor. Terry was waiting by one of the doors.

Had he been waiting that entire time?

Terry nodded to Will to confirm that the coast was clear and led us outside to open the car door. We both hopped in the back.

No fans today.

I dutifully put on my seatbelt, but Will had other ideas. He was on me before we'd pulled away. It was as if the tension from the night before, the post-show buzz, and the cupboard incident were too much to contain. While his kisses became more persistent, his hand disappeared up my top, pulling the cup of my bra down. I glanced over at Terry, but he was looking straight forward at the road ahead.

'Don't worry about Terry,' Will said, sensing I was feeling uneasy. I didn't want to know how he knew Terry wouldn't mind. Will started to unbutton my jeans.

'Will, we are not doing it in the back of a car.'

I sounded a bit more pissed off than I had meant to. I sat myself up and did my button back up, as he moved to his side of the car like a puppy scolded, and then he leant back over, kissed my neck, and said, 'when we get back, I have plans for you.'

Oh.

I sat there patiently waiting for the journey to end, wondering what those plans might be. And wondering just how British I was?

Chapter 12

Thankfully the house was quiet when we arrived home, and Terry could drop us off at the front. Before I had even got the key in the lock, Will had me pressed up against the wall kissing me deeply. Then, the dogs started barking, sensing someone outside, and Will pressed his forehead against mine, sighing. I quickly unlocked the door, fussed the dogs, and let them out. While I was waiting for them to do their business, Will decided to go up and have a shower. I probably needed one too, and that gave me an idea.

After locking up, I quickly darted upstairs, but having undressed, I suddenly felt exposed and wondered if I was being too brazen. Will was half-humming, half-singing something in the shower like he was trying to work out the lyrics to a song. I quietly opened the door and pulled the light cord.

'Lucy? I think the power's out?'

I went in and closed the door.

'Lucy, are you in here?'

'Yes,' I whispered.

He pushed his hair out of his face to see what was going on and, realising my intentions, pulled me into the shower. We kissed with the water running between us, but it was slow and lazy, with no time constraints or anything holding us back. He turned me around and kissed my neck. I could feel him growing against the small of my back. He hummed a low hum, then took his hands up into my hair and scrunched it up into his fists, pulling it slightly and making my head jolt back. Releasing me, I heard a bottle open, and he massaged shampoo into my hair. The suds ran down my back, making our skin all slippy. His hands travelled down over my shoulders and onto my breasts, kneading them gently.

'These are amazing,' he said, and I could hear the smile on his face.

I smoothed my hands down his thighs and slipped one between his legs, cupping and massaging him. His dick was hard against my back. Still kneading one of my boobs, his other hand travelled between my legs, and his fingers circled me. It felt so good, he knew exactly where to put them, and I could feel my insides waking up. He moved his other hand up from my chest and under my chin, pulling my head back onto his shoulder.

'I really wanna bend you over and fuck you right now, but I didn't bring the condoms in.'

Bloody condoms! I exhaled in frustration.

'Come on.'

He switched the shower off, guided me out, and pulled me in for a kiss. I was freezing in seconds, and my skin was covered in goosebumps. He leaned over and grabbed a towel from the radiator, and wrapped it around me, trying not to break the kiss and failing. I took the towel and quickly tied it at the front above my tits while he did the same around his waist. I smiled, thinking how it reminded me of him standing in the kitchen, wringing his shirt out just over a week ago. And now we were here.

So much had happened.

I watched as water dripped off his fringe down his torso.

'Are you just gonna stand there?' Will asked, looking at me as if he was looking over an invisible pair of glasses, hands-on-hips.

I looked down, embarrassed for the second time that day.

He caught my chin with the cup of his hand and lifted my face back up to his. He kissed the tip of my nose, and I scrunched it up and followed him into the bedroom.

Sitting on the bed, he rifled through his bag and then chucked a fresh packet of condoms on the bedside table. He stretched his arms behind himself, propping himself up on the bed, and looking up at me. I stood there, staring at the rug. I had completely lost my nerve and wasn't feeling brazen at all. The alcohol had clearly worn off. It felt like I was on stage, and he was spectating. Sensing I wasn't going to make the first move, he held his hand out for me to take.

I hesitated.

'Come here,' he coaxed.

I took his hand, and he pulled me down on top of him. I straddled him and kissed him, but my confidence was waning. I wasn't as experienced as him. He had had many women in his bed, and now he wanted me to entertain him.

'I'm sorry, Will, I'm not very...'

He wrapped his arms around me, rolled me onto my back, and kissed me softly.

'You are beautiful. You know that, right? Stop thinking so much.'

He kissed me again, delicately. He was smoothing my hair back from my face and trailing kisses down my neck to my shoulder. Will's hand glided down my arm making my goosebumps return. He linked fingers with mine and slowly lifted my hand above my head, leaving it there as he stroked my arm on the way back. I wriggled when he reached my armpit, making him stir. His kisses became slower, more sensual. He trailed his fingers down my neck, along my collar bone, gently undoing my towel.

It fell open, exposing me.

'Stop thinking,' he said.

Will's fingers continued their journey, gently stroking down my side to my hips, bypassing my breasts, but my nipples hardened all the same.

'You really are beautiful.'

As his hand reached my knee, he carefully lifted my leg out to the side. His fingers traced my inner thigh. He was hardening. I lifted my arm to touch him, but he caught it and firmly placed it back where it was. My insides contracted, and I raised my hips into him, all the while, our kisses became more intimate, our tongues exploring each other. His fingers started to move back up my body, and I was more than disappointed that he wasn't touching me where I needed him to.

I lifted my arm again to move things along a little faster, but he caught me again, pushing it back more forcefully this time and securing it there with his other hand. His fingers walked slowly back up over my hips and danced over my nipple. He pinched it, and I bucked my hips. I was so wet, and he hadn't even been there. I was completely trapped, pinned down. I couldn't talk for his relentless kissing, and my nipple was burning from the gentle pinching and pulling.

All I could do was lie there and accept his tender assault, but man, I wanted him so much.

Finally, he broke away from the kiss. 'Are you okay?' he asked.

'Will, I want you.'

I sounded flustered and needy. He slowly pushed himself onto his knees, removed his towel, and reached for the condoms.

Note to self, book a doctor's appointment on Monday.

Once it was in place, he resumed his position, holding my arm back up and kissing me slowly. I was getting agitated and cross. Why wasn't he giving me what I wanted? He began to trail his fingers back down my side, and the slower his fingers became, the angrier I became, but at least they were going in the right direction. Before they reached their goal, he lifted his hand to the top of my knee and started the slow descent again.

For Christ's sake.

Without thinking, I used all my strength to push him off and onto his back. I think I may have growled doing so. He looked up at me, smiling, biting his bottom lip. Was this his plan all along? I didn't care. I lifted myself and held him in place before slowly lowering myself down on him. Oh, the relief.

He held my hips in position and pulled my head down to meet his, 'I want you too, Lucy.'

He let go, and I started to move. This was fun, I could move at my own pace, fulfilling my needs, but I needed to prove something. I sat back further, taking him in deeper, leaning back and holding on to his thigh with one hand and teasing his balls with the other. He groaned. It felt good. I pushed back a little more, throwing my head back and lifting my chest in the air. Will was watching me, I could feel his eyes on me.

Suddenly I felt his thumb circling me. I was building, and Will was meeting me with every bounce. Eventually, he grabbed hold of my hips, and I threw myself forward, bracing myself on his chest. I rode him, but he stilled, and I looked down at him.

'I'm gonna come. Are you there?' he asked.

'Yeah, don't stop.'

Moving his hands to my lower back, he pulled me down with force each time I descended, and simultaneously thrusted upward, the additional leverage making it deeper. Our climaxes crashed together, the ripples of mine, and the pulses of his milking every last moment of ecstasy. His jaw was tense, and his arms were rigid, but not once did he take his eyes off me.

I collapsed on top of him, and he laughed. My legs were killing me. He rolled me over and gently pulled away to sort himself out.

'I should really go on the pill,' I mused.

'You really should,' he said. 'I know I sound like a broken record, but that was amazing.'

'I'm thinking of selling tickets,' I joked.

'I'll buy them all. You're all mine,' Will said with a wicked glint in his eye, enveloping me again.

Chapter 13

It was Sunday, and neither of us had any commitments. Although I woke up late, well, late for me, Will was still fast asleep. He looked so peaceful. I smiled to myself as memories of last night washed over me. Mike and I had had a good sex life, or so I thought. We did it fairly regularly when things were good between us, but it was always the same. It wasn't passionate, exciting, or carnal, but I guessed I didn't know what I was missing.

I slipped out of bed and went downstairs to make a coffee. Rooting around in the fridge, I found some bacon. My mouth instantly watered at the prospect of bacon. If that wasn't going to wake him up, I didn't know what would. While the bacon was in the oven, I nipped into the garden, cut a couple of roses off the bush, and inhaled deeply. They smelt so lemony. Setting the table with napkins, water, and a jug of orange juice, I placed the roses in the centre. I turned to find Will in the kitchen doorway, leaning against the frame and yawning.

My plan had worked! He looked lanky and stood there with his hair messed up in his t-shirt and boxers. All broad-shouldered and skinny legs.

'Hungry?'

He tried to stifle another yawn, but his eyes said yes. I buttered some bread, fetched the sauces, and we sat opposite each other, making our bacon sandwiches. I spent quite some time picking all the rind off mine, and then licked my fingers before squirting some tomato ketchup. I looked up to find Will watching me with a half-smile.

'Have you finished slaughtering your sandwich?' he asked.

I smiled back, yes, yes I had!

'What are we doing today?' Will asked before taking an enormous bite out of his sandwich.

'I thought we could go on a day trip,' I announced.

'What does that involve?' Will enquired.

'Well, we have a choice... we could pack a picnic and head into Bristol and go for a long walk, or we could take the campervan and head over to Exmouth, and have fish and chips on the beach?'

'You have a campervan?' Will asked, surprised.

'Yes, she's in the garage.'

'She?'

'She, as in Billie, that's her name.'

'Well, if it means I can take two girls out at once, then Exmouth it is,' he said.

I laughed.

'I'll call Terry,' Will muttered, and I felt my face fall.

I watched him as he got his phone out of his pocket. When he looked up, he realised I was struggling with the concept.

'He can travel behind us,' he said, waving his hand and then taking my hand, interlacing our fingers. 'He's very discreet.'

I chewed my bottom lip. 'Okay,' I said, looking at our hands.

Is this how it was going to be? Terry trailing behind us everywhere we went? I didn't want the day to start on a downer, so I kept my thoughts to myself.

The van took a few attempts to start, but on the fourth go, she roared into action. The dogs in the back were pacing, wondering where we were going. I loved our van. We had had so many lovely family holidays and last-minute weekends in it that I'd lost count. She'd been a bit unreliable but comfortable to sleep in and easy to park. I had a feeling Frankie would want to drive her when he passed his test. But, of course, that's if we didn't have to sell her. Oh, God. I pushed my thoughts away.

'Have you been to Exmouth before?' I asked as I spotted Terry pulling in behind us on the motorway.

'No, but I've been in plenty of vans, and I have to say that Billie is far better equipped than most vans I ever used to tour in.'

What a life. I had always thought I might drop sticks and take the van on a UK or even European tour, but the opportunity never arose.

'How long did you tour in vans for?'

'Quite a while, the first few years at least, and then eventually proper tour buses. I'm not sure we'd do another tour if it meant driving again. Don't get me wrong, we had some amazing times, but it was exhausting, and well, I like a bed.'

I took the junction and followed the windy road toward the beach. I drove to the very end of the promenade, past the tacky amusements and pretty little beach huts, knowing that this section of the beach was dog friendly. The dogs knew where we were and were going crazy in the back. I backed into a free parking spot overlooking the beach, and Terry pulled into one a few spaces down. Rain clouds were starting to appear over Dawlish, and I was keen to get the dogs walked before a shower. So, we all headed down onto the beach. Grayson immediately ran off towards the water, so we followed. It was breezy, but I had my rain jacket. Will put his arm around me as we walked. Luna was splashing about in the water, flicking a piece of seaweed up in the air and catching it. Grayson just stood in the water, waiting for one of us to throw something for him to swim after. I thought I would feel like we were being followed, but Terry had the whole discreet thing down, and I forgot he was even there after a while.

'I don't intend to go swimming today,' Will warned. It made me chuckle, and he pushed me, causing me to stumble. Then, after playing fetch with Grayson for a while, we continued along the shore. 'Look at that dilapidated building,' he nodded towards the headland.

'That's View Point, it used to be a really chic hotel in the 1930s, but it fell into disrepair in the '60s, I think.' However, you could still see the art déco curves and turrets despite having no roof.

'What a crime,' Will said thoughtfully.

The clouds were getting darker, and we decided to turn back. The rain started to fall about two minutes short of getting back to the van, so we ran the last bit. We all hopped in the back, and I towelled the dogs down while Will opened cupboards and drawers to see what equipment we had.

The windows started to steam up, so I pushed the seats down to make a bed and pushed the back door open creating a storm porch, allowing us to look out over the bay. We both lay on our fronts, watching people on the beach frantically gathering their things and others dashing to their cars. The dogs fell asleep at the foot of the bed, and as the beach cleared, the rain eased a little. We lay there in comfortable silence. The waves lapped, and we listened to the rain pitter-patter on the van. This was my happy place, people-watching with a beach view, and Will seemed super chilled too.

'I guess you don't get many opportunities to do stuff like this,' I pondered aloud, moving onto my side to face him, aware that he hadn't been stopped for a selfie or an autograph since we'd arrived.

'Not on tour, no,' he admitted, still looking out to the beach. 'It's not so bad at home, people know who I am, and they tend to leave me to my own devices. It's normally tourists that stop me, I think,' he surmised.

'Do you get homesick?' I asked.

He pushed himself onto his side.

'Not when I'm with you,' he replied, looking at me.

I smiled and then looked away. Sometimes, Will said things with such weight it caught me off guard. Will ducked his head to catch my gaze again.

'You ground me, Lucy. Don't take offence to this, but I crave normality, and you, your life, and your world is everything I want,' he said.

I swallowed, trying not to look away, and took a breath but did not know how to respond. Will laughed a little, shaking his head, and interlaced my fingers with his.

'What's so funny?' I asked.

'You! You become so timid when we're talking about our feelings,' he said, smiling.

'I think you'll find you were talking about your feelings,' I replied, biting my lip to hide my smile.

He shook his head again, lifted our interlaced hands, and pushed my hand back, my body following. He closed the gap between us, hovering above me.

'What *are* you feeling?' he asked.

Despite trying to lighten the intensity of the conversation, he wasn't going to give up, but I was so crap at putting my feelings into words.

'Ummm... hungry?' I said to wind him up.

'Lucy...' he pleaded as he completely rolled on top of me, and I became conscious of our surroundings, but his fringe created a mini confessions box between us. He was looking me straight in the eye.

'Okay, okay...' Honesty is the best policy. 'I feel pretty....' The pressure was consuming. '... sick when I think about you.' Will tried to stifle a laugh. 'Bloody hell, I can't do this,' I said, trying to wriggle out from underneath him, but he held me there.

'I'm sorry, but this is gold... go on,' he said, releasing my hand and using his to physically wipe the smile from his face. I couldn't look at him. I looked through the tiny gap in his fringe at the top of the seatbelt strap.

'Not sick, something similar. Anyway, when I'm with you... that feeling goes somewhere... else, and I feel....' What did I feel? 'Whole.' I didn't know how else to describe it.

Will didn't say anything.

I looked back at him, and he was staring at me, his expression serious. I looked into his eyes, thinking I'd cocked up and failed the honesty test. But then he kissed me with such force I moaned as I released my breath. I returned his kiss, closing my eyes, not caring that we were lying in the van with the door wide open, Terry a few cars down. When our kiss came to an end, he said, 'so. I make you whole. Is that what you meant?' Will asked, trying to clarify my messed-up explanation.

'Yeah, I think that's what I meant,' I said, frowning a little.

'Okay, I'll take that,' he said, nodding, and I sighed contently, and my tummy rumbled. 'Happy?' Will asked.

'Very. Although I am getting a bit hungry, and I know an amazing place for fish and chips,' I said.

Will smiled.

We shut the back and climbed back over to the front. When we pulled up, Will asked what I wanted, but I looked at the queue and then back at him, and I said I'd go. Eventually, I left carrying the salt and vinegary lushness.

Arriving back at the van, Will was on his phone.

'Well, you'll have to cancel it,' he said irritably. 'No, I'm not there, and I wouldn't get back in time, anyway.' He sighed heavily. 'Okay?' Then he hung up.

'Everything okay?' I asked as the van filled with the smell of deliciousness, making the dogs stir.

'Yeah, that was Alysa. She wants me to do an interview this afternoon.'

'Well, we could head back. It won't take long,' I offered.

'No, it's fine. I explained I was with you.'

'Oh dear...'

'Why, what? Has she said something?' he asked.

'No, I just get the feeling she's not my biggest fan.'

'She's... just... highly strung.'

I thought he was going to say something else but decided better of it. I handed over his warm paper package, and he opened it enthusiastically. It was so good. The fish was perfect, super flakey. The chips were a bit soggy, but I didn't care. The dogs waited patiently for a chip, drooling like a pair of goons.

'Should I have bought Terry some?' I asked.

'No,' Will replied with a laugh. 'He's working.'

I frowned, thinking that was not very fair. He must be starving.

Arriving home, I was feeling a bit down, knowing that I had to return to work the next day and Will had other gigs to do next week, which would mean him staying away. I'd had such a fantastic weekend, and I didn't want it to end. Will seemed to read me and gave me the biggest hug.

'I've had a great time. Next week is gonna be pretty busy, but we'll find a way, okay?'

I reached up and kissed him. We would find a way. Somehow. But I had a sinking feeling that our drug-fuelled, speed-dating honeymoon had ended.

That night neither of us slept much, dozing and then waking and finding each other again. It was like the most prolonged goodbye. He had gigs in Manchester and London.

He had to leave for Manchester for rehearsals, meetings, and interviews the next day and then to London for more of the same. He wanted me to come to the gigs, but I was working, and the boys were home at the weekend. Besides, Mike and I had some hard decisions to make, so seeing each other would be tricky.

Terry had been waiting for several minutes, as we were still saying our goodbyes at the door.

'I'll call when I get to Manchester.'

One final kiss, and he was gone.

If I didn't have anything better to do, I would have collapsed on the floor in a sobbing mess, but reality came crashing down. That night I cooked a pasta bake for the boys and me, but I was just pushing Fusilli around my plate.

'Has he gone then?' Paddy asked.

Oh God, was it that obvious?

'Yes, he's got some other gigs to do.'

'You could always leave us here if you wanted to go and see him, Mum,' Paddy suggested.

'Yeah,' Frankie said as they exchanged a look. Any switched-on parent would identify the look as the *house party* look.

'I can't trust you to tear yourselves away from your gaming long enough to walk the bloody dogs, let alone remember to feed them.'

The dogs looked up from their beds, hopeful at the mention of a walk. Then my phone rang.

It was Will.

'Hello.'

'Hey, it's me. Sorry it's taken so long to ring, we had a meeting in Bristol before we set off, and annoyingly, Alysa cocked up, and the interview here is actually tomorrow, so I could have come back.'

Alysa cocked up? Hmmm.

'That's a shame. Are you okay, though? What are you up to tonight?'

'We're all heading out to dinner. Alysa has booked some Indian place she knows.'

I pursed my lips. Her name was beginning to grate on me.

'That sounds good.' I could hear he was with other people.

'Listen, I've gotta go, but I just wanted to let you know I was here. I'll call you tomorrow, yeah?'

'Tomorrow,' I confirmed.

I was sure I could hear Alysa laughing in the background.

'Okay, have a good night.'

This was going to be much more challenging than I had thought. I cleared away the dinner things, made a cup of tea, and sat on the sofa staring off into the distance. And then they came, the tears, silent tears rolled down my cheeks and clung to the bottom of my chin before dripping onto my top. Dark thoughts of not being cool enough, Will having a girl in every port, or thoughts of Alysa whispering into his ear kept swirling around in my head. Later, I woke up on the sofa, and everything was dark and quiet. I heaved myself up and went upstairs. Glancing at Will's room, I was tempted to sleep in there, but I'd only toss and turn.

The next day wasn't much better, it was like I was mourning him, and I couldn't quite find the enthusiasm to do anything. All my clients were eager to know if what they had read was true. I followed the instructions from Will's media team and made sure I didn't say anything that could be misconstrued.

Steph had texted to ask if I fancied going to the quiz night on Thursday, and I had politely declined. Mike had texted to say he had an interview on Friday but wasn't holding out much hope, so could I contact the local property agents to get the house valued? Will had texted to say he was crazy busy and would phone when he could. He hadn't called by ten-thirty, so I went to bed.

The following morning was a beautiful sunny day, too bright for my mood, but it did make me want to get out in the fresh air. Seeing the sea glittering in the sunshine was refreshing, and it was doing its best to lift my spirits. I walked past the spot where Will and I nearly got caught canoodling at sunset and past the pub we had food at, towards the pier.

Occasionally I'd spot someone do a double take or whisper something to whoever they were with, and one person actually pointed. I kept going, doing my best to ignore them, and I walked along the pier, following our first date in reverse. I took the steps to the café two by two to see if they had any marble cake left. I was in luck, so I bought a piece and went and sat on the bench that Will and I had shared. Will was right. It was delicious. I couldn't help but think about what the boys had said. Could I leave them? Maybe my mum wouldn't mind checking in on them? I was so desperate to see him. Just then, my phone sprang to life. It was him.

'Hi!' I said as brightly as I could muster.

'I'm so sorry. The rehearsal went on until the early hours, so it was too late to call, and I've only just woken up. Anyway, I miss you. What have you been up to?'

I smiled for the first time in days.

'Um, just working and...' moping around and constantly thinking of you and feeling pretty sad that I can't see you, 'well yeah, not much else.' I thought that was certain to lure him back into my arms, looking up at the sky.

'Well, I can't stop thinking about you, but admittedly it's not when you're working!' I smiled, wiping a stray tear from my eye. 'There's a chance I can pop back before we head to France.'

'Really? I would love that... I was just mulling over whether I could leave the boys for a night,' I said, still torn about whether that was the best parenting decision.

'Come to London! I'll send Terry. You can hang out with Hannah while we play, and then I can make you whole,' he said.

I could hear the smile in his voice, and I laughed. It felt good to laugh.

'I don't know for sure, I need to put a few things in place, but if I can make it work, I will,' I said, wondering what Mike would think.

'I can't promise anything either, our schedule is filling up, but I've told Alysa to keep it free. And Lucy?'

'Yes?'

'Did you find something on my bedside table?' he enquired.

No, because I can't bear to go in there for fear of falling to pieces.

'No. Did you forget something?'

'Well, go look already.'

'I can't. I'm not at home.' I'm on the pier eating the cake you had, like a love-struck teenager.

'Well, when you get home, okay?'

'Okay.'

'I'm being stared at by everyone waiting in the car. I think I need to go. Text me later, yeah?'

'I will, bye.' He had gone. What was it with him not saying goodbye to anyone, I thought, as I started to walk home at speed.

On the bedside table was an envelope with a simple kiss on it. I carefully opened it, and inside was a return plane ticket to Portugal.

Oh, my God!

There was also a note.

I told you I would buy all the tickets. I took the liberty of asking Steph if she could look after the dogs. Will X

I quickly checked my calendar on my phone. It was the weekend that Mike had the boys. Had he known? God, if I'd opened this on Monday, maybe I wouldn't have spent the last few days feeling so low. I hugged the ticket to my chest and then allowed myself to lie on the bed and roll myself up in the duvet like a Swiss roll to smell him. Not a love-struck teenager at all.

When the boys returned from school, I spoke to them about London, and then rang my mum. She would be happy to check in on them. I decided not to contact Mike. I was worried he would disagree, especially as I was going to see

Will. And besides, if my mum thought it was okay, it must be.

That night, I knew Will would be playing, but I dropped him a text.

Possibly the best thing I have ever discovered on a bedside table. Thank you. I hope the gig went well. p.s. See you in London X

That night I had the most rejuvenating sleep. It may or may not have had something to do with the fact that I slept on Will's pillow.

Chapter 14

I had just over a week to prepare for Portugal. The gig was in Lisbon. Checking online for the temperature for this time of year, it was going to be hot. Really bloody hot. I didn't even have a bikini. I had a tatty old Speedo swimsuit that had lost all its elasticity from wearing it under wetsuits. I was going to need to go shopping, but the funds were low. While showering, I made a mental note to check the B&B account. Maybe I could use some of the holiday funds, it was a holiday after all, but that was really for the boys.

Dilemma.

A text was waiting for me when I returned to the bedroom.

It was from Mike. *Have you phoned the estate agents yet?*

Shit. I needed to get on that. And while making phone calls, I must ring the doctors too. But, unfortunately, I had a full day of clients, so all this would have to wait.

'We would love to assist you, Mrs Daniels. Would you be available next week for us to pop round to carry out the valuation?'

I checked my diary, but I was stacked out. The publicity generated from the poorly reported scandal had put a lot of traffic through my website. Will's media team had removed my mobile number from view, but potential clients could send me a message which I could screen and respond to if I felt it was genuine. I was still getting messages from non-work-related people, but that had died down. I was a bit worried that some people had booked an appointment hoping they'd see Will, but my business was flourishing either way. Don't they always say there's never bad press or something?

'Umm, I could do after four on Tuesday?'

'Super, that's all in the diary for you, and Matt will be delighted to meet you then.'

I'm sure he bloody would.

After phoning a couple of other agents and organising more appointments, I rang the doctors.

'Yes, I'd like to speak to someone in Family Planning?'

Is that what they call it these days?

Clearly not, when the receptionist asked if I was planning on having a family.

'Erm, I just need to go on the pill.'

'Okay, well, you will need to make an appointment for that, so let me have a look.'

I rolled my eyes. Did they not just dish these things out to teenagers nowadays?

'The only appointment I have is at four on Tuesday.'

Bloody typical. I'd have to change the appointment with the agent.

'Yes, could I book that, please?'

'Of course, make sure you come with a full bladder as the nurse will need to carry out a pregnancy test.'

What?

'Okay, thanks.'

I looked at my watch. I needed to get the dinner on. I put the oven on for jacket potatoes. Steph had texted to double-check if I had changed my mind about the quiz. Another text came through as I was typing back.

It was Will. *You're the best thing I've discovered next to that bedside table. When can I send Terry to pick you up? X*

I smiled, remembering that night. He made me do things I wouldn't dream of usually doing.

Let me get back to you xx

I responded to Steph. *I can't. I've got too much to do, I'm off to Portugal, but I think you knew that already. X*

She replied. *He's clearly in to you!! X*

I told the boys at dinner, and they were genuinely excited for me and maybe just a bit miffed that they weren't coming to Portugal. Paddy ate an obscene amount of tuna mayo with his potato. He was obviously going through another growth spurt. I asked the boys to clear away so I could call Mike. I needed to tell him about Portugal in case something happened to the boys while I was away, and I headed into the lounge.

'Have you called the agents yet?' He asked. No *hello*. He sounded stressed.

'Yes, I have three coming here to carry out valuations next week.' I looked at the ceiling, feeling like I was being checked up on.

'Right, well, I have to go. I'm trying to prepare for this interview tomorrow.'

I could hear papers being shuffled.

'Okay, but hang on... I just wanted to let you know that I'll be away the weekend after next.' There was a pause.

'With him?' he asked with an obvious note of anger, which riled me immediately.

'He does have a name, you know.'

'Oh, believe me, I know,' he responded bitterly.

'Why are you being like this?'

'Well, I don't think all the press last week will help me get this job.'

Oh, come on.

'The only people who would recognise you from that picture are people we know,' I said defensively.

'Lu, the interview *is* with people I know,' he said with a sigh and then asked, 'where are you going?' I was hoping he wasn't going to ask.

'I'm going to Portugal,' I said quickly, hoping it wouldn't quite sink in.

'Portugal?' He spat. 'And while we're trying to put the house on the market?'

I took a steadying breath.

'Yes, I can't imagine the house will be on the market by then, but I have everything in place next week,' I countered and started to pace around the lounge. 'You could always stay here?' I suggested, trying to temper the moment. He sometimes stayed when I was away with the girls, giving him the opportunity to go out with his friends locally.

'What, in the bed you've been shagging him in?'

Whoa! I stood still, my mouth open, but unable to speak.

'I've got to go,' he added a few moments later and hung up.

Jeez, was he jealous? Surely not. If he was, he had no right to be. I was really wound up.

I quickly text Steph. *See you at the quiz. X*

Sod it, I needed a drink, so I'd go to the quiz after all, and I bounded up the stairs to get changed quickly.

I texted Will between applications of make-up. *Would 4 pm be ok for Terry? xx*

I could see he was texting back. *How about 3 pm?*

I frowned. I wasn't sure whether he wanted me there earlier or whether it was more convenient for Terry. I had to get the house ready for the estate agents, but I was sure I could do that and get ready by three.

3 pm xx

Half an hour later, I sat in the pub with Steph and Claire. Zara wasn't there, and I didn't want to think about what that meant.

'Totally jealous,' Claire said. 'What an arsehole. It's nothing to do with you, though, babe. It's totally because you're getting some, and he isn't,' she said, and Steph nodded.

'I'm just really hacked off with him. I know he's stressed, but the annoying thing is, Will and I haven't even done it in my bed,' I said in a whisper, suddenly aware that there was a chance someone could listen in.

'But you've totally done him, right?' Claire nudged me with a massive grin and a sparkle in her eyes. I rolled my eyes. 'Of course, you bloody have,' she confirmed to herself.

'In which year did Margaret Thatcher come into power?' The quiz master asked, and everyone in the room began to have hushed conversations. Two hours later and I was feeling the effects of the alcohol. Having epically failed the first two rounds of the quiz, we'd all but given up, and we were chatting, much to the annoyance of the other patrons.

'The boys will be absolutely fine tomorrow night,' Steph said.

Remembering that I'd need to tidy the house from top to bottom the next day, and was already likely to have a hangover, I decided it was time to go. Claire and I walked back together, she was more drunk than me, and after rummaging around in her bag for a while, she pulled out a vape and took a long drag. Clouds of strawberry-scented smoke surrounded us. It reminded me of the smoke machines at the school disco.

'So, he's taking you to Portugal,' she slurred. 'You'll be living together before you know it.' Pronouncing the T a little too specifically.

'I doubt that. He lives in Brooklyn. But, to be honest, it's difficult to see too far into the future, and we've only known each other for a couple of weeks.'

It was two weeks today.

'Well, if what Steph said is true, I'm sure you'll figure something out.'

'Why, what has she said?' I enquired.

'That you two are loved up to the max, and he can't keep his hands off you.' I smiled. 'And she told me about the cupboard. You little minx!'

'Nothing happened in that cupboard,' I said honestly. We were nearly outside my house.

'Whatever you say, girlfriend.' And then she squeezed me. 'I'm really happy for you.' She turned a little too quickly but managed to right herself before gliding down the road, with a plume of smoke in her wake.

Chapter 15

I had worked my arse off to get the house sorted and be ready by three. I had even left a note for the boys to make sure the house stayed tidy and reminded them to look after the dogs before I saw Terry pull up outside. He hopped out and opened the back door for me, 'Hi Terry, how are you?'

'Very well... Ms Daniels.' I smiled because he wasn't sure how to address me.

'Lucy, please,' I implored, and he nodded and waved me in. There, on the seat, was a little gift bag. 'Is that for me?' I asked.

'I believe so,' he said, looking at me in the rear-view mirror with a smile in his eyes.

Inside was a box wrapped beautifully in tissue paper, about the size of a brick but not nearly as heavy. I carefully picked at the stickers while Terry pulled onto the M5. I slid the lid off to find a pair of sunglasses. They were lovely, brown tortoise shell frames with huge lenses, but a bit random. I couldn't think of the relevance a pair of sunglasses had. It wasn't even sunny. I put them to one side and looked out the window for a bit.

Was I supposed to chat with Terry? I didn't know the etiquette of sitting in the back of a chauffeured car.

'Do you have a family back home, Terry?'

He glanced at me via the mirror again, and I could see the smile in his eyes returning. By the time we got onto the

M4, I had learnt that Terry had a wife, two daughters, and a son. His eldest daughter had already married and left home. His wife worked with children who had special education-al needs at the local school. And they had a dog called Will, named after Will!

'So, have you worked for Will for a long time?' I asked.

'Yes, quite a few years now, maybe seven?' he recalled.

'Wow! You enjoy it then... driving?' I asked, and he chuckled.

'It started with driving, but the role has become more varied over the years. I am a trained bodyguard.'

My eyes widened, and he caught my reaction.

'Personal shopper.' I looked at the gift bag. 'And other odd jobs upon request.'

I looked out of the window again. Like, picking women up from their homes and taking them to Will? He must have witnessed all sorts of stuff. Will must really trust him.

'I haven't had to do this before,' he said, interrupting my train of thought and trying to make me feel comfortable.

'Am I an odd job then?' I asked, and he laughed then.

'A special request,' he confirmed as we whizzed past where the old Lucozade sign once stood.

'Where are we going, by the way?' I suddenly realised I hadn't even asked Will.

'Shangri-La, The Shard,' he confirmed, and my mouth popped open.

I was wearing jeans. Holy moly. Okay, now I was ner-vous.

'I'm afraid word has got out, though.'

I slowly looked over at the sunglasses. Oh, God. I stared out of the window again. He could have warned me.

'You'll be fine.' Terry assured me, but I didn't reply, my nerves taking hold.

We pulled up outside the revolving doors. There was a bank of fans on either side. I found it strange that the fans were so obedient, staying behind the barriers with their arms hanging over, holding their phones out, ready if they caught a glimpse.

'It's unlikely they'll recognise you, so I will come and open your door, and you will step out and walk straight in. I will be behind you. Put the glasses on,' he said, giving me a firm nod via the mirror, and he got out.

Oh Em Gee.

I slipped the glasses on and then slid across to the other side. As Terry opened the door, the crowd of fans went quiet in anticipation, and I all but ran across to the revolving door. I concentrated hard on the substantial bonsai trees on either side of the door, not wanting to look at anyone in the crowd, but as soon as they realised that I was nobody, they started talking amongst themselves again.

I sighed in huge relief as we reached the vast marble foyer. Terry moved in front of me and guided me over to the lift. He pressed the button, and my stomach flipped as the elevator started to move. I wasn't sure whether it was because of the motion or the excitement of seeing Will. The doors opened into a suite, and I pushed my sunglasses onto my head. It was all clean lines, blue swathed carpet, marble counters, and floor-to-ceiling windows. I could hear Will talking on his phone in another room, but I was immediately drawn into the room to look at the view. Wow, there it was, London in all its glory. I could see the Walkie-Talkie building, the Gherkin, forgetting for a moment that I was at the Shard.

'What do you think?' I span around to see Will. Terry had disappeared.

'It is...' I turned again, unable to tear myself away from the view. 'Wow.'

'Cool, huh!?' he said, placing his hands on my hips and kissing my neck, sending tingles all over me. 'So, you managed to get in unscathed?' I turned to face him and looked him straight in the eye.

'You could have warned me,' I said seriously.

He bit his bottom lip. 'I didn't wanna put you off,' he said, taking my sunglasses off my head and placing them on a nearby counter.

'If I'd known, I would have worn something different...' I started, but he interrupted me.

'If you'd known, you would have been overthinking it.'

He kissed me, but I pulled away. 'If I'd known, I would have worn a balaclava,' I stated, and he dropped his head to one side, half smiling.

'Just a balaclava?' he questioned.

I went to slap him, but he caught my wrist and kissed me again, pushing me back against the cupboards. He lifted me so I was sitting on the counter. The marble felt cold on my thighs, but Will stood between my legs, and he was warm, so warm. I was wearing a silky green blouse, and he was already making light work of the buttons.

'I have missed these,' he said as he stepped back to get a better look, and I rolled my eyes. As I did so, I spotted the

London Eye, distracted. 'Do I need to shut the curtains?' he asked.

'Maybe,' I joked, looking back at him and smiling.

Suddenly he grabbed me, I had to wrap my arms and legs around him to stop myself from falling to the floor, and he carried me into the bedroom and placed me on the bed.

'Keen,' I said, still smiling.

'I want to make you whole,' he said, pulling his t-shirt off and climbing on top of me, kissing me from my waist upwards as he did so and then undoing the button on my jeans. I couldn't help but wonder if this was the reason he wanted me here an hour earlier than I had suggested.

'I'm not sure I have much choice in the matter,' I said while I smoothed my hands down his back, onto his arse. He had something in his back pocket, and I instinctively went to put my hand in to see what it was. He quickly pulled away and stood up, removing his jeans himself. I looked at him inquisitively, and he smiled, shaking his head.

'What was that?' I asked.

'Nothing,' he replied as he pulled my jeans down, grabbed hold of the bottoms, and whipped them straight off.

'It wasn't nothing,' I said, pushing myself up on my elbows, but Will was already climbing back on top of me and pushed me back down.

'Okay, it was something but not for now.'

He kissed me before I could ask any more questions. He was hiding something, but as Will gently pulled my knickers to one side and slid his finger inside me, I didn't care. His pace was slow but not frustratingly slow, just thorough. I attempted to take the lead several times, but he gently pushed me away. It was as if he wanted to touch, lick or kiss every part of me, and then, just as I was starting to become a little restless, he removed my knickers, put on a condom, and pushed himself inside me. He watched me as he did so, and I held my breath, waiting for my insides to adjust. Would I ever get used to the size of him? Thank God I was so wet.

His pace remained consistent. We didn't change positions or do anything else. We just kissed until I began to build. I kept building, and I wanted Will to speed up, but he was in one gear and one gear only. I began to pant, and he just watched me, slowly coming undone, and when I came, Jesus, it was incredible. Will put his forehead against mine, and we stared at each other, moving in unison, my orgasm setting his off. It was so intense. It wasn't just the orgasm. It was a moment in time that we were experiencing together. I was his, and he was mine, but there was something else there, and I couldn't put my finger on it. Will discarded the condom somewhere in the vicinity of the bin and resumed his position. 'Are you okay?'

'Yes, why wouldn't I be?' I said, wondering why he asked.

'Are you whole?' he asked, and I smiled at him, an enormous Cheshire cat grin that I couldn't seem to wipe off my face.

'Yes,' I said, biting my lip. 'I felt whole when I walked in the room,' I admitted, and he smiled.

'Come shower with me. I need to get ready.'

We hooked up with Paul and Hannah in the lobby an hour later. Paul nodded hello, and Hannah gave me the biggest hug.

'It's so wonderful to see you again,' she said enthusiastically. 'I've got so much to tell you. We went to Buckingham Palace. Those red guards are stern, aren't they? I wanted to see the corgis, but I didn't even catch a glimpse.'

Was she always this full-on? She was drawing so much attention from everyone in the reception area I felt slightly embarrassed. I saw Terry out of the corner of my eye standing by the wall, trying to hide a smile, I caught his gaze and smiled, and he had to look away. He observed the greeting, and I wondered what he thought of Hannah. Will saw the exchange, too, and the slightest frown passed over his face.

I noticed Will was remarkably hands off in the lobby, which felt strange after being in such proximity. Jake joined us, followed by Alysa, and was it, Bill? The other security guard person. Alysa clocked me and was surprised to see me. She smiled the most enormous, fakest smile I've ever seen and then said something in Bill's ear.

'Okay, people, I think it's probably best to split this girls and boys. Terry, you take the boys. Bill, you're with me,' Alysa said, and then Will looked over at me. I looked back, wondering why we were being split up.

Alysa looked at her watch and then clapped her hands. 'Come on, people.'

Before I could even speak to Will, Bill was whisking us out the door, past the fans who appeared to have doubled since I arrived. Hannah flipped her glasses down onto her face. Damn it, I had left mine in the room, but the crowd did not seem interested in us, and before I knew it, we were in the car.

As we pulled away, I heard an eruption of screams and shouting as the band left the building. 'So...' Alysa said, looking at me. 'When did you get here?'

'Um, a couple of hours ago? Terry picked me up at three,' I explained.

'Terry?' she asked, 'our Terry?' As if no one was allowed to use Terry's services without her say so. I nodded slowly and looked at Hannah as if I'd done something wrong. She looked at me confused, and then once Alysa's eyebrows had moved back down her face, she started looking at her phone. I looked out of the window. She had managed to create such an awkward atmosphere within the space of a few minutes.

When we arrived at the car park, Alysa hopped out like a bolt of lightning, and disappeared through a door. Bill got out and sparked up a cigarette.

'What was all that about?' Hannah asked.

'I was going to ask you the same thing. Have I done something wrong?' I asked.

'Not that I know of, but she is pissed about something.' Hannah took a compact mirror out of her bag to check her perfect make-up and moved a couple of hairs on her perfect head before snapping it shut and throwing it back in the bag. 'Come to think of it, she's always pissed about something.' She looked at me then. 'How are you feeling after all the press stuff?'

I looked at the floor. 'Um, not great.' I shrugged my shoulders, not really knowing how I felt. 'I mean, my friends and family are cool... on the whole,' I said, thinking about Mike. 'But... I've had some horrible messages from people I don't know, and concerning my business, I don't know who is genuine and who isn't,' I admitted. It was the most honest I'd been since the news broke. Hannah smiled a sorrowful smile.

'I think I'm quite lucky that I'm with Paul. The fans are far less infatuated by him. Will has always had all the attention, so apart from the occasional picture, I haven't had to deal with any fans personally. Sometimes, Paul will get asked for an autograph if we're at a local gig, but poor Will takes the brunt of it.'

'I know. We can't seem to get through a date without someone stopping him for a selfie,' I said, and just then, the door opened, and Will leaned in.

'What are you hanging out in here for?' he asked, putting his hand out to help me out and then doing the same for Hannah.

He was such a gentleman. She spotted Paul immediately and joined him.

'Sorry we couldn't travel together. It was easier with the fans outside.'

'It's fine, although I think I've already managed to get into Alysa's bad books,' I grimaced.

'Nope, that was my fault too,' he said, looking around and then pulling me into him. 'Apparently, I should have asked her if I could use Terry to collect you.'

'Oh, well, I may have dropped you in it,' I admitted.

'You haven't done anything wrong. It's cool.'

He kissed me. Not in the lobby, but okay in a car park. I couldn't get my head around it. Someone cleared their throat, and we both turned. It was Alysa with the passes. She had a face like stone, handed all the triple A passes to Will, and then walked off. Will bit his lip and scrunched his nose up at me, and I couldn't help but giggle. He took my hand, and we headed into the building.

It just seemed to be a maze of corridors and doors. I tried to recall which direction we were travelling, but there was no use after a while. We eventually arrived in a room with two bright pink Chesterfield sofas and a couple of low coffee tables. There was a dressing table bench with three stools set up against the back wall and in the corner was a small bar with wine, spirits, and an ice bucket—a fridge with more wine, beer, and soft drinks. The walls were covered in posters of gigs gone by, and they were overlaid one on top of the other. I couldn't see any wall for posters.

Will walked over to the bar. 'What would you like?'

'Just a lemonade,' I said, and he looked at me.

'A lemonade?' he said disbelievingly.

'I haven't eaten anything. If I start drinking now, I'll be wasted by....'

I looked at my watch. It was twenty past eight.

'Eight-thirty.'

He laughed.

'Lucy, I'm so sorry, we should have got some food at the hotel. I never eat before gigs, so it didn't even cross my mind. You want me to see if I can get you something?'

I shook my head.

We all sat about on the sofas, enjoying our drinks. Alysa was nowhere to be seen. Hannah was holding court, telling us all about their trip to The Ritz to have afternoon tea. Will had his hand up the back of my top, gently caressing my spine. It made me feel awkward, but I could tell Will was doing it on purpose because he was watching me with a glint in his eye.

'What are you girls gonna do while we play?' Paul asked. Hannah looked at me, and I shrugged. 'There's a really nice bar here if I remember rightly, and it won't be swamped while we're playing.'

'I'm happy with that,' Hannah said. 'I don't fancy getting all sweaty tonight.'

Jakes's eyes lit up. 'If you two are gonna get all sweaty, is it too late to cancel the show?'

The guys laughed while Hannah and I shared a look of disdain. They were such schoolboys sometimes. Alysa came charging in.

'It's time, boys.'

We all stood up, and Will gave Terry a look, who nodded in some kind of silent agreement. Will kissed me goodbye, and I wished him luck before Hannah grabbed my hand. She gave me a packet of what looked like mini Haribo, but it was a pair of earplugs. We wandered along the maze of corridors until we bumped into a member of staff who pointed us in the right direction.

The venue was much bigger than Bristol, but Paul was right, the bar was pretty quiet. The stage was miles away, but I was glad Hannah placed our drinks order before they started to play because, my God, it was loud. Hannah had automatically ordered me a glass of wine, so I felt obliged to drink it.

'So, how are things going with Will?' Hannah shouted once we had settled ourselves on a couple of bar stools.

I instinctively looked around before replying and noticed Terry standing on the periphery. Had Will asked him to follow us?

'Well, it's early days, and it kind of feels like there's a time limit on our existence but other than that... I do like him.' I could tell I would have a sore throat in the morning.

'Well, he is smitten with you! You can totally see it, and Paul said he hasn't stopped talking about you.' I looked at the floor, a little embarrassed. 'I have to admit, I'm kind of glad.' I looked up then, puzzled as to what she meant. 'He was in a bad way before. He was drinking way too much and was turning up to rehearsals late or half cut. That's why they didn't tour the last album. Paul had started looking for other jobs. Will was calling in the middle of the night, and Paul or Jake had to go and collect him from random places a couple of times.'

I guessed this is what he was referring to when he mentioned his *dark place*. We had finished our drinks, and Hannah asked if I'd like to go backstage. I wondered just how many gigs she'd attended. She must be bored sick of their set. We finally found the room with the pink sofas, helped ourselves to more wine, and made ourselves comfortable.

'Anyway, Paul said he can always tell when Will is happy because he writes, and he's been writing the whole time I've been here,' she confirmed, and I smiled.

It was kind of reassuring to hear this stuff from someone else. For all I knew, Will could have been seeing other people. We hadn't made any formal commitment.

'I'm not surprised, really,' She carried on. She loved to talk, this girl. 'You're lovely, and Paul says you're different from the rest.'

Okay, maybe it wasn't so great hearing stuff from someone else.

'I'm just gonna head to the loo, back in a sec,' I said as I stood up.

Woah! That wine had gone straight to my head as I'd predicted. I opened the door, wondering whether I should go left or right, and stood opposite was Terry. 'Oh, hello again.'

'Ma'am.' He nodded, and I frowned at his formal greeting.

'I'm just heading to the Ladies,' I explained, unsure why I felt the need to tell him.

'Very good. I'll show you the way,' he said and lifted his right hand to direct me.

'Is this another one of Will's special requests? Babysitting the girls?' I asked as we walked, but then he stopped.

'The Ladies,' he said, but I wasn't sure if he was correcting my use of language or telling me we'd arrived at the loos.

I wasn't going to get anything out of him, and it was probably rude of me to ask. He wasn't going to confirm anything with me. He worked for Will. As I washed my hands, I stared at myself in the mirror. Was I one of many? And why was I different? I could hear the crowd shouting 'encore'. They must have nearly finished their set. I apologised to Terry on the way back, I didn't want to put him in an awkward position, but he just nodded and stayed silent. Hannah stood when I came in.

'I didn't say too much, did I? Paul always tells me off for saying too much. Are you okay?' She handed me another glass of wine, and I took a long sip.

'I'm fine, I guess Will and I just don't know each other too well yet, and I feel like I'm picking up bits and pieces about his past here and there. I overthink things sometimes,' I admitted.

'Oh, my God, me too but isn't that what women are supposed to do!?' she said, flopping back down on the sofa and sloshing her drink on the floor as I sat opposite her.

I could hear the crowd roar in the distance, which could only mean one thing. A few moments later, we could hear a hive of activity approaching the door, and they all came piling in, not just the band but a whole bunch of other people I hadn't met, maybe friends of theirs and the support band? Will entered a few moments later with a towel around his shoulders, followed by Terry. He wiped his face and scanned the room for me, silently beckoning me over by nodding towards a quiet corner.

'Hey, did you enjoy the show?' he asked, wrapping his arm around my waist. He was wet through with sweat.

'From afar, yes.'

I suddenly felt a bit rude that I'd missed the show. Will spied my glass of wine and cocked his head to one side. I couldn't quite make out his mood.

'I thought you weren't gonna drink,' he said, taking the glass from my hand and placing it on a shelf behind me.

'It was a means to an end,' I said.

He leaned into me. I thought he was going to kiss my neck, but instead, he whispered in my ear.

'Not babysitting, just looking out for you.' He had got the low down from Terry. He put his forehead against mine and looked deep into my eyes. 'Okay?'

'Okay.'

I sensed someone was waiting for us, and I looked over his shoulder. It was Alysa. I looked back at Will and then back at Alysa, and he turned to see who it was.

'Sorry to interrupt, but there's just a couple of people I need you to say hi to.'

She looked uneasy.

'I'll be there in a minute,' he replied, and I got the vibe that everyone in the room was half-listening. He turned back to me and, cupping my face in his hands, kissed me as if no one was watching. Then, he slowly pulled away and picked the glass of wine back up.

'I'll be as quick as possible, but you might need this.' Will handed my glass back, giving me a wink, and headed out of the room with Alysa.

I weaved my way back over to the bar and refilled my glass.

Half an hour or so went by, and I got chatting to some guy, whose relatives lived in Clevedon and had visited on several occasions. He could remember walking along the pier when he was younger and dropping a pound coin. He was devastated because it disappeared between the wooden slats into the sea below, and he wanted to buy something from the gift shop.

'What would you have bought from the shop?' I enquired.

'Oh, probably one of those crappy gemstones. I was well into them when I was younger, like a little magpie,' he said as he waved his hands up and down like a bird, and I laughed.

Just then, Will flung the door open with force, nearly knocking the people over who stood by it, Alysa in his wake. He did not look happy. 'Who in the hell is leaking this shit... it's someone close.' He wasn't really talking to Alysa. He was kind of addressing everyone in the room. Paul stood up and put a hand on Will's shoulder, guiding him away from the main throng of people.

'Oh dear, that doesn't sound good,' magpie guy said. 'The crap they've been printing about him is off the scale, and he seems like a nice guy. Do you know him?' he asked.

I wasn't sure what he was referring to because I had made an effort not to look, but whatever Will had discovered did not sound good. He was waving his arms around aggressively in the corner while Paul did his best to calm him down. I noticed Alysa had disappeared. I wasn't sure whether to go over or not.

'Um, yeah, I do... I'd better see if he's okay, actually. It was good to meet you.'

I kind of bowed out of our conversation and weaved my way back to the other side of the room.

'Hey, what's going on?' I asked, looking at them from one to another. Will looked at the floor, and Paul looked at me with compassion as I frowned. What on earth was going on?

'I'm gonna leave you to it,' Paul said and stepped away.

Will was still looking at the floor and I was starting to feel on edge.

'Should I go?' I asked, for want of a better suggestion. Will looked at me, surprised, and took my hand.

'No!' he said, pulling me towards him, and I brushed his fringe out of his eyes to see him properly.

'Have we reached a room service situation?' I asked with a smile, desperately trying to lighten the mood.

It worked, he chuckled, but his eyes were still dark.

'Something like that.' He looked beyond me and nodded to someone, and within seconds Terry was by our side. 'We need to go.'

'Give me a few minutes,' Terry said and disappeared out of the room. Will turned his attention back to me and put his forehead against mine. I was beginning to realise that this was his way of blocking everything out, taking a moment to focus and zone out of everything that was going on around him.

'Okay, so don't flip out.'

Why did people say that? When they are about to tell you something terrible, no good would ever follow a statement like that. So, I didn't respond. I just waited.

'There are some pictures in the press of me with someone else.'

So, there were others. I'd had my suspicions, but this was a gut punch.

'They're old, but they've been made to look current because we're in the same location.'

I was starting to feel a bit unsteady on my feet.

'How old?' I whispered, almost not wanting to know the answer. It wasn't until this very moment that I realised I would feel incredibly betrayed and stupid. Stupid for believing this was an exclusive arrangement.

'Like, a couple of years old... and the story goes that I'm cheating on you after breaking up your family. I'm thankful I'm being made out to be the scoundrel, if I'm honest.'

Will took my glass out of my hand for the second time that night. It was probably for the best, as I was shaking.

Terry appeared at our sides again.

'It's not looking good...' he said.

Will sighed and dragged a hand through his hair.

'We can access the hotel through the service entrance, so that's not a problem, but the press are here in the car park. I've managed to park as close as possible, but we'll need Bill.'

Terry looked at me. I must have looked terrified because his face dropped. Paul, Hannah, and Jake were all looking on with concern while the rest of the crowd sensed there was a problem. If the ground could have swallowed me up, it would have been a great time to do it. I was petrified. This wasn't just a bit of local press. This was the paparazzi.

'Okay, come on, let's get this over and done with,' Will said, and put his arm around my waist, pulling me towards the door.

'Can we not just wait until they've gone?' I asked desperately. I didn't even know if I wanted to go back to the hotel. Or be with Will. Or be in London. 'Can't I just go, get a cab? Go home?'

Will had pulled me into the corridor, away from all the onlookers, and took my face in his hands.

'Look at me. It's just you and me,' he said.

I was aware that my breathing was erratic. I couldn't quite find a rhythm.

'Everything else is just hearsay, remember?'

I was aware that Bill had joined us, and we were walking, but my legs were not acting normally. I kept stumbling, and I couldn't quite keep up. Eventually, Will picked me up and carried me along the final stretch to the door before placing me back down.

'We've got about twenty feet,' Terry confirmed, and I could hear the press outside, chattering amongst themselves.

'Lucy, you're gonna have to walk,' Will said. 'Come here.'

He pulled me into him, putting his arm around my shoulders and pressing my face against his chest. He used his jacket to cover my face as best he could. 'Put your arm around my waist.' I put both my hands around him, clinging to him. I was so nervous and scared.

'Okay.'

Terry or Bill opened the door, and we all moved forward as one. Then, everyone outside started shouting, and it was like someone had switched on a strobe light. I kept looking at the floor, and every split second, everyone's shoes would turn black and white. It was disorientating.

'Will, over here.'

'Lucy, how are you feeling?'

'Will, who's heart are you going to break?'

There was pushing and shoving, and I stumbled a couple of times, but then I saw the car, and Will pushed me inside, and he followed.

It wasn't until the car started to pull away that I realised I was crying, Will dragged me onto his lap, stroking my hair, and I listened to his heart beating as I started to calm down.

'I'm so sorry,' he said through a long breath.

Once we had been safely deposited back in our hotel room, it was like an actual elephant had joined us. Neither of us knew what to say to the other. I perched on the arm of the sofa and looked out at all the lights across London. Will broke the silence.

'Would you like a cup of tea?' he asked tentatively.

I started to laugh, but I must have sounded a bit crazy.

'What? Isn't that what you Brits do? Drink tea after a stressful situation.'

I sighed and pulled my phone out of my bag. Jesus Christ, I had no less than thirteen missed calls from Mike. The boys, my mum, Steph, everyone. I leaned forward, and an involuntary sob came out. Will was there in a second, dragging me up to my feet.

'I'm so sorry,' he said again. 'Listen... there is no one else, okay? There hasn't been anyone else since I met you. I know we haven't... made us official, and maybe you don't want to, but I do. I want you to be my girlfriend. I want you to tell everyone that I'm your boyfriend.'

I didn't know what to say to him. If he had told me that a few hours ago, I would have been delighted, and would have probably sung it from the rooftops, but life had become very convoluted all of a sudden and complex. I wanted to see the worst of it. I wanted to see the pictures, see how bad they were... no, I didn't. Why would I want to look at Will with someone else? I needed to ring the boys and Mike. Will was still looking at me expectantly, and I closed my eyes.

'I need to make some calls.'

His shoulders slumped, and he looked at the floor, shaking his head.

'I'm gonna go take a shower... don't run.' He looked at me troubled, and if I wasn't mistaken, it looked like he was welling up.

'I won't run.'

He released me and headed to the bathroom, and my whole body went limp as I sat on the sofa. I called Frankie first.

'Mum! Are you okay?' Frankie sounded worried, and I could hear Mike in the background asking if it was me.

'I'm fine, Frankie, absolutely fine. It's just the media making stuff up again. It's all rubbish.' I could hear Mike asking to speak to me, and there was a kerfuffle.

'Lucy, what the hell is going on? You left the boys on their own to see him? Your mum is here. We're all worried sick.'

I looked at my watch. It was nearly 1 am. I imagined the scene in my kitchen, everyone pacing around, my mum making copious amounts of tea, and Mike constantly refreshing his laptop to see the latest.

'Nothing is going on. I'm safe, I'm at a hotel in London, and the stuff in the news is just made up.'

I tried to assure him.

'Lucy, you're delusional. He's fucking you around. He's with someone else and just using you. You're making a mockery of yourself. Have you even seen these pictures?'

He was really cross. He never swore in front of my mum.

'No, and I don't want to...' I admitted. I heard Will finishing up in the shower.

'Well, the only person here having the wool pulled over their eyes is you!' he shouted.

I squeezed my eyes shut and massaged my forehead with my free hand.

'And you know, leaving the boys on their own... you could have run it by me. What were you going to do, sneak off to London for the night and hope I wouldn't find out?'

He was really starting to piss me off.

'I wasn't *sneaking* anywhere. I don't have to answer to you.'

Will came out of the bathroom and looked over at me, but I looked away and sighed.

'You do when I get a phone call from our son who's worried about you because he's seen some pictures of his mum's boyfriend with someone else online.'

I put my hand over my mouth and looked at the ceiling, I could feel myself welling up, but I did not want Mike to know I was crying.

'Have you finished?' I managed to say. 'Can I speak to Mum now?'

'Whatever, I'm going home.' The line was silent for a moment, and then my mum picked up. Just as she said hello, I heard the side door in our kitchen slam.

'Hi, Mum, I'm really sorry it's so late. Are you going to stay?'

'No, I'll head back. It will only take five minutes. Are you okay?'

It was such a loaded question tears began to track down my face, and I brushed them away.

'I'm fine, Mum. Please just give the boys a kiss goodnight from me, and I'll see them tomorrow,' I said thickly.

'Of course, I will, goodnight darling.'

I hung up and lobbed my phone across the room before hugging my knees into my chest. It bounced off the carpet and skittered along the marble floor towards the window. It wasn't long before I felt the sofa depress next to me, and then Will fed his arms around me and picked me up. I instinctively put my arms around his neck, and he carried me to the bedroom. He laid me down and then pulled the duvet over me without even undressing before wandering off to turn the lights out. I felt him get into bed, but he made no effort to touch me.

'I'm sorry,' he whispered.

He sounded so sad, but I had nothing left. I was done in. I reached out and found his hand and held it. Two bodies lying in a vast bed with London laid out beneath them, almost hanging on to each other.

When I opened my eyes, the first thing I saw was London Bridge and the Thames winding its way through London like a long thick worm. My first thought was Will, and the conversation we'd had last night, or rather what he'd said, and I turned quickly. He was lying on his side watching me. He looked tired, like he hadn't slept. I reached out and put my hand on his cheek, and he covered it with his own and closed his eyes. He was still waiting for me to respond. Was I being a fool to trust him? Had I had the wool pulled over my eyes? I'd only known him for a few weeks. Yet, I had faith in him, and I was drawn to him by some unspoken calling. Above all, I wanted him, and despite the media coverage, what was life without risks? I wriggled over to him until I could feel the heat from his body, and he opened his eyes.

'Who do you want me to tell first?' I asked, and he frowned. 'That you're my boyfriend.' I clarified.

He looked at me, went to say something, and then stopped. And then took a breath in to say something but nothing came out.

'Are you serious?' he said, eventually. 'After yesterday?' He dragged his hand through his hair. 'I have Terry on stand-by to take you home.'

'Well, I do need to go home, I've kind of been made to feel like the worst mum, but I get the feeling that the boys will be pleased for me.'

He allowed himself to put his arm around me.

'Because they would obviously be the first people I'd want you to tell.'

He rolled me onto my back.

'Seriously?' he asked again, smoothing my hair out of my face, and I nodded.

It was so good to feel his body against mine. He had evidently felt so incredibly insecure last night, it was as if he couldn't believe his luck. His luck? I mean, I was the lucky one, right?

'I can't believe you're taking this on,' he said, waving an arm around to signify all the other stuff.

'But it's just you and me. Everything else is hearsay... isn't that right?' Will laughed and shook his head, and his eyes looked glassy. I cupped my hands around his face and kissed him, and he deepened the kiss, pushing himself against me.

Chapter 16

Terry escorted me from the room to the car. There was no need as all the fans had gone, but Will insisted. I slid in the back, and once again, there was a little gift bag on the back seat, *Stephen Webster*? I'd not heard of him. The gift card was handwritten, and I couldn't help but notice that his handwriting was expressive, just like the note he'd left on his bedside table.

To my girlfriend. I hope you like it. See you in Lisbon. Your boyfriend x.

The word girlfriend and boyfriend were in italic and were particularly swirlier than the rest.

I smiled.

He was certainly making the most of our new status. Is this what was in his back pocket? The little black box had its own outer casing. I pushed the box out and opened it. Wow! My jaw dropped. It was a beautiful black butterfly necklace encrusted with black pavé stones, the silver chain attaching at the tip of each wing. It was delicate but had a rocky edge and a certain weight to it that suggested it was expensive. I had never been given something so exquisite, and I tilted it from side to side to see the stones sparkle before carefully laying it back in the box.

When did he expect me to wear it?

When I got back, the boys were both at home, I told them about Will and me, and we chatted about the media. I didn't want them searching for information that would likely be made up. To be fair, it had mainly been their friends messaging them, and they were undoubtedly worried. I promised to try to check my phone more regularly and to message them to let them know I was okay in the future. I didn't ask them about Mike. Frankie couldn't understand why he'd flown off the handle so much. I put it down to stress about the job, which seemed to appease him.

Thank you for my beautiful gift. I miss you already xx

It was pathetic, I'd only been home an hour, and I could not stop thinking about him. I just wanted to cancel all my appointments and fly out to France with him next week.

'Cooee.' Steph wandered into the kitchen. 'Just wanted to check in on my famous friend,' she joked, squeezing me.

'Oh, don't, I haven't looked, and I don't want to know.' I sighed, squeezing back.

'I don't know how you manage it. I'd be refreshing the gossip pages every half hour,' she admitted. 'Is it too early for a gin?'

'It's never too early,' I said, collecting a couple of glasses and filling them with ice before heading into the lounge.

I told Steph everything, I needed her perspective, and she gave it. I was thankful that she thought Mike was being a dick. I needed reassurance that he was blowing everything out of proportion. And although she'd only met Will briefly, he seemed trustworthy to her, and the press was very good at distorting the truth.

'I really can't believe you've bagged Will Reynolds as your boyfriend. I don't mean that you're not worthy, but it's absolutely crazy, right?'

She waved her hands around as she said it, and I laughed.

'I know... I feel lucky, but Will can't believe I agreed to be his girlfriend after all the hassle he'd caused.'

I shook my head, still thinking I would wake up and it would all be a dream.

Steph ended up staying for dinner, and we shared a bottle of wine which was probably a mistake after all the gin.

I woke up at about four in the morning, desperate for a pee. It was always the same when I had been drinking. My head felt like someone had secretly stuffed cotton wool into my ears overnight, but thankfully I didn't have a headache. As I walked back across the landing to the bedroom, I thought I heard something downstairs. I froze, my ears suddenly searching, and I held my breath. Was it the dogs? Something shuffled, and the dogs started to bark, so I used the opportunity to leap back into my room. Oh, my God, was it a burglar?

Both boys' bedroom doors were shut, so I figured they were asleep. I grabbed the cricket bat from under my bed and hid behind the door. I had put it there after Mike moved out, but I had no idea what to do with it if I ever needed to use it. It just gave me peace of mind all the same. I pressed myself against the wall, hugging the bat and trying to control my breathing. It sounded like I was breathing really loudly. Someone was coming up the stairs, and as they approached the open door, I held my breath again.

'Lucy?' Came a hushed whisper. I released all the air in my lungs and dropped the bat in relief upon hearing Will's voice. Unfortunately, it landed straight on my big toe, and I yelped, hopping around like a lunatic.

'Mum?' I heard one of the boys call as Will said, 'Shit.' And turned the light on.

'It's okay. I stubbed my toe,' I called to whoever it was as I sat on the edge of the bed.

Will shut the door, dropping down to inspect my toe.

'What are you doing here?' I asked as I held my toe tight while it throbbed.

'I had a window,' Will said, staring up at me, looking a bit sheepish. 'I wanted to see you before we went to France, so I thought I'd surprise you.'

'Will, it's...' I glanced over at the clock on the bedside table and then looked back at him. 'Ten past four!'

'I know.' He smiled. 'I got your text when I finished up with the band, so I called Terry to bring me here.'

He removed my hand from my toe to check for damage, but it didn't look too bad. He kissed it.

'Do you want me to grab you some Advil?'

I shook my head, looking into his eyes. It was pretty sweet that he'd made an effort to see me.

'Good because I haven't got long!'

He stood up and took his jacket, shoes, and trousers off. Oh.

'Scooch up,' he said, waving me onto the bed. He engulfed me.

'That was very presumptuous,' I said as he rolled me onto my back, leaning on his elbows, his fringe tickling my nose.

'I was willing to take the risk,' he replied before going in for a kiss, 'I don't think there's going to be any need for these panties.'

I cringed—*panties*—I hated that word.

'You can't call them panties, you're in the UK remember?'

He laughed quietly before cupping me between my thighs, making me gasp at his boldness.

'I suppose you're gonna tell me I can't call this your pussy either.'

I put both of my hands over my face with sheer embarrassment as Will chuckled some more. I couldn't work out whether I was uncomfortable with the word or just not used to the language.

Two hours later, I was dozing, Will's arms and legs draped all over me. I felt something vibrating. What the hell?

'Aww, that's me,' Will said sleepily, 'I'm gonna have to make a move.'

It was his watch, alerting him it was time to go.

'Really, so soon?'

I was more than gutted.

'I'd love to stay for one of your slaughtered bacon sandwiches, but I have a plane to catch.'

I watched him as he got up and tried to locate his clothes in the half-light. I could feel his boxers were by my feet. I got hold of them by scrunching my toes and lifting them out at the end of the bed. He took them and smiled at me, and I watched him dress. He was so lean.

'I won't see you until you fly out to Portugal, but I'll meet you at Lisbon airport, okay?'

I nodded.

'I've booked us a hotel. I think you'll like it.'

'Do I need to pack anything in particular?' I asked as he put his jacket on, and I wrapped the duvet around me like a cone.

'You don't have to pack anything. Just come as you are.'

I giggled, and he swooped in to kiss me.

'Where's your necklace?'

I bit my lip, and then he saw the box on my dressing table.

'It's so beautiful. I'm worried I'll damage it,' I said as Will picked the box up and got the necklace out. He leaned over me and attached the clasp before looking at it. I stroked it carefully.

'If you damage it, I'll get you another one. Wear it,' he said sternly before kissing me again.

I saluted Will before he disappeared out the door.

I rolled back and looked up at the ceiling, was that what they called a booty call?

———◦———

I logged on to the B&B account to check the balance. I really needed to go shopping and get some bits and pieces for the trip. I didn't even have a nice pair of flip-flops. There was more money in there than I had thought—a lot more. I looked back through the visitors to determine if there had been a mistake. I thought my eyes were deceiving me, but I realised that Will had left a tip. A thousand-pound tip. I couldn't believe it. He never said. I hoped he didn't think I'd seen it and not said anything to him about it. A grand was a lot of money and way too much for a tip. Blinking a few times to check I wasn't going mad, I transferred the money to my current account. And text Steph.

Fancy a shopping trip? I need a bikini. X

Steph texted back. *Yes! Shall I ask Claire and Zara if they'd like to come? Girls' day out and then drinks back at mine?*

Yes and yes! Sounds perfect.

I was rather excited. It would be the first time ever that I could go shopping and not have to count the pennies. I would, of course, save most of it. Maybe I could book a little holiday cottage for the boys and me in the summer. Make a change from using a campsite.

That evening I was exhausted, what with the early wake-up call, my mild hangover, and all the housework I'd done. But, of course, once I'd gotten into bed, I couldn't sleep, so I checked my phone. Mike had texted to say he had a second interview on Tuesday, with no apology.

Will had too. *This morning was... amazing x*

It was always amazing.

Chapter 17

I woke refreshed and was looking forward to our girls' day out. Steph had texted to say Zara was a maybe. I really hoped she'd come. It would probably do her a world of good.

Steph came to pick me up, and I was thrilled to see Zara in the car. We then popped round the corner to scoop Claire up. Everyone had made some effort, although Zara still looked a bit washed out. We arrived at the shopping centre mid-morning. I had a list that the girls thought was hilarious.

'I don't want to forget anything. I haven't got time to come back before I go.'

'Right ladies, shall we stick together or split up and meet back for lunch? I've booked us a table at the Thai place at one,' Steph announced.

We were all there for different things, so it seemed best if we went our separate ways to get what we needed, and then we could browse together after lunch. So, I went straight to the department store. I might as well start with underwear and work my way out. I bought a couple of new bras with matching knickers and a pack of five cotton plain black Brazilian pants. I hadn't treated myself to new undies for such a long time. The elastic was starting to go on the ones I had. As I wandered towards the tills, I spotted a beautiful night vest, it was black with deep red lace accents, and it boasted 'cooling' material.

'Buy it,' Steph said, who had crept up behind me.

'Oh, I don't know. It's quite expensive, Steph.'

She took my shoulders in her hands.

'He's flying you out to Portugal. Give him what he wants.' She picked it up and put it in my basket.

'And you can put these back.'

She picked up the set of pants.

I swiped them back off her.

'Those are not for the weekend. They're for everyday,' I said as I put them back in my basket, glaring at her.

'Ohhh, someone's on a spending spree.'

I didn't want to mention the money Will had left. It felt weird telling her and somehow wrong, so I ignored her comment.

'Erm, Lucy?' I tore myself away from my list to look at her. 'Is that *Stephen Webster*?' I stroked my necklace again and coloured up.

'Is he famous?' I asked.

Steph rolled her eyes. 'That is expensive shit!' she confirmed, lifting the pendant to take a closer look as she whistled and then looked back at me.

'A gift?' She guessed, and I looked at the floor as she puckered her lips, knowing I wasn't going to confirm or deny.

'What else do you need?' she said, more determined to help me get what I needed.

'Um.' I pulled my list up on my phone again. 'Flip-flops, a bikini, sun cream, some shorts, a skirt, and a dress, maybe?'

We meandered around the shops together. I picked up shorts, and flip-flops while still in the store, and sun cream from the pharmacy. So that left the bikini, the skirt, and the dress.

'What is the dress for?' Steph asked.

'Well, something that's smart enough to go out to dinner and relaxed enough to wear on the beach. He's booked us a hotel, and judging by the last hotel we stayed in, it will be a posh one,' I explained, and she thought for a moment.

'I hate my boobs!' I said, trying to shove them down into another pretty little dress. They weren't suitable for delicate clothing. They needed structure and support, otherwise, I looked like I was wearing a sack.

'Okay, let's think outside the box here... why don't we get you a supportive bikini and then like a sheer beach dress to pull over the top? You could also pop it over those shorts.'

So, we altered our search, and while I tried on several bikinis, Steph went on a hunt for the dress. I found a lovely bikini with a fun tropical print. It lifted my boobs and covered them enough without creating the dreaded four-boob look. I was delighted to discover the set had options with several types of bottoms. I opted for the low-rise shorts. I was not about to parade along a beach in a thong, and the high-waisted version made me look frumpy.

'I bought you this, we can always take it back if you don't like it, but I think you will.'

It was a light green cotton floaty number. Steph held it against me, and I looked at myself in the mirror. It had little cap sleeves that would protect my shoulders from the sun, a loose V-cut neckline, and a string tie waist so I could pull it in under my boobs for a more fitted look. It was perfect.

'They've got a long version if you'd prefer, but....'

'No, it's just right—thank you.' The hemline would hit just above the knee. Steph winked. 'How much do I owe you?'

'Oh, don't worry about it.' Waving my offer away. 'Consider it an early birthday gift. Now come on, we're gonna be late for lunch.'

During lunch, Zara updated us about everything that had been going on with Andy, he wanted to split up with the woman in Cornwall and make another go of it with Zara, but she had rightfully refused. Good for her. They were due to break it to the kids the following day, and my heart went out to her as I remembered doing the very same thing eight years ago.

The conversation moved on, and I filled them in about Mike flipping out, and they all agreed with Steph. We had a lovely lunch and a second visit to the shops. I picked up a couple of pretty bangles, a denim skirt, and a new lipstick. An hour later, we all piled back into Steph's car, and we were on our way back to hers for drinks.

When we got in, Steph popped upstairs to drop her shopping off, Zara went to the bathroom, and Claire popped into the garden for what I guessed was a drag on that vape thing. I noticed that I'd missed a call from Will, so I called back, it took a while to connect, but it started to ring.

'I need to take this, Hi!' I heard Will say. 'What have you been up to?'

'Shopping! A guest of ours left a rather large tip, so I thought I'd treat myself.'

He laughed. 'What an awesome guest. I'm glad you've put it to good use.'

'Thank you.'

'It's nothing, really.'

'What are you up to?'

'Ah, just in a meeting trying to sort out the logistics for the festival back in the UK. Actually, could you come?' he asked.

It would be over a weekend, meaning I wouldn't miss any work. I guessed it would depend on whether the kids were with Mike or not and if the kennels were free. The girls gathered back in the kitchen, Zara and Claire sitting at the breakfast bar and Steph fetching glasses. 'I'd really like you to be there, and I could get extra passes so you could bring some friends.'

'Um, when is it?'

Steph looked up from making some G&Ts, a little glint in her eye.

'It's the weekend after Portugal.'

Hmmm, I'd have the kids. Could I leave them for a whole weekend?

'Um, could you get three extra passes?' I asked tentatively, Steph looked up again, and Zara and Claire turned on their stools to look at me.

'Sure, if it means you being there, I'd get twenty extra passes,' he declared, and I smiled.

'Okay, let me see what I can do.' I looked back at the girls with an excited smile.

'I'd better get back to this meeting. Text me the names.'

'I will.' He was gone, so I ended the call and looked up at the girls. 'Fancy going to a festival, ladies?' They all chimed in with yeses and claps of glee as Steph handed out the drinks.

'To super-hot boyfriends with benefits,' Steph said, and we all clinked glasses. 'So, when is it?'

Everyone checked their phones to see if they were available. Steph and Claire were already adding it to their calendars, but Zara looked up at me, hesitant.

Before she said anything, I said, 'It would do you a power of good.' She looked back at her phone and slumped her shoulders.

'It's Toby's swimming gala on Saturday and Henrietta's ballet exam.' Claire reached over and pinched Zara 's phone out of her hand.

'So, you message that dickband of yours and tell him he's on duty.' She started typing out a message.

'Claire, don't. Please give it back.' Zara looked panicked, and I took the phone back off Claire and gave it back to her.

'Look, I'll text Will back with our names, and you see what you can do,' I said to Zara. 'But honestly, I think he should totally be on Dad duty.'

Steph picked up her glass again and said, 'To Dads on duty.' Everyone laughed, and I quickly texted Will back with our names.

It was one in the morning, and I was wasted. The G&Ts had moved on to Cosmopolitans and then to wine, a terrible mistake, and I was standing at Steph's kitchen sink with the hiccoughs, trying to hold my breath and drink water. Steph walked back in after seeing Claire and Zara off.

'Do you wanna stay here?'

I tried to say yes, but a hiccough replaced it.

'The spare room is made up. Come on, grab your bag and bring that glass of water.'

Steph got me upstairs, and I collapsed on the bed, but as soon as I lay down, I sat straight back up. The room was spinning. Jesus, it had been a while. I got back up and, half staggered, half used the wall to guide me down the landing into the bathroom. I went for a wee and thought, 'Oh God', and whizzed around quickly to be sick. What a state. I finished my business and then splashed my face with water. Thankfully, the room had stopped spinning when I got back, but I could hear something in my bag. It was my phone.

'Mello?' I slurred.

'Hey, it's me,' Will announced.

'Ohhh, it's my super-hot boyfriend with benefits,' I slurred, and Will laughed.

'Oh, someone's had a few drinks.'

'Mmm hmm. I'm at Stephs.' My lips got stuck together each time I pronounced anything with an M.

'Well, it sounds like you've had an excellent night.'

'Aha, aaand I think I'm falling for you.'

'Ooookay, maybe a conversation to have when we're both sober?'

'Maybe,' I whispered.

'Listen, I'll call you in the morning. You get some sleep.'

I took a deep breath and looked at my phone with one eye shut so I could focus. He had hung up.

'Everything okay, sweetheart?' Steph stood in the door-way. I fell back onto the bed and started to undo my jeans. 'Do you need me to get a bucket?'

'Nope,' I said over pronouncing the P. 'I've already been sick, and now I need to sleep.' I struggled to get my jeans off, so Steph grabbed hold of the bottoms and pulled them off, laughing.

'Okay, babe, see you in the morning.'

Chapter 18

Oh my actual God, my head was in a vice. I scrunched my face up and opened one eye. Where the hell was I? Oh, Steph's.

I looked over at the bedside table to locate my water and noticed two painkillers beside it. Bless her, she was a good friend. I took them straight away and then headed to the bathroom. I didn't have anything with me, so I had a quick wash using the soap and used my finger to circle some toothpaste around my mouth.

I gingerly ventured downstairs. Steph sat at the breakfast bar, sipping a coffee. 'Morning, sleepy head. Do you want a coffee?'

My stomach turned, and I shook my head. 'No, I should get home. I didn't tell the boys I was staying.'

'Don't worry, babe, I text them. Do you want me to drive you back?'

'No, I'd better walk. At least I can throw up in a gutter if I need to.'

'Oh dear, you'll feel better once those painkillers have kicked in, and you can go back to bed when you get home.' I picked up my coat and bags and gave her a big hug.

'Thanks for last night... I think.'

'No problem, it was a lush evening, although before you go, you might wanna know that you told Will that you were falling for him last night.'

'What?' I dropped my bags. 'I didn't.'

'Yeah, you did.'

'What did he say?'

'I don't know, but the conversation was over pretty quickly,' she explained.

'Oh, God...'

What did I do that for? I mean, it wasn't as if I hadn't had those feelings, but it was way too early to say anything to him.

'Bollocks, bollocks, bollocks.'

I looked at the ceiling and then at Steph.

'Don't worry too much. I'm sure he's feeling the same.'

I bent down and picked up my bags as Steph guided me to the door. On the way home, I wondered whether I should call him. Or maybe text him. Or not. For goodness' sake. What an idiot. I've probably scared him off. I resolved not to do anything. I would wait for him to call me.

And wait, I did. By the end of the day, I was sure I would never hear from him again. I was so tired. I hadn't gone back to bed and had powered through, taken the dogs out, and even managed to empty and reload the dishwasher without being sick.

By eight-thirty, I was in my PJs with herbal tea in hand and heading to bed. I took two more painkillers to knock me out, hoping I would wake up tomorrow and realise it was a terrible dream.

When I woke up the following day, I checked my phone straight away, but there was nothing, no missed calls, no text. I got up and put the dogs in the boot of the car. I needed to clear my head. I drove to the next town. I didn't want to see anyone I knew, so I took the dogs for a walk along the coastal path. It was a refreshing change, but my head wasn't any clearer. Maybe I should just call him and get it over and done with. Not speaking to him would only delay it. I got back to the car and stared at my phone. I looked out of the windscreen and then back at my phone. I took a deep breath and was about to call him when a text came through.

It was Will. *Gonna be pretty up against it over the next few days. I'll see you at the airport on Friday. We need to talk. X*

I reread the text several times. I couldn't determine whether he was off with me or just being practical. He had put a kiss at the end, but what did he mean by *we need to talk*? Did that mean he wanted to end it? Would he really make me go all the way to Portugal to tell me that? Maybe not. Was he honestly trying to tell me he was too busy to speak to me until I got there? What did it mean? And what was I supposed to reply with? *Great, see you Friday*? No, too happy. *Ok*? Too blunt. Ahhh, in frustration, I threw my phone onto the dashboard, and it clattered into the passenger footwell. I quickly picked it back up to see my screen was cracked. Great. And it wasn't responding. It was just stuck on the text message. I switched it off and back on again, but it wouldn't come back on. I kept pressing and holding the button, but it was no use. Fuuuuck. My phone was broken.

I drove home. There was no way I'd have time to get that fixed before the weekend. I was way too busy. What did it matter? He was too busy to speak to me anyway. The dogs raced back into the house, and when I walked in, I realised why. Mike was in the kitchen. I took a long, steadying breath. This was all I needed.

'Hi,' I said. I was still pissed off with him.

'Hi. I just wanted to come and apologise for the other day. I was just really stressed about the interview, and it was out of order. I'm sorry.' He looked at the floor.

'It's ok, I should have checked my phone earlier, but it was all a bit full-on... do you want a coffee?'

We sat at the table with our coffees.

'So, how do you feel the interview went?' I asked.

He took a deep breath. 'It went okay, I mean, I'm up for a second interview, but I don't know whether that's because they thought I was good enough or whether they had to pull a few strings.'

I nodded slowly.

'Is it serious? With Will Reynolds?'

That was not what I had expected him to ask, but I guess he had a right to know, we were still married. But actually, I didn't really have an answer for him because I didn't know.

'It's complicated.' I sighed. It was his turn to nod. 'Actually, he's asked if I want to go to a festival he's playing at the weekend after next. Do you think the boys will be okay on their own for the weekend?' I asked, realising that this was what I should have asked him the other day.

'Frankie is an adult now,' he said gently, knowing I didn't want to admit it. 'I think they'll be fine, and I'm only a phone call away.'

Our spat was over, and we finished our coffees. Before Mike went, I wished him good luck for his second interview, and he wished me a good time in Portugal.

Monday arrived. I went back through the entire house, ensuring everything had been put away. I lingered in Will's room, still a bit numb about the situation but excited about Friday. I had decided to go, even if it was to see him, talk and then fly straight home. We needed to see each other, no matter what.

The doorbell went. It was one of the agents. I let him walk around the house, taking measurements and making notes. He then had a look around outside. It was weird and slightly awkward. He eventually came back in.

'When was the last time you had that roof replaced?' he asked, pointing to the flat roof.

'Erm, about six years ago, I think.'

'And do you have a HETAS certificate for that log burner?' I nodded to confirm we had.

'Great, well here is our sales pack. It includes all the details you'll need, including our commission rate. We have a fantastic reputation for completion, so if you'd like to use Matt Thomas as your agent of choice, we can arrange for one of the team to come and take photos.' I took the pack. 'Are you and your... partner looking to move up the ladder because we have several properties on our books that may interest you.'

'Um, actually, we would be looking for separate properties.'

'Well, we have some very prestigious properties that might be of interest,' he said, and I looked at him. Did he know I was with Will? Did he think we were moving in together? 'I will email you with our valuation.' And I can ignore it, I thought. He left, and I watched as he climbed into his sporty Mercedes, and I hoped I would never have to see him again.

The rest of the day flew by with clients, a few enquiries, and running the boys around after school. I was just making dinner when I heard,

'Cooee, only me.' Steph was at the side door.

'Oh hi, are you okay? Come in.'

'More to the point, are you okay? I've been trying to phone you,' she asked.

'Oh yes, my phone's broken, and I haven't got time to fix it this week, too much on,' I explained.

'That's a bugger. I might have an old one you could borrow. I'll have a look when I get home.'

'Thanks, that would be great. I don't fancy going away with the kids not being able to contact me.'

'So, you're still going then? What was the outcome after your drunken call?'

'Well, actually, I don't know.' So, I explained what had happened, how it had been left, and all the possible scenarios of what could happen and that I'd come to the conclusion I should go, anyway.

'Definitely, you have to go. It will all sort itself out when you get there,' she agreed.

Chapter 19

'Great, well, that's all updated on the system. Here's a pot. If you'd like to make your way down the corridor, the loo is through the last door on the left.' The nurse said, who had just rinsed me for my entire life's sexual history. I took the pot and peed. Suddenly I was overwhelmed with worry that I could be pregnant. Not that I was late or anything, but there was a chance, I guess - a 1% chance. I took the pot carefully back through to the nurse. She popped the stick in, and I waited with bated breath. 'And that's negative, so we can look at options.' I was more than a little relieved, but she didn't seem to notice. 'Do you have a preference for either the combined or the mini-pill?'

'No, I don't think so.'

'In that case, considering your age, (I managed to refrain from rolling my eyes) I would recommend the mini-pill, so you take one tablet every day rather than having a break. Are your periods regular?'

'Yes, I mean, I don't take much notice of them these days, but they seem to come every few weeks.'

'Well, you should take the first tablet on the first day of your next period, and then you will be covered from the moment you start taking them.'

I thanked her for her time and then left. The next stop was the pharmacy. It had been another crazy day of clients, and I was looking forward to getting home and having a nice cup of tea. Once home I sifted through all my enquiries for treatments through my website, still receiving the odd, weird one and deleting them accordingly. By the time I had finished, my tea was cold, and it was time to make dinner.

'Dad's been trying to call you apparently,' Frankie said. It was his second interview today. I wondered how it went.

'Could you text him and tell him that my phone isn't working? I managed to crack the screen the other day, and it died.'

'Sure,' he said absentmindedly.

That evening I couldn't settle. I kept wondering what Will was up to, what he was thinking and what would happen when I got to Lisbon. I tried watching a film and reading, but it was no good. I just wanted it to be Friday already.

It was official. All estate agents were the same. I shut the front door a little too hard when he left, the condescending dickhead. What business is it of his whether I was happily or unhappily divorced? Suddenly the bell went again, and I thought it might be the agent complaining that I'd practically shut the door in his face, but it was a delivery man. I quickly scanned him for large cameras, but he held out a package for me with a dull look on his face.

'Lucy Daniels?'

I took the jiffy bag. Hmmm, I hadn't ordered anything. I wondered what it could be. I ripped it open there and then, and inside were four passes for the festival. A great big grin appeared on my face and a frisson of excitement.

I decided to take a bath. I was unlikely to have enough time to have one after work the next day, as I needed to pack. As I lay there, I tried to get my ducks in order. The last agent would be the next day, and then I had to work, then I needed to drop the dogs off, pack, sleep, and get a taxi to the airport. Damn! I hadn't booked a taxi. I quickly washed and got out.

'Paddy, can I borrow your phone? I need to make a call,' I said as I was drying myself.

'That's all booked for you, Friday at five o'clock.' Why were flights always so early? But at least I wouldn't have time to worry more about seeing Will.

Thursday arrived, and when I woke up, I thought, this time tomorrow, I'll be in the air. I hadn't flown for such a long time. Despite being super busy, the day dragged. Once I finished, I dropped the dogs round to Stephs, and she handed me a mobile phone. 'It's pretty old, and the battery doesn't last long, but at least you'll have a form of communication. It's one of the girls' old ones, so it's probably best to keep it off until you need it.'

'Thank you so much, Steph.' I took it gratefully.

'Are you excited?'

'Yes! Excited and nervous. I still don't know what to make of Will's text, but I guess I'll find out tomorrow.'

'You will, and it will be fine. You'll have a fab time, and you can tell me all about it on Monday, and then it won't be long before the festival.' She winked and clapped at the same time.

'Yes, the passes have arrived. Do you know if Zara managed to sort everything out?'

'I believe she did, so it should be the four of us.' That was great news, I was worried she'd bail, but she bloody well deserved a few days to herself. 'I'd better dash. I'm on my way to the supermarket, have the best time.' She pulled me in for a big squeeze.

When I got back, I raced upstairs to pack, simultaneously getting the boys to pack for their weekend with Mike. I lay everything out on the bed, the two sets of underwear and a spare pair, bikini, the pretty sundress, shorts, skirt, vests, a cardigan in case the evenings were cool, flip-flops, sandals, toiletries, passport, ticket. Was that everything?

I put everything in the case. I set my alarm, took a deep calming breath, and then went downstairs to make herbal tea. Before heading to bed, I made sure the boys were sorted and gave them both a hug. It would be weird going away without them. I knew it was only for a couple of nights, and they often stayed with Mike but going away and not being able to nip back if there was a problem was hard.

'We'll be fine,' Frankie said, ruffling Paddy's hair which Paddy was not impressed with.

'I know, but I'm going to miss you all the same.' So, we had a little joint hug, and then I climbed into bed to read my book.

Chapter 20

My eyes flickered open as my alarm beeped softly. It was four o'clock. I stretched and then crept into the bathroom for a quick shower. I couldn't believe the day had finally come. It had been the longest and most stressful week I could remember. After brushing my teeth, I put on a pair of light cotton trousers, a fitted t-shirt, my jacket and a pair of flats. I sneaked into the boys' bedrooms to say goodbye and give each a kiss on their foreheads, both mumbling their goodbyes in their half-sleep. I grabbed my bag, checked for the millionth time I had my passport and ticket, and went downstairs to wait for the taxi. It arrived a few minutes early, which I was relieved about because at ten to five, I was convinced it wouldn't turn up and I'd miss the plane.

It didn't take long to get to the airport as there was no one on the roads, and soon I had paid the driver and was pulling my little case along in the cool morning air. It was quite a long walk to the entrance from the drop-off point, and the undercover walkway was doing little for the cool breeze, but I eventually made it through the large rotating doors. The airport was pretty busy. Some people were dashing about, others were waiting at the exchange counter, but most were standing in queues, so many queues. I stopped to look up at the large board to find out where I was going and was immediately shoved in the back by someone walking behind me. He tutted me, and I muttered an apology. I was being *that* person, I thought, and I pulled my case in close.

I eventually worked out where I was supposed to be and boarded the escalator. At the top was a bank of checkpoints to scan my ticket, so I moved to the side to get mine out. I held my ticket over the infrared window, but nothing happened. I did it again, but the little doors stayed firmly shut. The person behind me gave an audible sigh, so I stepped to the side, a little flustered, and looked around to see if there was an information desk. I went back down the escalator and rushed over to the desk. There was a bit of a queue, and I was getting worried I would miss the flight, but I finally reached the counter. 'Hi, my ticket doesn't seem to be working,' I said, sliding it over to her. The lady took my ticket and tapped away on her computer.

'I'm sorry to inform you, Madam, but your booking has been cancelled.'

What? This couldn't be happening.

'There must be some kind of mistake. I haven't cancelled my booking. I'm due to meet someone in Lisbon.'

She tapped away again.

'I have just double-checked. It was cancelled a few days after the booking was made, and a refund has already been processed. I have just checked to see if any other seats are available on that flight, but sadly it is full.' I stood there looking at her as if she was going to offer me an alternative solution but clearly not, as she was simply staring back at me.

'Um, are there any other flights today? Or tomorrow even?' I asked in desperation. More tapping.

'The next flight leaving Bristol flies out on Tuesday at 10:40 am. Would you like me to book that for you?'

'That's too late,' I said in barely a whisper. I could feel my eyes starting to burn.

'Is everything all right, Madam?' I heard a distant voice say as I started to back away from the desk, realising that I was not going to get on that plane, I was not going to Lisbon, and I was not going to see Will. And then the darkest thought arrived, had Will cancelled the booking? The tears came, and I stood in the middle of the concourse, amongst the people queuing, clinging to my case. I had never felt so deflated in my entire life. Finally, I pulled my phone from my purse and made a call.

'Hello?' came a sleepy voice.

'Steph, it's me,' I said, my throat straining while holding the tears back long enough to speak. 'I need you to come and pick me up from the airport.'

'What?' she said, suddenly sounding very awake.

I repeated myself.

'I'll explain when you get here, but please come quickly.'

I was sitting on a bench at the side of the concourse with a cup of tea in one hand, and the phone that Steph had leant me in the other. I was gazing at a picture of a Pikachu on the screen saver. I'm not sure how I got there or who had given me the cup of tea, but I had worked out that I'd get through to Steph if I called *Mum* on the phone.

It was over, Will and I were over. And it was all down to a stupid drunken conversation. Suppose I could just turn back time. I felt so heavy, physically and emotionally heavy.

All the stress and preparation were wasted, pointless. I just wanted to go home, climb into bed and never get out again.

Chapter 21

A period of mourning followed. After Steph had dropped me home, thankfully just missing the boys as they left for school, I cried myself to sleep and woke at about three in the afternoon. I thought everything was okay for a few seconds, but as I came to, a dark blanket of gloom silently covered my entire body. I rolled over and looked at my case, standing in the middle of the room, looking depressed. I continued to roll out of bed to go to the loo, unbelievably ecstatic to find my period had arrived.

Great.

I hadn't eaten or drunk anything all day, but I wasn't hungry. I wrapped a blanket around me and went downstairs to get some water. It was cold on my lips. My entire face and neck were red and blotchy. I stared out towards the garden, completely numb and barely having enough energy to hold the glass. Will had stood there once, I thought, wringing his t-shirt out after saving Luna, and without hesitation, the tears came flooding back.

After a fitful night, I watched as dawn broke through the crack in the curtains. Whenever a thought of Will came into my head, I felt sick. I blew my nose and added the tissue to the small mountain I had created next to the bed. I got up, dragged my sloppy joe's on, grabbed my keys, and as I left the house, I pulled my hood up and started walking. I walked where my legs took me, I could feel the sun's warmth on my back, but it did nothing for my mood.

I reached the sea wall, pushed myself up, and sat cross-legged on the deep coping stones. I wondered how many broken hearts the wall had coped with in the past. I looked across to Wales. Some of the tiny buildings glistened in the morning sun. The sea lake below me was calm, and a few early morning swimmers were getting ready to take a cool dip. A few dog walkers strolled by behind me, and I wondered what Grayson and Luna were up to. Eventually, as the promenade slowly began to get busier, and the café owners arrived to open up for the day, I unfurled my legs, slid back down onto the prom, and walked home.

When I got there, I made myself a coffee and then ran a bath. All the curtains were still shut, but I didn't care. They could stay that way. I had a long soak, the bath water swallowing up yet more tears. They were like two little rivers flowing into the sea. My fingers and toes had turned spongy, and the water was cold when I hauled myself out. After carefully patting my face dry, I slathered it with cream, which stung a bit because my skin was sore. Putting my sloppy joe's back on, I went down to find some food I didn't think I would immediately puke back up again. I ate a Gingernut biscuit.

There was a gentle tap on the door, 'Cooee, are you in there, Lu?'

I opened the door. Steph took one look at me and stepped in to wrap me up in a huge cuddle. I just stood there with my arms by my side while she held me, and I wept some more. 'I had a funny feeling you'd be doing this.'

'Doing what?' I sniffed.

'Sobbing in a darkened room.' She lifted a bag and put it on the counter. 'This is your getting over a broken heart emergency kit.' And she started to unpack. A box of tissues, chocolates, some homemade chicken soup, a bottle of wine, and even some biscuits and a pack of tea. 'If it's any consolation, apparently the gig in Lisbon was crap.'

I frowned. 'What do you mean?' I asked as I immediately opened the tissues to blow my nose again.

'I searched it up, you know, on the in-ter-net...' she said slowly like I was a complete imbecile. 'The gig had awful reviews. Apparently, Will was drunk, and they didn't even bother coming on for an encore.'

Will was drunk? Maybe he was in one of his dark places.

'Oh.' Was all I could muster to say.

'Come on,' she said, beckoning me into the lounge. She flung the curtains open, and I squinted while my eyes adjusted to the light. She looked at all the tissues on the floor and sighed. 'Right,' she said with her hands on her hips. 'You're allowed another twenty-four hours.' I frowned again. 'You have to put a time limit on this wallowing, so...' She looked at her watch. 'by eleven tomorrow, you're to pick yourself up, brush yourself down and do the British thing - carry on.' She added to clarify. I couldn't help but think she looked like Mary Poppins, and a small smile found its way onto my lips. 'You see, there you go, you just have to try. So, get those tears out, watch some soppy romance films and eat those chocolates until you feel sick.' She bent down and picked up all the soggy tissues. 'I'll keep the dogs for as long as you need but

I've got to take the girls to netball now. Do you think you'll be okay?'

I didn't answer. I just said, 'Thanks, Steph.' With that, she was gone.

I followed her instructions to the T. I watched Me Before You, followed by A Star is Born, and finished with Ghost, interspersed with several bouts of sobbing and sniffing. By the time I took myself off to bed, I'd eaten two-thirds of the chocolates and polished off the wine. The soup would keep until tomorrow.

I slept reasonably well, considering, but the cloud of doom engulfed me again when I awoke. I lay there for a while. Time was hard to pass when you had nothing to do. And then an idea came to mind. I quickly showered and got dressed, brushed my teeth, and jumped in the car.

I picked the dogs up from Stephs, they were so pleased to see me that they nearly bowled me over, jumping up and licking my face. I laughed, trying to steady myself and keep them under control while I thanked Steph.

I drove to Sand Bay, one of their favourite places, and I took them along the shore from the car park to the little coffee shop. They bounded around, clearly happy to be free to roam where they liked. I bought a takeaway coffee from the café and walked back to the car, a good couple of hours in total. When I got into the car, I noticed it was eleven, and I took a long breath in through my nose and a slow breath out through my mouth.

It was lunchtime when I arrived home, so I warmed up the soup and toasted some bread from the freezer to dip in. After that, the dogs settled down for a sleep, and I spent the rest of the day pottering, doing the odd bit of house-work, and checking my diary for the forthcoming week. It was pretty much full again, which was no bad thing. It would be easier to pass the time.

I was just about to watch a movie when the front door flung open, and Frankie and Paddy came bustling in. 'Mum! What are you doing here?' I had forgotten that Mike was dropping them back this evening.

'Um, I didn't go in the end.' They looked at me, confused, but Mike came in before they could ask any more. 'Hi,' I said, but he looked pretty fed up. 'Is everything okay?'

'I didn't get it, the job, they gave it to Tom. I left a mes-sage for you, but you didn't reply.'

Ooh crap.

'I'm so sorry. My phone is broken. Didn't the boys tell you?' I'm not sure I had it in me to deal with more bad news. The boys pegged it upstairs, having dumped their coats and shoes all over the entrance hall. 'Is there not anything else you can apply for?'

'There is, but I'm worried I won't find out in time to save the house, so can you send me all the valuations so I can take a look?'

'Yes, I'll send them over now.'

'I've left the car running, so I'd better go.' And then he added, 'I thought you were coming back tomorrow?'

'Change of plan,' I said as he said his goodbyes.

Chapter 22

Monday arrived, and it was the usual rush in the morning, packed lunches, errant PE kits, and dog walks, all before my first client walked through the door. Busy was the way forward. Thoughts of Will would drift in, and I'd push them right out again by concentrating on something else. It wasn't until I was doing my banking and preparing for the next day that I couldn't push them away any longer, and a few stray tears appeared, so I started preparing dinner to keep myself occupied.

Tuesday was much the same, however, just as I was setting up for the next day, there was a knock at the side door. It couldn't be anyone I knew. Otherwise, they would have walked in by now, but I could hear whispering. I opened the door to find Steph and Claire, one holding a couple of bottles of wine and the other holding what looked like a Chinese takeaway.

'Hiya, we thought we'd come round to cheer you up. Have you eaten?'

'No, I haven't, actually,' I said as I waved them in. Steph dumped the bottles on the side and walked straight into the walk-in cupboard to collect plates, cutlery and glasses.

'Sorry to hear about the trip, babe,' Claire said as she gave me a side hug.

'Well, it obviously wasn't meant to be,' I replied, swallowing back the tears. It was so lovely of them to come over.

I think any gesture of kindness would have made me cry at that point, but I did my best to keep it together. Steph was setting the table, so I carried the wine through while Claire carried the food. I hadn't eaten much since Friday, but I had to admit it smelt good. We all sat down, and while we served up and poured the wine, it was clear I would have to tell Claire the blow-by-blow account of what happened on Friday. I managed to get through the ordeal without allowing a tear to escape.

'So, let me get this straight. The booking was cancelled?'

I rolled my eyes, really not wanting to go over it again, and tried very hard not to sigh. 'That's correct.'

She put her index finger out as if she was starting to count. 'But you don't actually know for sure if it was Will that cancelled the booking?'

I frowned. 'No, but who else would have done it?'

She added her middle finger. 'Well, it could have been a clerical error, and am I right in thinking that you still haven't sorted your phone out?'

'I haven't, but he said he was busy, and we'd see each other on Friday, so I wasn't expecting a call.'

'So, there is a chance that he was expecting you to arrive, and you didn't turn up, and he hasn't been able to contact you.'

I blinked, and my face followed into a scrunch while I tried to process the information.

'She's got a point, babe,' Steph added.

I started to shake my head. I didn't even want to consider the possibility because if it weren't true, I'd be back to square one, grieving what could have been all over again.

'You need to get that phone fixed,' she said, raising her eyebrows.

'Do you want some more wine?' Steph asked, holding the neck of the bottle over my glass.

'Please,' I said, shaking off the thought.

We had a pleasant evening. The boys were gutted to find they had cheese on toast for dinner and not Chinese, but they soon got over it when Claire handed them the remaining pack of prawn crackers. Steph told us about her plans for their bedroom, which was next on the list for an overhaul, and Claire told us exactly what she thought of Zara 's husband Andy, who, it was fair to say, she had an immense hatred for.

Just as they were getting ready to go, Claire spotted the lanyards for the festival. 'Oh, my God, are those the passes? Are we still going?'

I hadn't thought about it since Friday, but I sure as hell knew I wasn't going.

'Um, well, I won't be, but you're welcome to go without me. It seems a shame to waste them,' I said, shrugging.

'You could totally go. We don't have to go backstage. We could just go and enjoy the festival and see all the other bands,' she said hopefully.

'My head's just not in the right place, and the thought of being in the same vicinity as Will is making me feel a bit sick.'

For breakups, it was easier living in different countries. I picked up three of the lanyards and gave them to her.

'Do what you want with them but don't tell me anything about it when you return.'

Realising her insensitivity, she looked up with a sad face and puppy dog eyes. 'Sorry, babe.' She gave me a quick hug and then pulled straight back and held her hands out in front of my boobs, air squeezing them. 'Those wangers frighten me.'

Steph shoved her out of the way and pulled me in for a hug, 'Night, sleep well, okay?'

I waved them off, locked up, and yawned. I was tired.

It was the middle of the week, hump day, and another day of clients to get through. It was hot already, and they were reporting on the radio that temperatures could sore at the weekend, potentially making it the hottest day on record. As I was carrying out my first treatment of the day, my thoughts drifted back to what Claire had said. Could it have been a clerical error? I didn't ask the lady on the desk who had cancelled it or even know whether they'd have that information. It was almost annoying that there was a glimmer of hope, and it was niggling me. I must get my phone sorted out, but when would I have time to go to Bristol? Friday maybe?

Mike had sent an email back recommending that we go ahead with Matt Thomas estate agents. Typical, I would have to deal with that pretentious twat, but I wasn't going to argue with Mike; knowing him, he would have worked out the best deal. I couldn't believe we would have to sell this place. After Mike left eight years ago, I didn't want to stay. There were too many bad memories, and I wanted a fresh start, but over the years, as time had moved on, the house had become a happy place again, and I couldn't even imagine selling now, not until the boys had moved out and started their own families. I'd have to call the agency tomorrow and arrange for them to take pictures.

Bloody hell, that would mean more cleaning.

That evening at dinner, Frankie was acting weird. He'd been back late the last couple of evenings, and I couldn't work out whether he was tired or agitated. Paddy went off to use the loo as we were clearing up, and Frankie said, 'Mum, can I have a word?' The first thought that went through my head was that he'd got a girl pregnant. And then, he's gay, although my gaydar had been terrible recently.

'Of course,' I said, trying not to sound hesitant or worried.

'You know Emily from the pub, (I nodded to confirm I knew of said Emily) well, we've been seeing each other for a while now, and I wondered if you would be happy if she stayed over sometimes?' I tried to conceal my sigh of relief that I wasn't about to become a grandparent, and at the same time proud, at how grown up he'd become.

'Frankie, if you feel that it's the right time to ask her to stay, I fully respect your decision.'

The relief dropped off him like an apple falling from a tree.

'As long as you're safe and respect our home, Emily is welcome,' I confirmed.

'Thanks, Mum.' And then he paused. 'How are things going with Will?'

I was not expecting him to ask that, and a big lump appeared in my throat.

'Um, we split up,' I managed to say through the constriction.

'Shame, he was cool,' he said, giving me an awkward half-hug and a peck on the cheek.

Then he bounded upstairs. Oh, my baby boy was growing up. I mentally flagged the little episode to tell Steph the next time I saw her and then wondered how I'd tackle the subject with Paddy. I didn't want him to think he had the green light to bring whoever he wanted back too. Mind you, he didn't seem particularly serious about dating yet.

Once I'd finished cleaning the kitchen, I sat on the sofa with the dogs on either side of me, with their heads on my lap, enjoying a stroke. I sat there and realised I had managed to get through the day without crying. One step at a time, I thought.

The following afternoon, when I had finished work and done my banking, which I admitted was looking somewhat healthy, I made the call that I had been putting off all day.

'We would be delighted to showcase your home, Ms Daniels. When would be convenient to come and take footage?'

Ms, grrr, he was so tactless. I needed time to tidy and wanted to sort my phone out.

'Saturday?' I suggested.

'I'm afraid our videographer doesn't work at weekends. Are there any other days of the week that would be suitable?'

Videographer? What the hell? I just thought they were going to take a few snaps. I swiped through my calendar on my phone.

'Monday afternoon, after three?'

'I have a quarter-past three appointment available on Monday. Shall I book that for you?'

'Yes, please,' I confirmed, unsure I wanted the house filmed at all.

I added it to my diary. I put the phone down, and my heart sank. It was happening. We were putting the house on the market. I suddenly felt a little overwhelmed thinking about all the crap we had in the loft, the garage, the shed, and every cupboard in the house. It would all need to be sorted. I imagined sitting in the queue for the dump and rubbed my eyes to remove the thought physically.

I then remembered I needed to book to get my phone sorted, so I searched for the mobile store. Within a few clicks, I was booking an appointment. They made everything so easy. Repairs and physical damage, screen and display, schedule a repair—booked. Five o'clock on Friday gave me enough time to walk the dogs and clean the house before heading into Bristol.

Joy.

'Cooee.'

There she is, checking up on me again. Despite the few heated words a couple of weeks ago, she was such a supportive friend.

'Hi, I'm in here.'

She appeared in the doorway of my treatment room.

'Do you want a cuppa?' I asked.

'You're looking perkier,' she replied, searching my eyes for any trace of tears.

'You'd be proud of me. I managed to get through the whole day without crying yesterday.'

She smiled and gave me a quick hug.

'I'm always proud of you... You're a constant pain in the arse, but I'm willing to put up with it.'

I rolled my eyes at her and poured the water into the kettle.

'I've popped over to ask you something.'

'If you want a treatment, it's a no. This week has been backbreaking.'

'No... it's about the festival....'

I stopped tea-making proceedings.

'I just wanted to double-check if you meant what you said to Claire the other night?'

'What, that you should go?' I wasn't sure how I felt about it, but I couldn't put my finger on why.

'It's just that Zara has spent the entire week reorganising all the kid's activities, arranging lift shares, adjusting times, calling in favours, and when she called to find out what the plan was, she was so excited, I didn't have the heart to tell her we weren't going.'

I'm not sure I'd ever actually witnessed Zara being excited, she was always so busy.

'As I said, the tickets would be wasted if you didn't go,' I said with as much airiness as I could muster.

Steph took my shoulders in her hands. 'I know that's what you said, but what are you actually feeling? I know you too well, Daniels.'

'Well, I can't deny it feels a bit weird, but Zara is going through a shit time. She could do with letting her hair down.'

'And what are you going to do this weekend? If you are going to sit here in a darkened room for forty-eight hours, I'm going to stay here and sit with you.'

'Actually, I've got quite a lot to do this weekend. We've got to put the house on the market, so I'm going to start sorting the shed and the garage out. Apparently, it's going to be hot, so I may as well get everything out and decide what needs to go to the dump.'

'Shit, babe, I'm sorry. No luck with the interview then?' she asked.

'No, he got through to the second interview, but they gave it to someone else.'

'Let me chase up those emails I sent the other day.'

The tea was ready, and we sat in the lounge. Steph told me all about the plans for the bedroom, from wallpaper to flooring to furniture. She loved a project, that girl. I told her about the conversation with Frankie, and we both oooh'd and ahhh'd about the fact our babies were growing up. Before I knew it, the boys started sniffing around to see what was for dinner. Honestly, they couldn't get out of bed on time, but they were like clockwork when it came to food. Forget Greenwich meantime, it should be Daniels mealtime.

'Are you sure you're sure?' Steph asked again.

'Will you just go, and if you decide to call me to tell me how great it is, put your phone back in your back pocket and zip it, Sister.'

After seeing her out, I whacked the oven on and got some pizzas out of the fridge. That will have to do. I hadn't had time to cook anything. It was a balmy evening, so I flung the back doors open to try to circulate some air. I had a feeling it was going to be a muggy night.

Chapter 23

Despite it being warm, I slept well and woke up feeling refreshed. While showering, I pushed the thought of Will heading to the UK right back out of my head. I just needed to get through this weekend, and then I could get on with my life, knowing that he was thousands of miles away.

Doing the housework in the cloying heat was not pleasant, and I had to have another shower before heading to the mobile store. Thank God they had air conditioning. I was also thankful I had booked an appointment because it was jam-packed. The guy took my phone and asked if I had mobile care, I couldn't remember, so he looked up to check my details.

'It looks like you have, so let me take this out to the technicians and see what they think.'

I hung about, fiddling with the tablet in front of me while I waited. My mind drifted to the girls, as they would have arrived at the festival by now. I wondered what bands they were going to see.

'Your phone is good to go!'

I jumped, not expecting the sales assistant to arrive back so soon.

'The screen has been replaced for you, which is covered under your package, and it would appear that your phone died purely because it was out of battery. We've been charging it for the last 5 minutes, but you'll need to put it on charge when you get home, and it should be fine.'

He gave me a broad smile while handing it back to me. I couldn't believe it. I could have charged it last weekend. Why didn't I try that? I thanked the sales guy and headed home, stopping via the corner shop to pick up a bottle of wine.

Once I'd cleared the dinner things away, and the boys had disappeared upstairs, I put my phone on charge and settled in the lounge with a glass of wine. I switched the TV on and was aimlessly flicking through the channels. I had a funny feeling in my gut, but I couldn't quite place it, and it was making me restless, so I poured myself another glass.

When I realised that I hadn't actually decided what to watch half an hour later, and the wine glass was empty again, I switched the TV back off and let out a big sigh. I was irritated, but why? My thoughts kept drifting back to the girls and wondering what they were doing at the festival.

Maybe I was jealous?

Either way, I couldn't get the festival out of my head, and if I was really honest with myself, I couldn't stop thinking about Will either.

Had he landed? Was he at the festival with someone else? Had the girls bumped into him?

I stared at my laptop while I tapped my Grandmother's eternity ring against the side of my glass. Was I going to be like this all weekend? Fuck it. I opened it up and searched the festival's website. I had a little peruse of the line-up. The 'king Band were headlining tomorrow night, but there were so many other good bands. I was about to flip it shut again when I noticed a live announcement section at the bottom of the page. It was a scrolling banner.

The 'king Band confirm last ever UK show.

What? There was a link to a report, and my stomach knotted as I hovered over it. I couldn't resist. I clicked.

There in front of me was a picture of Will. I took a prolonged breath in, trying to cleanse my mind and soul and keep my composure. It was like a stab in the heart, but I forced myself to read on.

Lead singer Will Reynolds said, 'Yeah, this is probably the last UK date we'll be doing.' When asked why, he said, 'Love has been lost on British shores.' We tried to get more details out of him, folks, but he refused to comment further.

I sat there looking at the screen, searching the picture of Will's face for answers. What did he mean? *Love has been lost*?

I sat there for a long while thinking about the trip to Lisbon, Steph's comments about how bad the gig had been, Claire's hypothesis about the cancelled flight, and my gaze slowly drifted to my phone. I suddenly launched across the sofa and picked it up. As I suspected, I had tons of messages. I scrolled past the ones from Mike, the boys, Steph, various clients, and a whole bunch of numbers I didn't recognise and read the one from Will,

But I'll try to call tomorrow. I think there are a couple of small gaps in the schedule. X

It had come through seconds after the previous message, which I read again.

Gonna be pretty up against it over the next few days. I'll see you at the airport on Friday. We need to talk X

Then there was a simple text a few hours later.

Lucy? Are you getting my messages? What's going on?

Oh God. Maybe he cancelled the flight after that because I wasn't replying. I dialled my voicemail.

Mike said he hadn't got the job. Steph asked why I wasn't replying to her messages. My mum asking if the socks were the right fit, and Will...

'Hey, it's me, have I said something out of turn? You're not replying to my messages.'

I closed my eyes, the burn of tears threatening. It was so lovely to hear his voice.

'Lucy, I'm at the airport.'

I sat up suddenly.

'Where are you? Call me when you get this.'

Shit, shit, SHIT! And then another.

'Okay, I don't know what's going on. Call me.'

He sounded cross, defeated, and cross. And he hadn't cancelled the flight. He had been at the airport. Oh, God. I tilted my head towards the ceiling and pointed my bottom jaw out to save myself from screaming.

I stood up, and as my head spun, I sat back down. I'd finished the bottle of wine. For fuck's sake, all I wanted to do now was jump in the car and find Will, but I couldn't because I was over the limit. I could call him. But I was drunk, and I couldn't help but feel this needed to be an in-person conversation. I tried to call Steph, but it rang out. She was probably pissed and unable to hear, so I messaged her.

I'm coming to the festival tomorrow. I need to speak to Will. Hope you're having fun x

There was nothing else I could do. I might as well take myself off to bed, sleep this bottle of wine off, and then get up in the morning, drive to the festival and find Will. My heart was racing at the prospect, and I had the most fretful sleep, tossing and turning, thinking about all the possible scenarios and outcomes. It was so hot, and just before six am I decided to get up.

At least there was one bonus, I didn't need to pack! My suitcase for Lisbon was still stood in the middle of my bedroom, untouched. Once I'd sorted the dogs out, got myself ready, and collected the festival pass from the hallway, the boys were still in bed, so I left them a note.

Decided to go to the festival, look after the dogs and look after each other. My phone is fixed, call me if you need me. Love Mum x

When I eventually joined the queue at the festival, several stewards were directing the festival-goers. One of them approached me and asked to see my ticket.

'I don't have a ticket. I just have this.' I lifted the lanyard to show him.

He took it and then nodded to a colleague and held up three fingers, a bit like a boy Scout. His colleague then hoisted a makeshift gate open and ushered me through. I pulled out of the queue and headed along the dirt track to another tall barrier where several stewards were standing. They rechecked my pass, and I suddenly panicked, thinking that maybe Will had cancelled it too, but he turned and collected a gold material band and attached it to my wrist. Meanwhile, one of them opened my boot and had a good nose around before slamming it shut and, again, signalling to the other stewards. The barrier began to open like a pair of giant MDF stable doors, and they waved me through.

As I drove in, I could see some Teepees on the left, some tents in front, and a few vans on the right. I couldn't see another steward, so I pulled up behind a big Hymer van making sure there was enough space for the other vehicles to get out. A few people were milling about, but it seemed to be quiet. I could hear the music thumping in the distance, but it appeared so far away.

I tried to call Steph again, but there was still no reply. It had only just gone ten o'clock, and they were probably still asleep, so in an attempt to deal with the already oppressive heat, I dug out my flip-flops, slathered myself in suncream, and wedged my rattan cowboy style sunhat on my head. I was only wearing a vest top and some denim shorts, and even that felt like too much. My stomach rumbled, I hadn't eaten breakfast, so I grabbed my purse and lanyard and headed down toward another set of gates. It was guarded by a steward next to a cabin, the sort you'd find on a building site, but before I reached my destination, my phone began vibrating.

'Lu!! Are you here?' Steph said excitedly.

'I've just parked up. Where are you?'

'We're still in the teepee. It was a heavy night.'

I looked back up the hill, eyeing the teepees, and began strolling back toward them.

'Which one are you in? I'm just walking up from the cabin.'

Before I knew it, I saw Steph frantically waving her hands. She looked tired. I pocketed my phone and squeezed her before she ushered me over to a deckchair.

'Claire and Zara are still sparko. I swear to God they were on something last night.'

'Oh my God! That's so funny.'

'Sooo... what made you change your mind?' she asked, settling down on a deckchair of her own.

'Well... I fixed my phone yesterday, and while it was charging, I wondered what you guys were up to. I ended up looking at the festival website, and I happened to see an update about The 'king Band. Apparently, Will had been quoted saying something about love being lost on British shores.'

'Right...' Steph coaxed, realising that wasn't the whole story.

'And then I checked my phone...'

I pulled my phone back out and showed her the messages.

'And then listened to my voicemail... he was there, at the airport.'

'I bloody knew it!!' I heard Claire call from inside the teepee before pulling the canvas door to one side. She looked awful, her mascara was mainly on her cheeks, and her hair was glued with sweat to one side of her face.

'Clerical error. I'd put money on it!' she declared before taking a long swig of water.

'So, what's the plan?' Steph asked.

'I don't know.' I admitted. 'Have you seen him? Is he here?' I asked hopefully.

'No babe, just call him, arrange to meet him,' Steph suggested.

'Yeah, maybe...' Suddenly I felt nervous, and I looked away, catching the inside of my cheek between my teeth.

'Let's go and get some breakfast first,' Claire proposed. 'Although I need a shower before that.'

'Me too,' called a weak voice from the teepee. Zara had awoken from her slumber.

I sat back, propped my feet up on a cool box, and pulled my hat over my face while they all got ready. I had a text from Frankie to say he'd seen my message. He promised to walk the dogs and wished me a good time. Eventually, after what felt like an eternity, we all headed back down the hill toward the steward by the gate.

'Where are you off to?' asked a man arriving at the gate at the same time as us.

'To seek out some food,' Steph replied.

'Oh cool, I'm headed that way, want a lift? It's a bit of a trek.'

I saw that his pass was also a triple-A and thought he must be staff of some kind. He was tall, with light brown wavy hair, not cut into a particular style, almost as if it was once in style, but it had grown out. He wore baggy jeans and a pair of beat-up old Adidas shell-toe trainers.

'That would be great.'

As we rounded the corner, the space opened out to a vast expanse with nothing but people walking with purpose from every direction, crisscrossing each other in the middle and towards the opposite sides.

'We call this the Millennium Falcon. We're in the engine room at the moment,' he explained.

A golf buggy was parked up, and he hopped into the driver's seat. Claire and Steph bagsied the seats next to him while Zara and I sat on the back, facing the opposite way. We gently pulled away, bumping over the uneven, dusty ground.

'There are a few of these on-site,' he said, raising his voice over the music. 'Just ask someone, and they'll take you wherever.'

The journey took several minutes, the festival site must be enormous, and as we crossed from one side to the other, the guy was explaining where everything was in a mock coach tour operator accent, making us all laugh.

'And this is where the food marquees are.'

He stopped by another gate. 'Enjoy the festival.'

I hopped off, thankful not to leave the skin from my thighs on the hot faux leather, and we all thanked him. Then, I walked through the gates and out into the festival. There were so many people. Some sat on the grass in small groups. Others stood about chatting, and across the way, between two of the marquees, was what looked like a road made up of humans. It was packed with people moving in both directions like a giant centipede. It took me a few moments to adjust to the culture shock before I began to meander along with the others.

Chapter 24

'Coffee and croissants?' Claire asked, pointing toward a stand with a queue slightly shorter than the rest. We all agreed and tagged onto the end. The girls filled me in on what they had done the night before and pointed out all the different areas of the site while we waited. Claire was peering over Zara's shoulder, both looking on the festival app to see what bands were due to play later.

'So, who are we seeing today then?' Steph asked, handing the coffees out.

'I reckon we should go and see PSB first because they're fun...' Claire suggested.

'What does that stand for again?' Zara asked.

'Personal & Social Behaviour,' Steph replied.

I always thought it stood for purple sprouting broccoli, but clearly, I was wrong.

'Then, after some dinner, we can catch Tootings as a warm-up for The 'king Band, who I'm guessing we're seeing as we have them to thank for these beauties,' she said, waggling her wrist about.

A wave of nausea passed over me as I thought about Will again, but suddenly Steph gasped, patting herself down.

'Damn it, I've left my phone back at the teepee!'

She looked at me with a pained expression and then added in a whiny voice, 'Would you come back with me?'

I rolled my eyes while taking a sip of coffee and nodded in agreement. We arranged to call Claire and Zara once we were on our way back.

It took us ages to walk back, it was so hot. I looked down at my feet, they were throbbing, and I could feel the heat from the ground radiating through my flip-flops. As I glanced back up, I stopped in my tracks.

'Steph?'

'Yeah?' she said, turning back.

'What is that in your back pocket?' I asked, and she pursed her lips.

'Okay, so I didn't leave my phone behind, but I'm not putting up with you all day, looking winded every time someone mentions Will or The 'king Band. You need to phone him... and I need a poo.'

I let out an exasperated laugh, but she was right. I didn't want to be a Debbie Downer and make everyone else miserable.

We eventually arrived back at the teepee, and Steph gave me the nod to go off and make the call. My stomach flipped. I took myself off to a relatively quiet space, away from the tents and teepees. I really didn't need anyone listening in. I took a deep breath and pressed call... and it went straight to voice mail.

Fuck.

I hung up.

I was going to have to find him, I thought. I walked over to one of the many gates and asked one of the stewards. 'Do you know where I can find Will from The 'king Band?' She looked at me and then at my wrist, sniffed, and said, 'You can ask in there.' She nodded over her shoulder to the cab-in being used as an office, so I wandered over and hovered in the doorway. A very officious-looking man was in deep dis-cussion with our golf buggy guy. The man looked scary, like the security guard of all security guards, overweight, skin-head, and enormous. He looked up from his desk, pissed off that I was essentially interrupting with my being there. The golf buggy guy nodded and smiled, which eased the pressure slightly but not much.

'Can I help you, Miss?' Officious Man said with a thick Liverpudlian accent.

'I need to get hold of Will from The 'king Band,' I said assertively.

'Don't we all, Queen,' he replied with a mighty belly laugh. 'I tell you what, if you get hold of him before me, be sure to let me know.'

Unsure what he meant by his comment, I rattled on.

'Well, I've tried to call him, but it's going straight to voicemail.'

He looked at his watch. 'They're probably in the air at the moment, if they're on their way, that is. They're not due here until four, but judging by the last couple of shows, who knows if they'll even turn up. And if they don't, that will make my job very tricky.'

'Oh, God,' I said, half under my breath, and sensing the conversation was over, I started to turn.

'Wait,' the golf buggy guy said. I turned back, hoping he had more information. 'You're the girl.'

'Yes, from earlier, in the golf buggy,' I said, realising it was just because he recognised me.

'No, you're *the* girl,' he said, nodding to Officious Man. I didn't know what to say.

They were both staring at me, so I nodded slowly and backed away. They must be on something.

'The girl that broke his heart.'

Wait, what? Broke his heart?

'No, I think you've made a mistake,' I said, forcing a bright smile.

'Ah-ah,' he said, disbelievingly and taking three cans of lager out of the mini-fridge by the desk. He opened one and passed it to me and one to Officious Man before opening the last one for himself. Ok, so I was staying for a drink. Twenty minutes later, I told them the whole story.

'And now I can't get hold of him,' I finished before taking a long swig of my beer.

'Well, Lucy, the word on the street is that he's not happy because you dumped his arse in Lisbon, and he's been like a bull in a china shop ever since.' Officious Man said.

I couldn't imagine Will being like that.

'As in violent?' I asked, and he could see I was concerned.

'As in, turning up late, getting drunk before shows, and not doing his fans any justice,' he clarified.

'Oh.' I said, wondering how he must be feeling after what I had been through. I took a deep wavering breath and then sniffed, brushing a stray tear away with the back of my hand.

'I'd better get back to my friend.'

'Oh dear, we're gonna have to look after this one,' Golf Buggy Guy said, giving Officious Man a pitiful look.

'Well, you're in luck. I happen to know Will personally, I got them a main stage slot when The 'king Band first came over to the UK back in the day.'

He picked up a cigarette packet and shifted his chair back, causing the whole cabin to rock, and he added, 'Let's keep in touch.'

After exchanging numbers, I walked back to the teepee.

'Christ, Lu, you've been ages. How did it go?' Steph asked.

I cast my eye around the teepee. It was pretty cool, four single beds wrapped around the edge with a little kitchenette area in the middle.

'I know, sorry, I got held up.'

Steph looked at the can in my hand and raised her eyebrows as if trying to telepathically extract further information from me.

'I met a guy who I think might be the festival organiser,' I said.

'Right,' Steph said slowly as if I hadn't given her enough information. 'What about Will?'

'Oh, it went to voicemail,' I said, gathering my lips to the side to signify that was all I had.

She looked a bit pissed off, so I elaborated.

'Officious Man—the organiser chap, and our golf buggy guy are going to keep me updated on their arrival.'

'Okay... so until then, shall we go and have some fun?'

I filled my lungs with air, satisfied that we had a plan, if somewhat vague, and nodded as I let the breath go out in a rush.

As we walked past the cabin on our way back, Officious Man called over.

'Hey Queen, I've had an email back from their Tour Manager confirming their attendance, so they must have landed.'

'Thanks,' I said. 'See you later?'

He nodded and went back to chewing his gum.

We continued the long walk back to find Claire and Zara. I wanted to try Will again, but now wasn't the time, and if I was completely honest with myself, I was nervous. Nervous about how he'd react. I tried to put myself in his shoes. He thought I just hadn't turned up, that I'd stood him up. I would have been mortified if I had been him, and I'm not sure if I'd like to hear from him. I needed to explain.

'Lu?' Steph said, waving her hand in front of my face.

'Sorry,' I said, giving her a big smile.

I linked my arm with hers in an attempt to rid my nervousness, and we marvelled at all the pretty flags and different food smells. I think every nationality was catered for. People were having a good time everywhere we looked, and there was no antsy attitude. It was just chilled, and it felt good.

By the time we caught up with the others, it had gone one o'clock, and it was clear that Claire and Zara hadn't wasted any time. They were already tipsy.

'Okay, let's grab some lunch before we go and see PSB.' Steph said, and everyone agreed.

It wasn't long before we found an old open-top red bus serving coffee and bagels. We arrived just at the right time as a group of four guys left their table on the top deck, so we quickly slid into their seats.

'What would everyone like?' Steph asked. 'My shout,' she added.

'No, don't be silly. It'll cost a small fortune,' I said, considering the price of the beer here.

'It's fine. You've essentially provided the passes, so please let me pay.'

So, we all gave her our orders and looked out across the festival site. It was a perfect viewpoint from up on the bus, and although we couldn't see the teepee, we could work out where it was in relation to the rest of the landmarks.

'It's like a small town, a really popular one,' Zara said, looking out, shielding her eyes to see further.

'You gotta look at the state of some people, though, guys. Look at him!' Claire said, pointing to a rather unfortunate man wandering along, dragging a coat behind him and covered from head to toe in leaves, wearing only one filthy white sock. Someone had spent a rather long time sticking them on. He was like a walking tree. And as we looked closer, there were quite a lot of people who were more than worse for wear.

After polishing off a smoked salmon and cream cheese bagel and a pint, we were ready to see PSB. I quickly checked my phone to see it was two o'clock. My tummy convulsed, and as time ticked on, I became more anxious.

Steph looked over at me. 'Come on, girls, it's time for a beer.'

Claire got to the bar first and ordered eight beers.

'Jesus Christ, Claire!' I said.

'Well, it will save us having to queue again.' She winked.

We carefully sipped the tops of both beers and walked towards the stage where PSB was about to start. Claire was right, they were fun. Lots of crowd interaction, and everyone was having a great time. The beers had gone straight to my head. Warm beer was disgusting, so I necked them quickly.

As PSB's set came to an end, I turned to see Claire and Zara giggling away, they had managed to acquire a spliff from somewhere, and I glanced at Steph, trying to suppress a smile. I was glad she was having fun, she was really letting her hair down, and she deserved it.

I was desperate for a wee.

'I don't know why I've never tried it before,' Zara said with a slur and a happy sigh.

She took an enormous drag and then handed it to Claire, but as everyone was filtering away from the stage to find the next band of choice, Zara came to a sudden halt and all the colour drained from her face.

Oh fuck.

Steph and Claire managed to grab her before she collapsed and slowly lowered her to the floor while I looked around in a panic to find help, but there was nothing, just people, thousands of people. I pulled my phone out of my pocket, but who was I going to ring? And then it came to me—Golf Buggy Guy. I dialled.

'Where are you?'

'We're somewhere between the main stage and the chill zone.' I shouted.

Apparently, that wasn't specific enough, and he told me to look up.

'What colour flags can you see?'

'Yellow.'

'Stay there,' he instructed.

'Okay guys, I think we've got back up coming.'

Zara started to come around as we waited, and I watched her face slowly morph from pale to green. I quickly shoved my empty pint cup under her chin, and sure enough, she threw up.

'Jesus Christ,' Steph muttered.

'Do you feel better, babe?' I asked Zara.

'A bit,' she managed.

A few minutes later, the golf buggy and its guy arrived like a knight in shining armour. Thankfully Zara appeared to have stopped throwing up and was just really sleepy. So, I got in the front next to our knight, Steph squeezing in beside me. Claire got on the back, clinging on to Zara to prevent her from falling out.

'Has she taken anything?' He asked. I shot a glance at Claire, who shook her head and demonstrated taking a drag of a spliff, not knowing whether she should say that or not.

'No, just a bit of weed.'

He glanced over at me and half-smiled, then widened his eyes, pulled a funny face, and said, 'White Out!'

I laughed. I liked him. He was funny and had a friendly face and a relaxed manner. He had taken his t-shirt off, and it was tucked into the back of his jeans. He was bigger than Will and had a lovely golden tan. As I looked down his arms towards the steering wheel, I noticed he had huge hands.

'Did you hear the big man got the email he was waiting for?' Golf Buggy Guy asked.

'He told me earlier,' I confirmed.

So, he must be the organiser.

'So, have you called him?' he asked.

'Nope, too nervous,' I said, chewing the side of my cheek.

'You should call him,' he said as he manoeuvred around the crowds carefully.

'That's what I keep saying,' Steph chimed in.

'I'm not convinced he's going to want to hear from me,' I replied.

'Course he does. He loves you.' He gave me a slow, knowing wink.

'And how do you know that?' I asked, laughing at him.

'Because no man acts like that unless they're heartbroken,' he declared, and draped his arm around the back of mine and Steph's shoulders as the crowd thinned out. He flicked his shades down, clutched the steering wheel with one hand as if he was driving an American Cadillac, and pulled away.

Chapter 25

The big gates opened almost automatically as we pulled up, and I told him all about the guy covered in leaves.

'... and all he was wearing was a dirty white sock,' I said as we all laughed, and then the golf buggy abruptly stopped. We lurched forward a little, making us giggle some more, and as the dust settled, there in front of us was Will, Paul, Jake, Alysa, Terry, and Bill, standing stock still.

I stopped laughing, and Golf Buggy Guy slowly moved his arm away from my shoulders.

For a moment, it was as if time stood still, I looked at Will, and he looked at me, and then the spell was broken as he turned on his heel and started marching back up toward the VIP camping area.

'Shit!' I said as I breathed out and almost pushed Steph out the way as I half slid, half clambered over her to get out quickly.

'Will!' I called as I started up the hill to catch up with him, but he did not stop walking.

'Will!' I said again as I began to run, trying not to wet myself. I finally got level with him and pulled on his arm.

'Will, would you let me explain?' I panted.

He suddenly stopped and turned to look at me. I had my hands on my hips, gasping for air, and he folded his arms across his chest.

'Explain?' He almost spat the word at me. 'Last Friday was the time for explaining, Lucy, last fucking Friday,' he shouted, lifting both arms in the air.

He was angry, furious, and he shook his head, looking up to the sky, anywhere but at me. I was shocked. I didn't quite know what to say. I don't think anyone had shouted at me like that before, and the sting of tears hit the back of my eyes.

I wanted to tell him that the flight had been cancelled, and I wanted to tell him how heartbroken I had felt all week - thinking that he had cancelled the flight following my drunken phone call. Still, nothing came out, apart from a frustrated tear that I swiped away as quickly as it had tried to escape. Will stood there looking at me expectantly, having refolded his arms.

'You wanted to explain, and now you won't talk. Well, I guess it makes sense. You seem to make a habit of changing your mind.'

I was speechless. He actually hated me.

'Don't contact me again.'

With that lasting comment, he walked back down the hill. I watched him disappear into the haze of the sun, and then I ran into the toilets and threw up three pints of lager, a bagel, and probably the can of beer I'd had earlier.

A few minutes later, Steph arrived. She crouched down to where I was slumped under a sink opposite one of the toilets. I looked up at her and then at the ceiling.

'He hates me,' I said, my voice wavering. 'He thinks I stood him up, and he hates me.'

There was nothing else to say. She grabbed a blue paper hand towel and dampened it down with some water so I could pat my face.

'Come on, let's get you back to the teepee.'

She pulled me up, and I was shaking. Steph guided me out and down the metal steps. Once we got to the teepee, she pulled all of their bags off the fourth bed and sat me down. I leaned forward, my head resting on my forearms, thankful that the teepee was cooler. I felt so weak.

'I'm going to find out where the others have got to,' Steph announced. 'Are you going to be all right on your own for a bit?'

She rummaged around in her bag, then produced a water bottle and handed it to me. I took it without speaking and put my head back down.

A while later, I sensed someone standing in the doorway and looked up, trying not to squint too much as the light shone in, so I could see who it was.

'Didn't quite go according to plan?' Golf Buggy Guy asked.

He came and sat next to me, putting his elbows on his knees and looking out down the hill. I didn't answer him. I just sat there twisting the water bottle cap on and off.

'I expect it was a shock seeing you here,' he added.

'He thinks I stood him up...' I paused, not wanting to relive the moment, and then I said with a constricted voice, 'and he shouted at me... he's really angry.'

The last word felt sticky in my mouth, and I couldn't stop them anymore. They didn't even wait to come out in turn. The tears started tracking down my face like they were in a race. Golf Buggy Guy put his arm around me, and we sat there until I couldn't cry anymore.

Then, in the distance, we could hear shouting, lots of talking, and plenty of swearing, and as the voices came closer, I could hear Claire. She was marching up the hill with Zara and Steph in tow.

'Nobody treats my friends like that. Who the hell does he think he is? He has no idea what she's been going through this week.'

As she approached the teepee and she could see me, she said, 'Lu, you're better off without him. What an absolute cunt.'

It was fair to say that if she didn't have the attention of the entire VIP camping area before, she did now. Steph physically held her arms down to stop her from flailing around. I think she would have used handcuffs had she had some available.

Golf Buggy Guy made his excuses and said he'd be back later. Steph took his place, and the girls sat on the next bed along. I took a deep nourishing breath.

'What do you wanna do?' Steph asked, gently nudging me.

'Nothing... I wouldn't wanna risk driving home, so I'll just stay here and drive home tomorrow.'

I took several glugs of water and then added, 'You guys go and have some fun. I'll be fine here.'

'No!' Zara said. 'We're not leaving you here. If you don't feel like going out there, we'll stay, and if you change your mind later, that's okay... besides, I could do with a lie down.'

'Hear, hear,' Claire said, and Steph squeezed me.

I was so lucky to call them my friends.

An hour or so passed. I was lying on my front on a picnic blanket, picking at the grass while the girls had a game of 'shithead' in the teepee. I could see Golf Buggy Guy approaching with a woman I didn't recognise.

He was carrying a large box.

'The boss man heard about your plight and has sent urgent supplies,' he said as he reached me and put the clinking box in front of me. It was a twenty-four pack of Corona, and the box felt cold. I pushed myself up onto my knees and shielded my eyes to look up at them.

'Thanks, that's very thoughtful.'

'This is Katrina. Katrina is the big boss's right-hand man.'

Katrina gave me a big, although slightly sorrowful smile.

'And you must be *the* girl,' she said, putting her hand out to shake mine.

'Lucy,' I said as the girls appeared, 'and this is Steph, Claire, and Zara.' They shook her hand before they all noticed the box of beer.

'Mind if we join you? We're on our break?' Katrina asked while Golf Buggy Guy tore the box open with a key.

'Ooh, don't mind if I do!' Steph said, diving in, and the girls followed.

We all sat enjoying a beer in the sun. For some reason, it reminded me of the scene in The Shawshank Redemption when they finished tarring the flat roof, and the officers gave them a beer. It went down surprisingly well, and before I knew it, I was already helping myself to another, beating Steph, which was unheard of.

In an attempt to entertain our guests, I leaned toward Katrina and asked, 'So, what's it like working for Officious Man?'

'Who?' Katrina looked confused.

'Sorry, I meant your boss,' I clarified, and she laughed.

'He's like a bear, grizzly on the outside, but he's a big softy once you get past the hard exterior.' She confirmed my suspicions. 'He just has to deal with a lot of shit, and if I'm not here to sift through the crap, he gets pissy.'

By the fourth bottle in, I was feeling the effects but not necessarily in a good way. I was really thirsty, so I just kept on drinking. My head started to bang, and my skin felt slightly sensitive to the sun.

After calming down and going over the scene in my head several times, I concluded that Will was being really unfair. He didn't even give me a chance to explain before he shouted at me. I was conscious that the evening was drawing in, and I didn't want to be in the VIP area before The 'king Band was due on in case I bumped into Will again. Katrina and Golf Buggy Guy had gone, and it was just the four of us who sat cross-legged on the picnic rug.

'Shall we go and find a band to watch?' I suggested suddenly. They all looked at me like I was insane. 'What?'

'I'm not sure that's a good idea,' Steph said, looking me straight in the eye.

'Why not? It will be fun, and you all said you'd be happy to go if I changed my mind,' I said, looking at them all as I made a circle with my hand, vaguely pointing at each of them.

'Okay, well, I'm not sure you're in the right frame of mind,' Steph said honestly.

I paused and then pushed myself back onto my hands behind me, effectively moving away from the group.

'I'm afraid I agree with her, honey,' Claire said, and Zara nodded.

I felt like a teenager being told what to do by their parents. I sat there for a while watching the first stars start to appear and then pushed myself up and made my excuses to go to the loo. While I was sitting there having the longest of wees, I had a thought. Just because they didn't want to go and see the bands didn't mean I couldn't. I washed my hands, checked I had some cash with me, and left the toilets, walking down the hill on the other side to the teepee so the girls couldn't talk me out of it.

Showing the steward my pass, I slipped into the main arena and went straight to the bar. Once I had a drink in my hand, I took myself to a marquee, but the DJ was playing some disco tunes, and although I loved disco, I was not in the mood for it, so I wandered off to seek out the other stages while sipping my beer. I wanted to get as far away from the main stage as possible. My head was banging, but I didn't care.

As I walked, I realised I'd left my phone in the teepee, but I didn't need it. At least it was safe. I didn't know the band's name playing on the other stage. It was heavy and fast, which is what I wanted. Before entering the marquee, I purchased another beer and stood on the periphery, sipping while I got my head into the music. I had a weird sense of being watched, so I gradually moved into the crowd as I drank my beer. It was fair to say that the people who were into this sort of music liked being super close to each other. My feet had already been stood on several times by great big black steel-toed boots.

Suddenly the music dropped out, everyone stopped, waiting in anticipation, and then the beat came crashing back in with strobe lights hitting the crowd. It was as if the whole group rose into a jump simultaneously, and then we all landed together. Little mini mosh pits were being formed all around me, and I was being pushed from one person to the next. The lights were making it difficult to get my bearings, and I was aware I was being sprayed with people's drinks, including my own. I couldn't quite get my balance, flip-flops were not the correct footwear, and I managed to lose one as I stumbled to the side. I tried to focus on the stage for a moment to work out where I was in relation to everything else. I made a beeline towards the back, eventually reaching the marquee's edge. I looked down at my feet. They were battered and bruised but had just about survived. I was covered in beer and sweat, and my top was ripped. I bent down, took my other flip-flop off, and headed out to find another bar.

On my way, I discarded my lonely flip-flop in a bin, but before I got to the bar, I rounded the corner and spotted another festival site area I hadn't seen before. I walked through the archway along a corridor of wind chimes, gently swaying and making an eerie noise. The lighting was dark, candles flickered in the distance, and then I stopped dead because I could feel something brushing against my face. I lifted my hand and realised it was feathers dangling down from what looked like a wooden pergola. While I waited for my eyes to adjust to the light, I realised I was alone. Maybe this was like a sensory place only used during the day. It was starting to freak me out, so I turned back and walked straight into someone.

'Oh, sorry,' I said.

Suddenly I was shoved with great force onto the floor. I looked up to see what had happened and who it was, it was the silhouette of a man, but I couldn't quite see as the lights from the festival were behind him. I was rapidly sobering up, and all of my senses were instantly on overdrive. My ears were straining for a clue as to what would happen next, and all the hairs on my body spiked. My natural reaction was to protect my head, and I lifted my arms across my face but allowing a gap to peek through for any sudden movement. I was waiting to be punched or kicked.

I allowed myself a split second to quickly glance to my left to see if there was anything I could use as a weapon, but all I could make out was the shape of a toadstool. When I looked back, I couldn't see him... had he gone? I sat up desperately searching the darkness for a clue, a sound, a movement. I wanted to scream, but I was too frightened. I could barely breathe, let alone make a noise.

I felt something next to my leg, but before I could put my hand down to feel what it was, I was hauled up to my feet from under my arms and dragged backwards. My heels were scraping along the rugged, dusty grass. An involuntary scream escaped me, and a hand was instantaneously shoved over my mouth. It smelt of cigarettes and felt greasy. After that, everything went into slow motion. I thought, this is it, I'm going to be raped or killed.

But then he stopped, righted me, and spun me around forcefully, shoving me up against something hard behind me. He lifted his forearm, pushing my chin up as my head crashed against the wall, and he held it there. 'I told you to steer clear of him, you stupid bitch.' He spat, shoving his body up against mine and pushing his arm up further still, causing me to catch my breath. My mind raced; it was an American voice I had heard before. Oh, my God, the man from the gig who warned me against Will.

'I'm, I'm not with Will,' I stuttered, trying to speak through the constriction he was causing against my windpipe, desperately trying to think of something I could do to escape. Instead, he brought his face close to mine, pushing even harder against my throat, and I could feel his stubble against my cheek and the bristles of his goaty on my ear as I struggled to breathe.

'Go home, leave while you still have the use of your fucking legs,' he whispered into my ear. I could feel his heartbeat against mine and his erratic breathing in my ear as I started to feel dizzy. He pulled his head back and looked straight at me. I could just about make out his features. His eyes looked completely black, dilated maybe, empty.

'You're not one of us,' he shouted.

He smelt of liquor, I don't know which, and then my ears started ringing... buzzing, I wasn't quite sure, and I could feel my eyes rolling into the back of my head, and then he moved his body away and just as I thought I was going to pass out he released me, causing me to fall in a crumpled mess on the floor. I stayed still and heard his footsteps getting quieter as he walked away. And then I started panting like I'd been for a run or was having an asthma attack, trying to open my mouth wider to accept more air into my lungs. Jesus Christ. Who was that guy? I started to shake and hugged my knees up to my chest, cuddling myself for comfort and safety.

I felt in my back pocket for my phone, but it wasn't there, and then I massaged my neck where he had roughly held it with his arm and then felt the back of my head to feel for any blood. My mouth was dry, and my palms were sweaty. Slowly, my breathing came back to a normal rhythm, and I tried to stand up, but my legs wouldn't allow me. They were trembling so much.

In the distance, I could hear an announcement being made, something about The 'king Band, but I couldn't quite make it out. I then heard booing, lots of booing. Had they cancelled the show? Had Will gone? I sat there for a while longer. And then I tried to stand again, but I was still shaking too much. I got onto all fours and crawled towards the lights of the festival, hoping that was where the entrance was. I finally reached the pergola and used it to pull myself up. I was pretty unsteady, but I figured I could use the pergola poles to support me as I edged towards the archway.

By the time I reached the wind chimes, my legs were too tired, and I decided it would be quicker to get back on all fours and crawl the rest of the way. The lights were getting brighter, and I could see people wandering this way and that. Despite feeling frightened and knowing I needed to tell someone... anyone about what had just happened, I suddenly felt exposed and aware that I looked in a complete state. So, I moved to my left and propped myself up against a wooden fence to compose myself.

I sat watching as people went about their business. So many legs and feet were moving in different directions at different speeds. I looked down at my own legs. I was covered in cuts and scrapes, my shorts were stained, and my feet were bare. My top was even more ripped, and my fingernails had dirt under them. I felt my face, it felt dirty too, and my hair was like a bird's nest of sweat and dust. I was in such a state.

I heard a ripple of cheers that seemed to spread all across the site. And someone strummed a testing cord. The band must be about to start. I thought I heard Will welcome the crowd, but the breeze had picked up a little, so I only heard some of the words. They would fade out, and then I'd hear a few loud and clear words. It was weird. The crowd went quiet, and I turned my head to point one of my ears toward the announcement. I heard the word *help* and *dan* maybe and *tickets*. He must be telling them about a competition or something, but why hadn't they started to play? My head was thumping, and I was so very thirsty.

Whatever the announcement was, it had finished, but something felt weird like the mood had changed, and I could hear shouting from a long way away, and the shouting was getting closer. Like a Mexican wave of shouts, I couldn't hear what they were saying. So many voices were mumbling at once like a strange pagan chant. It seemed to filter out towards the extremities of the site, and then I thought I heard someone call my name. I looked round to see if I recognised anyone, but no one was there, and then I heard it again from a different direction and with a foreign accent. And again. What on earth? Was I dreaming? Everyone was calling my name, literally everyone.

I searched the faces of everyone saying my name, but no one was actually looking at me and I didn't recognise anyone. I tried to call back to say I was here, but my voice had gone, and all that came out was a tiny squeak. I finally locked eyes with someone and lifted my arm. It was so heavy it flopped back down on the ground, but they'd seen.

She shouted, 'there she is!'

She came rushing over.

Within seconds there was a huge crowd around me, all asking me questions at the same time, but all I could do was look up at them.

Someone tried to lift me onto my feet, but I waved them off, knowing I'd fall straight back down. Instead, someone else shouted, 'she needs an ambulance,' and everyone called for doctors and ambulances. It was all too much, and I started to panic. I dragged my knees up towards my chest again and curled up like a ball, putting my forehead on my knees. I just needed them all to go away. I tried desperately to block the noise out. All I wanted to do was sleep.

Somewhere in the sea of voices was one I recognised, but I couldn't quite place it. My arm felt tingly, and someone was stroking it. 'Lucy, Lucy, can you hear me?' I tried to open my eyes to see who it was, but they stung like someone had poured dust into them. 'We're going to lift you now.' It felt like I was on a boat, bobbing along. Then, I could hear an immense roar in the distance, cheering and clapping. They were having fun, I thought.

'You drive. I'll sit in the back with her.'

'Officious Man,' I mumbled.

'Hang in there, Lucy, not long now.' The boat was getting thrashed around in the waves. 'I think she needs to see a doctor.'

'Hi, yep, can we have a doctor backstage asap, please?'

Stage? I thought we were on a boat. I was so confused.

'Okay, boss, man.'

There was a sudden jolt, and then I was bobbing again in the calm waters. I could hear a song I recognised, but it sounded strange.

'Jesus Christ!'

'Oh my fucking God!'

'Is she okay?'

Steph? Claire? What were they doing here? Where was I? I could hear lots of footsteps.

'I'm going to let Will know.'

'Will,' I whispered.

I heard a zip being pulled, and then the bobbing stopped, we had reached the shore, and I felt cool sheets against my skin. I felt safe, unfurling slightly, but my hands were still shaking.

'Okay, guys, move back, let the doctor through.'

'Hello Lucy, my name is Kate, and I'm a doctor. Do you mind if I check you over?'

I tried to say something, but I had no saliva left in my mouth.

'Can you get me a saline drip and some water, please?'

She picked up my hand and held my wrist. I managed to open my eyes very slightly. She had a pretty face. I thought she looked too young to be a doctor. She stuck something to my forehead. I felt really sleepy.

'Thank you. Lucy, I'm going to sit you up a bit. Can you help me? I need you to pull on my arm with all your strength like you're pulling back on a rowing machine.'

I did as she instructed, and magically something soft appeared behind me.

'Would you like some water?'

She held a cup up to my lips, and I sipped, the water reaching every crevice and fold in my mouth and every taste bud. I could feel the cool liquid going down my throat, washing and soothing as it went. She allowed me another few sips before putting the cup down on a bedside shelf.

'You'll feel a little scratch now while I attach you to this drip. It's just some saline to rehydrate you.'

I didn't feel anything apart from a cooling sensation in my hand. I looked at the cup, wishing I had a straw, and as if reading my mind, the doctor picked it up again and offered it to my lips.

She put the cup back and sat at the foot of the bed, pressing things on what looked like a tablet. I closed my eyes but could still hear songs I recognised in the distance.

'How's she doing?' I was sure that was Steph's voice, but my eyes were so heavy.

'She's doing fine, temperature's fine, blood pressure's good. She's a bit dehydrated and tired. I'm a bit concerned about some bruising on her neck, but other than that, she'll be okay.'

It was weird having someone talk about you when you were right there, but boy, I was tired, so I didn't care.

I wasn't sure how much time had gone by when I came round, but the doctor was packing the drip away and I realised I was in a teepee. She looked up.

'How are you feeling?'

'Okay,' I managed, although my voice sounded hoarse.

'Keep sipping on that water. That will help to keep you hydrated. I need to ask you about this bruising.' She pointed to my neck. 'Do you remember how you got it?'

A horrible feeling came over me, a darkness, I could smell cigarette smoke, and suddenly I heaved. She quickly passed me a cardboard bowl, and I spat up some bile. 'I'm sorry to push you on this, but did someone do this to you?'

I nodded. She gave me a knowing nod in return.

'And I'm sorry to ask such a blunt question but do you think you've been raped?'

I shook my head.

'Okay, I'm going to note the incident so that an officer can get in touch with you. Are you happy for me to do that?'

'Yes,' I croaked.

'Well done,' she said, 'I think several people out there would like to see you. Are you happy for me to send one or two of them in?'

I nodded again and smiled.

After a short time, Steph poked her head around the door. 'Hi, how are you feeling?' She stepped in and sat on the side of the bed.

'I'm not really sure,' I whispered.

My voice was still a bit hoarse, and I took another sip of water. Steph looked worried. She was looking at my neck and the rip in my top.

'I'm okay,' I assured her.

'We were all so worried about you, babe.'

'I'm really sorry.' I strained.

I had caused such a nightmare for everyone. Steph pinched her lips together with her fingers to indicate not to say any more, but I had so many questions.

'Has Will gone now?'

'Gone? No. He was the one that instigated the search party.' I frowned. 'He's just finishing the show, and I imagine he'll want to see you.'

'But he's so angry with me,' I said.

'Babe, so much has happened since you went missing. I'll explain everything tomorrow when you've had some rest.' Just as she said that, we could hear an almighty eruption from the crowd in the distance. 'They've just finished the show.' She confirmed.

'Steph?'

She looked up at me.

'I need a wee.'

She looked around for a moment, then stood up.

She secured the zip and pulled a little port-a-loo around to the side of the bed.

'Can you wriggle over to the edge of the bed?' I smiled and wiggled until my feet could feel the floor over the side of the bed, Steph helped pull me up to a seated position, and I undid my shorts. I tried to stand, wobbled, and then sat back down.

I began to giggle.

'For fuck's sake, Lu, will you just concentrate,' she said, but I could hear the smile in her voice.

I tried again, and she put her hands out to hold mine and steady me so I could lower myself onto the loo.

'How to be a best friend #22,' she said as she looked up to the top of the teepee while I peed.

'Okay, I'm done.'

She put her hands out without looking and hoisted me back up onto the bed, and I shrugged my shorts back up. She put the lid down and slid the loo back into place.

Just then, we heard a commotion outside as I managed to get myself back on the bed. 'Where is she? Can I see her?' It was Will. He sounded out of breath.

'Are you happy for him to come in?' Steph asked.

'As long as he doesn't shout at me again.'

'Noted.'

She undid the zip and stepped out.

'Is she in there? Can I see her?'

'Yes, she's pretty weak, no shouting.'

'No shouting,' I heard him confirm like he was making a Scout promise. Will appeared in the doorway and he took a sharp intake of breath before turning and closing the zip. I looked up at him, drinking him in. He was dripping with sweat, his fringe all matted together. He pushed his hair out of his face, holding his hands behind his head and looked straight back at me.

'Shit, Lucy, I'm so sorry,' he said, bringing his hands back to scrub his face as if he couldn't quite believe what he was seeing.

'Can you forgive me? I had no idea that the booking had been cancelled, and I should have let you explain.'

He hesitated a moment, putting his hands on his hips. His eyes roaming over my body as he moved closer to the bed. He put one knee on the edge of the mattress and then the other to get closer and sat on his heels like he was about to pray.

'What happened to you? Where did you go?'

'I went to see a band... and I was a bit drunk... and got a bit lost.'

My throat started burning, and I took a sip of water. Will shuffled across the bed and lay down next to me. I moved on-to my side carefully so I could look at him. I couldn't quite believe he was here.

'And yes, I can... forgive you, that is.' I whispered.

He moved closer still, and he looked down at me and frowned at the bruising.

'Did you get into a fight?' he asked, but I was too tired to explain.

'Something like that,' I said sleepily.

Will cautiously put his hand on my cheek and looked in-to my eyes.

'I really fucking missed you. I was going crazy not being able to speak to you,' he admitted.

'I... I was heartbroken.'

Will kissed me then. It was so good to feel his lips on mine, and it was about then that I fell asleep.

Chapter 26

When I woke, Will was asleep beside me, and I cast my eyes over our surroundings. We were in a double bed and there was a little kitchenette area to the side, just like the girls'. Will looked so peaceful, still fully dressed in the foetal position. I felt horrible and in dire need of a shower or, better still, a bath. And a cup of tea. I slowly sat up and gingerly swung my legs to the side of the bed, testing my feet on the floor.

I leaned across to the kitchenette and picked up the little kettle to see if it had any water, and I was in luck. I put the gas on and set the kettle down on the hob.

It was going to be another hot day.

While I waited for the kettle, I checked myself over. My hair felt like someone had back combed it, my skin smeared with dirt, and my clothes were ruined. The kettle started boiling just as Will placed a hand on my back and I leapt out of my skin.

'Hey,' Will murmured, cautiously lacing an arm around me, 'how are you feeling?'

I started to make the tea while I gathered my thoughts.

'Like I really need a shower. I feel grubby. A mess.'

I lay back down next to him.

'You were mumbling quite a bit in your sleep.'

'Oh God, sorry, I hope I didn't keep you awake.'

'No, I was just worried about you. You kept saying that we weren't together,' he confessed.

That's what I said to the man? I didn't want to go there yet.

'Where are the girls?' I asked, changing the subject.

'I think Gi drove them back to their teepee.'

'Who's Gi?'

'You know, the guy who works here and drives the golf buggy.'

Gi! That's his name.

'In fact, I thought you were together when I arrived. That's probably why I flew off the handle. I'm so sorry I shouted at you.'

'Please stop apologising. It was just a misunderstanding.'

'I know, but I kinda feel responsible... if I hadn't acted like an ass, you wouldn't have wandered off.'

Okay, well, that was probably true, but it was my decision to get caught up in a mosh pit and wander into a completely isolated area of the site.

I scrunched my nose up. 'It's done now, and it's in the past. None of it matters.'

Will stroked the hair out of my face, picking a small twig out of my fringe, inspecting it, and then throwing it towards the end of the bed. His hand then travelled down my face, onto my neck, and over my shoulder, making me feel all tingly.

'I know we've got a lot to talk about, but I just want you to know...' Will began, but suddenly, a slap on the canvas forced me to jump out of my skin again. Okay, so I was on edge.

'Lu?' I heard a loud whisper. 'You awake in there?' It was Steph. I sat up as the zip opened, and she stuck her head in. 'Sorry, babe, did I leave my phone in here?' She asked, spying it on the side by the hob. 'You look better.' She added before looking down at my neck and wincing.

'Thanks.' I said as she stepped in, and I stood to pass her phone. 'What are you up to?'

'We're just taking it in turns to shower, and then we'll probably grab something to eat.'

'Okay, cool, I could really do with a shower myself. Can I head over in a bit?'

'Of course, see you over there,' she said, zipping the door shut.

Will smiled as I turned back to him and sat up, swinging his legs onto the floor in front of where I stood. He took both of my hands and looked up at me.

'So, we're cool, right?'

I nodded down at him, and he slowly stood up, trailing his fingers up my arm, making me giggle, and then cupping my face bringing my lips to meet his. We kissed a long slow sensual kiss, his arms wrapping around me carefully, gently pulling me in close. His moves very considered, not his usual deliberate and commanding self. I traced my fingers around the top of his jeans and glided my hands up his back, feeling each rib and muscle. It felt so good, but then my legs started to tremble. I wasn't sure whether it was because of him or whether I was still feeling the effects of yesterday.

Will pulled back. 'Are you okay?'

'I need to sit down,' I said, my voice faint. Will turned me around and held my hands, letting me use them to steady myself as I sat.

'You need to take it easy today. Where's your shower stuff?'

We slowly wandered across to the girls' teepee, Will holding my things and my hand. Steph was rolling the doorway back to let some more air through when we arrived.

'You know what? I'm gonna go and find Paul and Jake, see if I can steal a shower myself. Shall I see you back here?' Will asked.

'Sure,' I said, and he gave me a quick peck on the lips and handed me my things.

'You sure you'll be okay?' he asked, tucking a stray hair behind my ear.

I nodded, almost embarrassed, despite only Steph being witness. He smiled and then headed off.

'Things are good with you two then?' Steph asked when he was out of earshot.

'They will be, we haven't had much time to talk, but I think we'll be okay.'

Claire wandered back into the teepee with her towel on her head.

'That was so good. Oh, hey, babe,' she said, giving me a gentle squeeze, and I retraced her steps toward the shower. It was a luxury shower for a festival, and you didn't have to keep pressing a button to keep the water on. It had a lever. I stepped under the water and let the water run all over me, and when I opened my eyes, the water in the shower tray was brown. Gross. I washed my hair. The back of my head was tender, and then I used shower gel for my entire body. Thoughts of the man came flooding in, and I quickly opened my eyes, steadying myself on the edge of the cubicle.

I never wanted to see him again.

I finished washing, brushing my teeth while in the shower, and patting myself dry. My skin was tight from the sun, and my neck was tender. I covered myself in body lotion and then in more sun cream and got dressed.

Claire was right, it was so good.

When I got back to the teepee, the three girls were sitting on deck chairs holding coke cans and various devices, catching up on the gossip pages or reading.

'Anyone would think you were on holiday!' I said. 'Hi Zara, you okay?'

'Yes, I'm good, thank you, more to the point, how are you?' she asked.

'Better, thank you.'

I dragged another deck chair out and sat down, pulling my mirror out to survey the damage. Gosh, my neck was quite bad, swathes of blue and black had started appearing, and the back of my head still felt tender.

'How did that actually happen?' Steph asked with concern in her eyes, but just then, Gi and Officious Man turned up on the golf buggy with delicious supplies.

'Hiya, Queen,' Officious Man said. 'We thought you ladies might like some pastries.'

I put my things down, stood up to take the tray, and popped it down on a log as the girls all leaned in to see what was available.

'How are you doing?' Gi asked, sounding concerned.

'I'm okay, I can't really remember what happened last night, but I get the feeling I need to thank you both.'

He wrapped me up in a friendly hug.

'Hey, hands off...' Will said cajolingly as he and Paul joined the group. '... ooh, pastries.'

We all sat around the log of pastries on various chairs and stumps, I sat sideways on Will's lap to make room, and the conversation quickly turned to the previous day's events.

'So, when we realised you'd wandered off without your phone, I went to tell Gi, and we drove around the site for ages looking for you,' Steph said. 'But you had completely disappeared.'

'Meanwhile, we had hung back here in case you came back,' Claire chipped in. She waved a hand toward Zara before adding, 'And I bumped into Will and went nuclear at him.'

Will cocked his head to one side and looked at me with a raised eyebrow.

'And then he made me explain what had actually happened last week.'

'Then we arrived back to tell everyone that we couldn't find you,' Gi said.

'I was being pressured by security to get the band on because the crowd was getting restless, so I told Will he had to go on with or without you,' Officious Man said.

'And that's when I came up with the idea to involve the crowd in the search.' Will added. 'When I got on stage, I explained that we wouldn't play until we had found you. I bribed them with tickets to the next show.'

'That's not quite right,' Zara said. 'He went on stage and told the crowd he had done something foolish. He'd shouted at a girl and told her never to contact him again, and that she'd disappeared and was on her own somewhere in the festival. It was very sweet. A picture of you appeared on the big screens next to the stage. The crowd wanted to help and asked for your name, and then everyone was calling for you, and I mean everyone,' she reiterated.

Will shrugged and smiled at me.

'We then got radioed to say that a girl had been found near the Soul Arena in a bad way, so boss man and I went off to investigate,' Gi said.

'Will wouldn't play until he'd heard that you'd been found,' Paul said. I was starting to colour up.

I had caused such a nightmare, and I was so embarrassed.

'So, once we got to you, we radioed back to confirm it was you so the show could go on,' Gi explained.

'I am so embarrassed guys, and I'm really sorry for causing so much stress.'

I started to well up, but we were interrupted by a loud cough.

'I'm sorry to bother you all, but could I ask if one of you is Lucy Daniels?'

It was a police officer.

'That's me,' I said, quickly wiping my tears away.

'I wonder if I could have a word, in private if possible?'

Everyone was looking at me, and I stood up, feeling shaky.

'Do you want me to come?' Will asked, and I nodded. 'Is that okay?' he asked the man.

'Of course,' he said kindly.

Officious Man showed us through to an empty teepee right on the edge of the site, and Will and I sat on the side of one of the beds while the police officer pulled up a chair to sit in front of us.

Chapter 27

After taking down my details for his records, he said, 'So, I understand that something happened last night which might account for your bruising.'

Oh God, I was going to have to tell him about the man. My jaw was tense, and I was feeding the hem of my skirt through my thumb and forefinger, back and forth.

'Take your time,' he said, gently coaxing me.

'I found an area of the festival that I hadn't seen before, so I went to look around. But I realised it was closed and was about to turn back.' I shuddered and Will put his arm around me. 'A man pushed me over... but I couldn't see because it was dark... he dragged me to the side....' Tears started falling onto my knees, 'and then he pushed me against a wall...' I waved my hands at the bruising while trying to cool my face down, 'and he gave me a warning.'

'You're doing really well. Can you remember what he said?' The police officer asked as he scribbled notes in his book.

'He told me to stay away from Will....'

'What?' Will said, looking at me, shocked.

'That he'd break my legs... that I wasn't one of them, I can't remember much else. I think I was losing consciousness.'

'He was strangling you?' Will asked, incandescent. I wasn't sure, so I carried on with my explanation.

'He was American... tall, dark, skinny... a goaty... and he smelt bad. Smelt of cigarettes and BO.' I shuddered again and wept.

'Is there anything else about him that you can remember?' The police officer asked once I'd managed to compose myself.

'He was... dirty, unwashed, wreaked of alcohol.' I didn't know how else to describe him.

'Can you think of anything else? Any distinguishing features.'

'Um, no, but it isn't the first time I've come across him....' The police officer nodded, encouraging me to go on. 'He approached me at a gig in Bristol.' I directed my gaze at Will. 'Told me that you would use me and then dump me.'

'Why didn't you tell me?' Will asked, tensing his shoulders.

'Because, because...' I stuttered. 'I didn't say anything because Steph thought it was probably a deranged fan. It was shortly after the cameraman incident.' I looked down at my knees, brushing the tears away.

Moving his questioning on to Will, the police officer asked, 'Is this something you have had to deal with before?' Will shook his head. 'Okay, well, I think I have enough information to be working on, and it would seem there is a high chance this man is still on the festival site.' I tried to shake the thought of seeing him again, and Will stroked my back reassuringly. 'I'm going to give you both my card, and if you have any further information and, more specifically, if there is a sighting of him, please call me.' He passed us both a card and gathered his things. 'Look after that one,' he said to Will before he left.

Tears were still popping out of my eyes like unwanted rain, and Will pulled me on to his lap, cradling me like a baby. 'I'm so sorry you had to go through that,' he whispered into my ear. 'I won't let that happen again.'

I'm not sure he had any control over that or why he was sorry, but he was trying his best to calm me down.

When I had composed myself, he slowly placed me back on the bed, got up, and carefully pulled me up to standing. Then, surveying the bruising in a new light, his eyes turned dark, and he put his hand over his mouth as if he was trying to stop himself from saying something.

'What's wrong?' I asked.

He exhaled sharply through his nose. 'I'm just angry that someone did that to you. Come on.'

He took my hand and started marching back to the teepee where the others were. He was going ever so slightly too fast, and I had to stop in the end.

'Will, what's going on?' I asked.

'I need to get back and speak to Paul.' He pulled me along. When we reached the teepee, Paul wasn't there. It was just the girls. 'Look after her, don't let her out of your sight.'

He didn't even kiss me goodbye. He just went.

'What's going on now?' Claire asked. 'I don't know if I can cope with any more drama!'

I took a deep breath and explained that I had been assaulted last night and that there was a chance the man was still on site.

'So now we're searching for someone else?' she asked.

'Is that where the bruises came from?' Steph asked.

'Yes, I'm not sure if it's a good idea that we search for him, but the police are,' I explained.

'Christ, Lu, from now on, we all stick together, okay?' Steph said, and everyone agreed.

'We saved you a pastry.' Zara pointed at the lone croissant, but I wasn't hungry.

I was a bit nervous about leaving the VIP area, but we couldn't keep ourselves cooped up all day, so we decided to walk around the site. We stopped to get a coffee and found a table to sit at. I couldn't help but notice how much rubbish there was. The bins, around the bins, and the tables were all full of garbage. There was at least one piece of litter in every square metre as far as the eye could see. There was a definite rise in wasted people too. Some were sleeping at the edge of the walkway or slumped on chairs. One man looked like he had severe heat stroke, and people were absentmindedly walking over him. It was a sorry sight. Then, out of nowhere, an utterly inebriated man plonked down on the chair next to me and slurred, 'Laaadiesz.'

He stank of urine.

I stood up straight away and suggested we head back. Thankfully everyone agreed.

⸺⚫⸺

'It's always safer on this side of the fence,' Gi explained. 'Here, grab some beers and go and chill.'

I wasn't sure whether he meant for her to do so, but Steph picked up the whole box and heaved it onto her shoulder, and we all walked back to the teepee.

'There you are!' Will said as we got back.

He'd obviously been looking for me.

'You know, they call these things mobile for a reason.'

In his hand was my phone which he handed to me.

'I thought you called them cells?' I said, trying to hide my giggle.

He put his forehead on mine and kissed me.

'Get a room,' Claire said almost immediately as Steph handed us all a beer.

We all sat cross-legged on a blanket that Claire had laid out, and Zara produced a bag. She began to hand out little pots of glitter, stick-on gems, and temporary tattoos.

'I couldn't resist,' she said, 'shall we all decorate each other, or shall I find a mirror?'

'Each other,' we all chimed.

I smiled, accepting one of the pots, and looked over at Will, but he seemed distracted. Like he was nervous and couldn't settle. He kept checking his watch and tapping his feet. I frowned at him, but all he did was kiss my knee. So, I turned, and Steph settled in front of me, offering me her face.

Paul came to join us a while later, he and Will shared a look, but I guessed it was band related.

'They've asked us to do a few acoustic numbers at the end before the finale,' Paul said to Will.

'Okay yeah, that would make up for last night, I guess. Jake cool?' Will asked, and Paul nodded.

'Beer?' Steph offered Paul before offering everyone else another.

'I'm gonna skip. I need the loo,' I said.

'I'll walk with you,' Will offered.

'Oh, would you listen to them?' Claire said, rolling her eyes.

We wandered up to the loos, and Will hovered outside while I went in. It was weird. We hadn't had the chance to talk about what had happened or what would happen in the future, but it was almost like the festival had created a little bubble in time around us, and I wasn't looking forward to it popping tomorrow when we had to go home. I washed my hands and headed out, wiping them on my skirt.

He took my hand and pulled me in close to him. 'I really just wanted to kiss you. Walking with you was a bonus.'

I smiled up at him, and he kissed me. He placed my hands up around his neck and then put his hands around my waist. Oh, I had missed this. Pulling me in tight up against him, he deepened the kiss. I was losing myself. We could have been anywhere. He dipped me backwards slightly, forcing me to cling to his shoulders, and kissed my neck gently. I closed my eyes, and then, suddenly, he was the man in my imagination. I quickly moved my feet backwards to right myself, pulling away and placing my hands on my thighs, gasping for breath.

'Lucy, are you okay?'

'I'm sorry. I. I can't.'

'It's him, isn't it,' Will asked.

I looked up at him. 'I could see his face for a moment. I'm still processing it. I'm sorry.' I straightened up as my breathing normalised, and I could see Will was concerned.

Then, reaching up to touch his face, he put his arms around my shoulders while I rested my head below his chin for a while.

We strolled hand in hand down to the teepee, 'So we're gonna play a few tunes tonight. It's the least we can do for them after last night's fiasco. Will you come and watch?'

'I'd love to, but I....'

'I don't mean out there. I mean upstage, on a stool, that I've glued your ass to!' I giggled.

'I know this sounds really lame, but I might have to have a little disco nap before that.'

'How about you go back to the girls' teepee, and I'll go find us something to eat because, if I'm not mistaken, all you've had today is a coffee and a couple of beers?'

'And a cup or tea.' I remembered.

'Oh, well, that's okay then,' he said with a sideways smile. 'Anything you fancy?'

'Well, apart from you....' I looked up at the sky, thinking, and he stopped and kissed me. I smiled. 'I don't know. Choose something for me.'

'Okay.'

He dropped me off and went off in search of some food. The girls were still decorating each other, and they were pretty merry. Over half of the beers had gone. I bypassed the girls and stepped into the teepee. Crawling onto the bed as if it was the last thing my body was capable of, I lay there listening to the girls laughing and chatting. I closed my eyes and drifted.

Chapter 28

I felt the bed sink beside me and suddenly opened my eyes. Will was holding two boxes of something delicious smelling with chopsticks poking out of the top.

'Sorry I took so long. The downside of being in a place where everyone recognises me, so I had to send Terry.'

I noticed it was getting dark and rubbed my eyes. How long had I been asleep?

'I feel like I've only just closed my eyes.'

Will smiled, waited for me to sit up, and we sat on the bed eating teriyaki noodles. They were so good.

'This is delicious, Will—thanks,' Steph shouted, and I could hear more mumbles of agreement.

Aww, he'd thought of everyone. We sat in comfortable silence for a while. I didn't realise how hungry I was.

A while later, I could hear someone running, and the footsteps were getting closer. 'Whoa, careful!' Claire shouted with a mouthful as Paul rounded the doorway.

'He's here,' he said quickly, entirely out of breath. 'Just walked in with her.'

Will suddenly dumped his noodles on the side and jumped up.

'I fucking knew it,' Will bit out, and they both started to run.

'Will!' I called. 'What's going on?'

It was too late. The girls and I looked at each other for a split second, and then we all put our food down and followed at speed. We ran through the tents to the other side, being careful not to trip over any guy ropes, and arrived in a large open clearing. A loading area maybe? We were just in time to witness Will walking towards Alysa and a man I didn't... wait... it couldn't be. It was him, the man. Paul had hung back, and we came level with him.

'Paul, what's going on?' I demanded between gasps.

'Just wait,' he said, putting his arm out as if to hold me back. I noticed Terry and Bill loitering, and it was as if they had them surrounded. Suddenly, Will started to run at full pelt towards them, and just before he reached them, he crouched into a rugby tackle, knocking the man over and down onto the floor. Alysa screamed and stepped back into the shadows to get out of their way. Will punched him, actually punched him while he was down. I gasped and held my hand over my mouth. Claire looked over at me with excitement in her eyes. What was going on? How did Will know he was the man? I could hear Will talking to him, but I couldn't hear what he said, and then the man spat in Will's face.

'Eww,' Claire said, and Zara clung to my arm.

Will pushed himself up off the man, wiping his face with the back of his hand as he walked towards us. The man said something that I couldn't quite make out, and Will stopped in his tracks. He slowly looked up at me, enraged, and his jaw was tense. I could see him take a long, steadying breath, and I thought he would continue walking toward us, but instead, he turned and kicked the man right in the bollocks, making him recoil and cup himself while he writhed in agony. But Will was not done with him. He jumped on him, laying into him, punching him, and at one point, Will reared up and landed back down on him with his elbow.

'Oh my God, I can't watch anymore.' I put my head in my hands. 'Paul, would you do something?' I shouted.

Just then, Jake came out of nowhere, running towards us, and said, 'Paul, come on, he's gonna kill him.'

The pair of them started to run towards Will and the man. They both grabbed Will, taking an arm each holding him back. The man on the floor was motionless, and Will spat back at him. I was shocked, my mouth open, and my breathing laboured. As Paul and Jake walked Will back, he spotted Alysa standing in the shadows. He stopped again, looked straight at her, and shook his head.

When they got to us, Will said, 'You can call that cop now. I'm finished with him.'

'Hey man, are you sure?' Paul asked.

Looking at me, Will replied, 'I'm sure.' I reached in my back pocket for my phone without taking my eyes off Will. His eyes were wild, and he stretched his hand out and wiggled his fingers, probably trying to deal with the throbbing.

'No need to call. They're already on their way.'

It was Officious Man. How long had he been standing there?

'I'm gonna be glad when this weekend is over.'

He directed the comment at Will. Will put his none throbbing hand out to shake his hand, and Officious Man pulled him in for a shoulder bump.

'There's ice on the buggy.' I was seriously missing something. How did he know? I looked up and saw the man lying on the floor, Alysa was nowhere to be seen. Officious Man started to stroll towards the man, Terry and Bill joining him to keep watch before the police arrived.

Will wandered over to the buggy to get some ice for his hand and sat on the back seat. I hovered, not knowing what to do because I felt entirely out of the loop. He beckoned me over with a flick of his head. I slipped away from the group, busy recounting the fight, and with his spare arm, he slipped it behind my waist, drawing me in between his legs. He looked up at me. Will was sweaty and had mud and possibly a smear of blood on his forehead. Using some blue roll and dipping it in the water from the melted ice, I wiped his face.

'I told you I wouldn't let that happen again.'

'Am I being really dumb? How did you know? I feel like I'm missing several pieces of the puzzle.'

He smiled and then winced as I steadied myself on his hand, forgetting he'd just used it to wallop someone.

'That's my brother,' he said, nodding towards the man.

I blinked several times, hoping it was a helpful piece in the puzzle, but if anything, more pieces were appearing.

'He used to be in the band when we were kids but left before we started getting successful. After a few years, he wanted a slice of the pie, but Paul and Jake didn't want him in the band. I had to respect that. I felt guilty, so I made sure he was sorted. Bought him a place to live and sent him money, but it was never enough.'

Will took his hand off the ice and stretched his fingers again. I sucked some air through my teeth when I saw the bruising. At least three of his knuckles were twice the size.

'Anyway, it all came to a head a couple of years ago when I caught him with Alysa, who I was seeing at the time.'

I knew there had been something there. It was like a girl's sixth sense with other women.

'We had a massive bust-up, and I stopped his payments. I hadn't seen him for months, but I'd heard he'd got himself involved in drugs, and all he wanted was revenge. I had to bail him out of the cooler a couple of times, Paul and Jake thought I was crazy, but I wanted to give him another chance.'

'So, he came over here for revenge... and Alysa?' I needed to know. I had waited long enough.

'Alysa and I split. I didn't speak to her for a year and a half until the tour was booked, and she wanted in. She promised me that she was rid of him and, what can I say? She's good at her job. From what I can gather, she's got herself mixed up with the same people as him, and she was doing him favours to get a hit.'

'For drugs?' I clarified.

'Yeah, and then when you told the officer what had happened, I knew it was him. I think he's been trying to sabotage our relationship since we met, getting Alysa to tell the press stuff, and I haven't checked, but I'm pretty sure she cancelled your flight.'

'How did you find him? How did you know he would be here?'

'I spoke to Jimmy, showed him a picture of Ben, and he shared it with his security team. Apparently, Alysa had been trying to get a spare backstage pass all weekend, so they gave her one, and sure enough, she brought him to us.'

'Jimmy being Officious Man and Ben being your brother?'

'If by Officious Man you mean the festival organiser, then yes, and Ben, yeah.'

He looked wistful. I stroked his fringe away from his face and lifted his chin, kissing him very lightly on the lips. He moved his arm from behind my waist and delicately traced my collarbone, where most of the bruising was.

'That was the final straw.' He looked up. 'It won't happen again,' he repeated, and then his hand reached up to my neck as he gently pulled me in for another kiss.

We heard some commotion, and we both looked up to see the scene unfolding as Ben was handcuffed and taken away by the police. Jimmy making a statement, as well as Paul. I thought it strange that they didn't want to speak to Will, and I had a funny feeling that a prior agreement had been made.

They both strolled back down to the buggy. 'I hope you're gonna be all right to play with that. We've promised the crowd something special,' Jimmy said, nodding toward his hand.

'It's an acoustic set. I'll be fine,' Will assured him as Jimmy and Paul climbed in the front.

'Hop on, Queen.'

Will moved back so I could sit on his knee, and Jimmy drove us the short distance back to the teepee. The girls were nowhere to be seen.

'See you in about half an hour,' Paul said as he went off to find Jake.

'Thanks, Jimmy,' Will said. 'See you after the show?'

Jimmy nodded and zoomed off.

Chapter 29

'Finally,' Will said.

'Finally, what?' I said checking the teepee was okay, and our belongings were still there after abandoning it earlier. I stepped in and started to clear away the cold noodles from the bed, but when I turned, Will took the noodles out of my hand, put them back on the side, and then closed the zip.

'I get you to myself,' he said, his eyes darkening as he rested his hands on my hips and moved forward so that I stumbled and practically fell back on the bed. My head smarting as it hit the mattress. Will followed, climbing on top of me, his fringe brushing the side of my face, which made me laugh. Without hesitation, he kissed me, immediately exploring me with his tongue, and his hand travelled down to the hem of my top.

'Is this okay?' he asked, breaking away briefly. I hummed some sort of response as he didn't give me the chance to reply. Lifting my top slightly to allow his hand to travel up my torso, he slowly pulled the cup of my bra down, exposing my nipple.

'Lu? You in there?' I heard as Zara rapped on the canvas a couple of times.

'Fuck!' Will whispered, rolling his eyes and collapsing on the bed beside me as I pulled my top down, trying to stop myself from laughing.

'Hi, Zara,' I said, sounding as breezy as possible. 'Everything all right?' I looked over at Will to check he had sorted himself out before hearing the zip.

'I just wanted to let you know that we're going to head out and catch the last band. Did you want to come?'

Will coughed quietly at the irony of her question, and I tried not to laugh.

'Um, I think I'm going to stay here, but you go, yeah? Where have you guys been?'

'Oh, just hanging out with Gi. Shall we meet by the cabin after the show?'

'Sounds like a plan. Have fun.'

She skipped off to catch up with the others. I flopped back down onto the bed.

'Are you sure you don't wanna go?' Will asked.

'No, it's fine. I thought you were going to glue me to a stool, anyway.'

He smiled. 'I'd glue you to this bed if I could.'

I laughed as he pinned my arms above my head and kissed me swiftly. 'But it won't be long before Paul, and Jake get here.'

'What are you going to do about Alysa?'

'I don't know. I need to speak to the others. Personally, it feels like a good time to let her go, being the end of the European tour, but it's not just up to me.'

I nodded, feeling a pang of sadness, a blanket of doom creeping over me, knowing that the end of the tour also meant the end of his time in the UK. When we spoke about it a few weeks ago, I thought our future would be clearer by now, but it feels like we're back to where we started.

'Are you okay?' Will asked.

'I'm good....' I pushed myself up onto my elbows, trying to escape the heaviness. 'I just feel... like time is running out.'

'Are we back here already?'

But I didn't need to answer.

'Look, it's been an eventful day, let me get this show out of the way, and we'll talk later.'

What exactly would we talk about later? I would talk about going back to work, and he would talk about going back home. My mood was getting darker by the second. How would we ever make it work? I pushed myself up further to sitting, I needed to freshen up. Will sat up too and then pushed me back down onto the bed and straddled me.

'I know we have a lot to sort out, but we will find a solution,' he said, gently shaking my shoulders as if trying to make the words more poignant.

'It just feels that everything is against us... maybe... it's just not meant to be,' I said flatly, desperately wishing a solution would pop into my head.

'Don't say that. I know that Alysa and Ben have been... less than helpful but look at what happened yesterday. Everyone on this entire site was helping us get back together.'

I looked up at him, his eyes pouring every kind of emotion into mine. He took my face in his hands. 'And... we haven't even talked about what you said on the phone last week.'

What did I say on the phone last week? I knitted my eyebrows together before realising what he was referring to.

Oh God, the drunken phone call.

I closed my eyes, not wanting to remember.

'Lucy, I feel the same way.'

Then, opening my eyes again, not quite believing what I was hearing.

'I'm falling for you too,' he said. 'You're thoughtful, forgiving, dedicated, loyal... shy, and you've taken the whole band stuff and everything that goes with it totally in your stride. I should have told you over the phone, but I had some romantic notion that I'd tell you over a candlelit dinner.'

I smiled, blushing a little.

'Maybe if I had, none of this would have happened.'

'Maybe... if you had, I wouldn't have spent most of last week crying in a darkened room,' I said with a smile to make light of the situation.

'Okay, so we both know how it felt when we thought the other person didn't care, and I don't wanna feel like that again.'

He kissed me on the nose, readjusting one of my stick-on gems, and pulled me up to sit.

'Let's get ready.'

I sat on the edge of the bed, reapplying my make-up, while Will grabbed one of the girls' magazines and flopped onto one of the other beds with a beer. I smiled to myself at his version of getting ready.

When we heard Paul and Jake's voices outside, I had just finished putting on some light foundation, hoping it was enough to cover my red nose and bruising. Will opened the door as I put my things away.

'Hey Miss Sparkly,' Jake said, 'cool set up.'

'Are you ready?' Paul asked.

'Yep,' Will said, stretching. 'Lu's gonna join us.'

Paul looked over at Will with a knowing nod.

'Serious then?' he said as I caught a look between the two of them while I checked I had everything I needed.

Will dipped his head with self-consciousness, not wanting to hold his eye, and then he put his arm around me, and we all headed off towards the stage.

It took a while to get there, and my sandals were starting to pinch my little toes, but we eventually arrived. It was loud, and there was lots of security to get through, high fives, *hey man,* and *hi,* but Will kept me close the whole time. Once we got to the edge of stage, the headlining band was coming to the end of their set, and Will found a spot for me to stand in the wings.

'We're only going on for a few songs, so we won't be long,' he whisper-shouted in my ear.

I nodded to confirm that I'd understood.

He went over to Paul and Jake, who were busy getting ready, and a spark of nerves came over me on their behalf. It was easy to pick up on the vibe. As the main act finished their final song, the lights went down on the stage, simultaneously highlighting the audience who went crazy. There were so many people out there. They all looked black and white in the lighting, cheering, clapping, and swarming like insects. More high fives as the band came off stage, sweaty but happy. And then the lights on the podium went up again, and someone approached a mic.

'We just wanted to say it's been lovely having you join us for this, our fifteenth year running.'

It was Katrina.

Lots of cheers and whoops. 'And it's fair to say it's been the hottest!' More cheers. 'We hope you're all hydrated out there because we've got one more little surprise for you. Please welcome back, THE 'KING BAND.'

Will glanced over and mouthed, *stay there!* to me as they walked on stage, and the crowd erupted.

They picked up their instruments, and the audience went quiet, waiting in anticipation.

Will pulled a stool up to the mic and perched, 'Good evening,' he said in a low, husky voice, making my knees wobble, let alone anyone else's.

A short burst of cheers spread through the crowd.

'We thought we'd come back and finish our set.'

He laughed, and the audience cheered happily. He gently played a few chords, almost testing the audience's knowledge of their tunes, and there were a few screams. He laughed into the mic again, and then they began to play. It was slower than usual, and the crowd loved it, swaying and hugging each other. All the flags around the arena were dancing in the breeze, and security was doing a marvellous job, handing out bottles of water to those at the very front of the crowd. The crowd seemed very loved up.

As they came to the end of the track, Will said, 'So thanks for all your help yesterday... as you probably know, Lucy was found, and she's doing okay.' The crowd cheered. He looked over at me, and I smiled. I noticed someone moving out of the corner of my eye as Will said, 'Do you wanna meet her?' It was Alysa, and she did not look happy.

I wondered if she had a hunch that Will wanted to let her go... hang on.

What?

The crowd went wild, banging on the railings at the front, whistling, cheering, and then someone started chanting,

'Lucy... Lucy... Lucy....'

It spread like a tsunami throughout the crowd. Will looked over at me, and I stared back in disbelief. He was waving me onto the stage, but my legs were not moving. Will started to walk towards me, but there was no way I was walking on that stage.

He took my hand, and I walked onto that stage.

Holy God.

'Thank you,' he said into my ear.

'Don't you dare make me speak,' I replied.

He smiled, and as we reached the mic, he lifted my arm up, 'Lucy Daniels, everyone.'

They cheered again, and my heart was thumping, my legs felt like jelly, and I hung onto Will's arm to stop myself from collapsing. Will picked me up and kissed me, the crowd doing a collective a*ww* before he carried me back to the side.

'That was so humiliating,' I said to Will before he literally handed me into someone else's arms. I turned to see who it was. Jimmy. I gave him a great big hug.

Will ran back to the mic and said, 'She's gonna kill me for that, so let's play another couple of songs while she calms down.'

He grinned over at me again, and I buried my face into Jimmy's chest while the crowd laughed and cheered again.

'You can put me down now,' I said.

'Nope, sorry, Queen, but you're staying here where I can see you. You've been a pain in my arse since the moment I laid eyes on you.'

I gave him a quick peck on the cheek and carried on watching the show.

As the final chord was played, Will turned and bowed to Paul and Jake, clasping his hands together in prayer to thank them, and then said, 'See you next year.'

The crowd clapped and cheered their final appreciation, and in perfect timing, a firework display began at the opposite end of the site for all the festival-goers to enjoy. Will walked over as Jimmy allowed me back on my feet. Will shielded his head with his arms in readiness for the onslaught of slaps that I felt duty-bound to give him, until he grabbed my arms and crossed them behind my back to kiss me. There was a little round of applause on stage, but I wasn't sure whether it was for us or the fact that it was the end of the show.

'Come on,' Will said. 'We're celebrating! It's the end of the tour.'

I wasn't sure whether that was a cause for celebration, but everyone was so happy. We walked back with a few of the others to the cabin, but as we got closer, it was clear that the celebrations were only just beginning. This was the after-party of all after-parties, and everyone was there. There was a little chill-out area with actual sofas and a rug on the grass, a DJ booth had been erected next to the cabin with a wide space for dancing, and there were lots of large logs, cut in half and set on their sides to create tables with log-rounds surrounding them for stools. I immediately looked for the girls and found them occupying one of the seating areas, drinks already in hand.

'I'm going to go and catch up with the girls,' I said to Will.

'That's cool. I should probably do some handshaking.'

'Oh, here they are, the happy ever afters.' It was Katrina. 'You do make a rather lovely pair.'

We smiled, but someone waved to her, and she made her excuses. I kissed Will and went over to the girls.

'Here she comes, the star of the show,' Steph announced.

I immediately coloured up.

'I've had enough embarrassment to last me a lifetime, thank you.'

Claire handed me a beer and then another one, 'Come on, you're on catch up!'

I took a long glug as if to prove to her I was catching up. Then, someone's head appeared on my shoulder, but it wasn't Will. It was Gi.

'Yay,' I said as I turned, and he gave me a massive hug. 'Have you clocked off?'

He lifted his beer to clink mine. 'Indeed, yes,' he said in the style of Yoda. 'How are you feeling now?'

'I'm good. Happy that the man has been caught and won't be doing a repeat performance with anyone else in the near future.'

'Am I right in thinking it was Will's brother?'

I nodded, unsure whether I should confirm that, but I guessed he must have spoken to Jimmy.

'Woah, he sure knows how to hit a man where it hurts,' Gi said.

'Hmm, I think Will knows how to do that too!' And we both laughed.

'So, what's next for you? Work-wise?' I clarified.

'We have another couple of festivals to run before the season is over, and then it will be on to planning next year.'

'And are all your festivals as crazy as this?'

He laughed. 'Yes, there's always something, but I'm not sure we've ever had such a romantic love story at one before.'

I rolled my eyes.

'Are things all good now?'

'Yeah, we still have a lot to talk about, but it's good. I'm not quite sure how it will work, but we'll see.'

'Love rules the world,' he said, and I smiled.

'Come on, Daniels, you're flagging,' Claire shouted.

'Actually, I'm not!'

I placed both bottles in the recycling box as she handed me two more.

Steph sidled up to me and gave me a sideways hug.

'Hey,' I said, squeezing her back. 'Don't feel like I've spent any time with you.'

'Oh, don't worry about me. You've kind of had it all going on.'

'I haven't even thought to ring the boys until now.'

'That's because you don't need to call them,' she confirmed.

'So, was the band good?'

'Yes, we had a great time. Claire went for a crowd surf, and then we couldn't find her for ages, but it all came together in the end.'

'That is hilarious. She's a wild card, that one,' I said, looking back at the girls. 'And she is a dark horse,' I said, nudging Steph to look and see that Zara was sitting on some guy's lap. 'Oh, it's going to be one of those nights,' I said, draining my third bottle of beer.

We spent the next hour or so mingling and chatting, and every time I looked up to see where Will was, he would catch my eye while talking to all the people wanting to speak to him. Gi dropped over another crate of beer to where we were hanging out, and someone cranked the music up. A couple of people sprang up to dance, making way for a little area to dance in, but a familiar voice came over the microphone before establishing their turf.

It was Jimmy.

'I just wanted to say a heartfelt thanks to everyone who has been part of the team this year, old and new. A special thanks to Katrina, Gi, Joe, and Steve, with who we wouldn't be celebrating another successful event. Now get your boogie on. Tonight is for you.'

There was a massive round of applause, and the music came back on.

'Aww, he's such a lovely chap,' I said to Steph.

'And strong,' she added with glazed eyes. 'I was well jealous when I realised he'd carried you all the way back.'

'He did?'

'He did, and I'm not saying you're a big girl or anything, but it was like he was carrying a baby.'

'Well, I was kind of acting like one. I'm really sorry I wandered off. I was being such an idiot.'

'Where did you go?' Steph asked.

'I went to see a band, no idea who they were, but they were really heavy, and I lost my flip-flops in the mosh pit.'

'What the new ones?' I nodded. 'Flip-flop sacrilege.'

'I know!'

'Shall we dance?' She asked.

We grabbed another couple of beers and joined the group already dancing. We were having a great time having our mini dance-off, Steph's moves becoming increasingly ridiculous as time went on. I was still aware that Will was keeping an eye on me, and I couldn't help but make my dance moves a little sexier than usual, but it was all in jest. I looked over to see if Claire and Zara wanted to join us and waved in Steph's face to get her attention again. Zara was now kissing the guy she was on the lap of!

'Fair play to that girl,' I said, 'she wanted to let her hair down.'

I looked over to see where Will was, but he'd disappeared.

'I'm just going to find Will,' I shouted

Steph was in the zone with the music and pretty much ignored me.

I wandered around the park's edge but couldn't see him. I was about to make my way back towards the girls when I heard raised voices. It was Will and Alysa. Gosh, their names sounded good together. How much had I had to drink!? I wondered what they were talking about, but I figured if their voices were raised, then it wasn't good. I lingered by one of the tents, wondering whether I should go over.

'Lucy has nothing to do with the decision,' Will clipped.

Shit, they were talking about me. I suddenly felt like I shouldn't be there.

'Oh, so it's just coincidence that she appears on the scene, and now you want rid of me?' she said, and I could hear she was seething. 'She's not one of us, Will.' she spat.

I was too frightened to move in case they saw me. That was what Ben had said.

'No, Alysa, *you* are not one of us.'

Woah, that must have stung, I thought, and she didn't reply.

'You revoked that right when you slept with my brother and then proceeded to tell the press about my upbringing and any other shit you thought they might be interested in.'

She went to say something back, but Will interjected.

'You had no right to do that. Now go and pack your shit up before I get Bill involved.'

I heard Will sigh, and I think I could hear Alysa sobbing.

'And Alysa... get clean.'

He started walking back towards the party, and I held my breath. Alysa began walking towards me, and I thought she would see me, but I heard a scream coming towards me that morphed into a roar. Gi came charging around the edge of the party, waving his arms around in the air with a ridiculous grin on his face. He spotted me, and I thought he was going to run past me, but instead, he scooped me up and over his shoulder and then carried on running.

I screamed with delight, 'Put me down!' I shouted in a non-convincing way, but he kept on running, throwing me around like a rag doll.

'Nope, you have to dance by order of the management!'

I laughed, and he eventually put me down in the middle of the dance floor, where many more people had joined the group. He grabbed my hands and lifted them in the air.

'I just got a promotion!'

'What, just now? It's two-thirty in the morning!' I said breathlessly.

'Yes! Katrina wants to go travelling with her boyfriend, so Jimmy has given me the job as his right-hand man.'

'That's amazing news,' I said, getting into the groove again. 'Congratulations!'

I gave him a great big hug.

'Thanks. You can call me Han Solo from now on. I'll be the Millennium Falcon's Commanding Officer.'

He hugged me back, and then we heard a very loud cough.

'Would you mind if I took this dance?' Will said to Gi, and Will looked at me with intent in his eyes. He put his hand out, and I took it.

'We'll celebrate later, Han Solo,' I said as Will pulled me in, nearly taking me off my feet.

'Do I need to be worried about him?' he asked with a smile in his eyes.

'No,' I said, frowning, and then asked, 'what's going on with Alysa?'

'She isn't our tour manager anymore.'

'Yeah... I kind of overheard... I didn't mean to. I just couldn't find you and....'

He kissed me, and I kissed him back, which I don't think he expected in such a public place, but the beers fuelled my confidence. He drew me in deeper, his hands exploring me as we danced. It was hot in both ways, and we were just about keeping it legal on the dance floor. He had his leg between my thighs, supporting my back with one arm as I clung to his back for support, holding my beer in the other. My skirt had ridden up, and I had way too much leg on show, but I was too drunk to care. He pushed me back over his knee, and I went with the move, my hair grazing the floor before he pulled me back up, our eyes locking. I felt like an extra from Dirty Dancing. I was by no means a dancer, but he knew what he was doing, and it was turning me on.

He moved his knee back, so that I was standing upright again, and grabbing my beer, he took the last swig and then tossed it into one of the boxes. His hands wrapped back around me and into my hair, our hips and lips moving together in time with the music. My hands travelled down, over his butt, and as I took one of my hands around the front to travel up his t-shirt, I accidentally, on purpose, grazed him with my fingernails.

He pulled back from the kiss, laughing a little through his nose, and shook his head slowly against the top of mine, as if chastising me for my brazenness. I looked straight back at him with longing and a little smile on my lips.

'You do realise several hundred people are standing around us?'

'I thought you liked an audience?' I said cheekily.

'Not in public with my girlfriend,' he said resolutely.

'Oh, but you were happy to drag me out onto that stage earlier.'

He went to say something and then stopped, and I smiled again, holding my own.

'So, are you trying to get me back...?'

Was I? I was trying to test him, I suppose.

'Because I can play that game.'

I wasn't sure what he meant by that, but it sounded like he was encouraging me, so I grabbed his waistband and pulled him towards me. He laughed again and kissed me, holding my head in place with both of his hands, being more forceful this time. I was starting to lose myself, and I wondered what my next move would be, and then I went for the kill, taking his jeans button fastening in my hands to undo it. He stopped, stepped back, and said, 'Okay, you win.'

I tried to stop myself from laughing when he bent down and grabbed my legs, lifting me over his shoulder. I squealed as we left the dance floor, and then he marched over to the teepees, walking further and further into the forest of tents until we reached an archway draped in white material. I was vaguely aware of additional security flanking the entrance, but not a word was exchanged.

'Can you put me down?' I was struggling to breathe normally and half laughing.

'Only if you promise me not to do that again.'

'Okay, okay, I promise.'

He stopped and let me slide down his front. I couldn't work out if he was actually cross with me or not.

'Listen...' he said, looking around to see if anyone was about. 'I love it when you do those things to me, but we just have to be careful. Imagine the story they could tell with those pictures.'

It was a sobering thought. Will bent down, and I thought he would do his shoelace up, but instead, he unzipped one of the teepees. I took a moment to study our surroundings. I noticed that the teepees were much bigger, and much further apart. I could see a large marquee in the distance with more security at the entrance, disco lights shone beyond, and I could hear the slow beat of some trance-like music.

'Whose teepee is this?' I asked.

'Mine,' he said, with a glint in his eye, taking my hand and pulling me inside. I realised in that moment that we were in the *real* VIP area. I looked around while he secured the zip.

There was a massive bed in the middle with proper bed linen and swathes of silk hanging from the frame of the teepee and down to the bed for privacy. There was a sofa with sheepskins thrown over it and so many fairy lights. Before I'd even finished taking it all in, Will grabbed me and tossed me onto the bed effortlessly. He was on me and kissing me before I could blink.

Now that we were behind closed doors Will did not hold back, tracing his fingers down my neck, his lips following in close pursuit. Catching the strap of my vest and bra as he passed and yanking it down, pulling the cup with it before seizing my nipple in his mouth. I yelped at the ferociousness of it, but that did not deter him.

As he continued down, I grabbed the hem of his t-shirt and pulled it up. Will lifted his lips and hands momentarily, allowing me to yank it free. His hands landed on the button and fly of my skirt, undoing them, tugging it down and off, pulling my sandals off with it.

He was standing now at the foot of the bed, shucking his jeans and boxers off while using his opposite heel to take off each shoe. He raked a hand through his hair, taking a moment to look at me lying there, all dishevelled and wanton. I stared back at his taught, impressive lean body, standing tall with confidence, completely unaware that the sight of his steel-like erection was making me ache inside.

'Fuck!' he murmured. 'Take off your tank.'

I assumed he was referring to my vest, so I peeled it off and looked back down, but he was already crawling up the bed after me, like a tiger approaching his prey. He hovered above me, millimetres away from my lips, as I lay there in anticipation, holding my breath. He held himself there for so long, watching me, I had to exhale quickly, and as if that had broken the spell, he kissed me with such force he took my breath away.

Our kissing was heavy, and our tongues intertwined as I wrapped my legs around him like ivy. I could feel him hard against me. I loved having the ability to turn him on like that. I pulled him in closer with my legs, pushing him against me, and he pulled away.

'Jesus Lu, we need to slow down... I need to slow down.'

I looked up at him, confused.

'I thought this is what you wanted?'

'It is, it totally is, but you are gonna undo me at this rate.'

Oh.

He knelt up, his eyes slowly roaming down to my lips and then over my tits.

'Appease me, take your bra off,' he said, climbing over my leg to roll onto his side, leaning on his hand.

I stretched my arms behind me, fumbling with the clasps, and then had to half sit up on my elbows to finish the job. Will was laughing, and I threw the bra at him.

'I'm glad I didn't have to take that off.'

'What can I say? A girl of my size needs support.'

'And I am totally in support of them.'

I laughed, really laughed. It was so easy to be around him when we had no other distractions.

'And these... *knickers*... are very sexy,' he said, running his fingers along the lace edge, making me cinch my tummy in and trying not to laugh as he tickled me.

'I bought them for the trip to Lisbon, actually.'

We were quiet for a moment.

'I was so gutted when you didn't get off that plane, I thought I'd cocked it all up, and you were ghosting me, and there was nothing I could do.'

'Well, I thought I'd said too much too soon, and you'd bolted.'

A few moments passed while we thought about the horrible week we'd had.

'I'll take you back there one day, the hotel was amazing, and hopefully, they'll have replenished the minibar.'

I raised my eyebrows, guessing he'd drained it after I didn't show. It was consoling knowing that he'd felt as sad as I had. I wish that circumstances had been different and neither of us had had to go through that pain. I kissed him and wriggled up closer to him, my nipples hardening as we were finally skin-to-skin. It was so pleasurable, just lying there next to him, heat radiating off each other, warming the other person. He kissed me lazily, and his hand travelled up my waist and then onto my boob. Taking it in his hand, he gently squeezed my nipple, making me break away from his kiss. He looked at me, watching my face as he did it again, and I had to bite my lip to stop myself from moaning. He smiled satisfyingly, knowing he had that power over me before doing it again, and a gasp escaped me.

He pushed me onto my back and bruised my lips, his hand travelling down my body over the lace of my knickers, coming back up slowly between my legs and then stopping. I broke away from his kiss and looked up as I panted, and then he pushed the heel of his hand down on me and kissed my neck simultaneously.

'Will!' I pretty much wailed, almost trying to get away from him before I came unceremoniously.

It was shameful, but I didn't care. He knelt back up and whipped my knickers off. I looked down at him, kneeling there, and allowed my fingers to caress him gently. He was pulsing at the slightest touch.

'I really don't need any help,' he said smiling, reaching over to grab a condom. 'I'm guessing we still need these?' he said, holding the condom up before placing my middle and index fingers in his mouth.

'I... went to the doctors but I...'

I lost my train of thought as he positioned my fingers between my legs, watching me stimulate myself with hooded eyes as he put the condom on, and then he lifted my knees. He crawled between my legs and leaned forward, kissing me and pushing his fingers inside. I was so wet, his fingers exploring every part of me and using the heel of his hand again to press against me. I was desperately trying to hang on, and in an attempt to stop myself from coming, I grabbed his hand, pulling it away, and he didn't hesitate, he pushed himself into me, filling me, and I threw my head back into the mattress. He stilled.

'Fuck, Lucy,' he looked down at the connection between us and bit his lip before looking back up at me, 'your pussy is...'

I closed my eyes, shaking my head slightly with embarrassment, moving my face to the side, but he took my jaw in his hand, bringing my gaze in line with his, forcing me to look and listen.

'Sublime,' he said with definition.

He was smiling, knowing I was finding his words difficult to accept.

'You good?' he asked, checking I had adjusted for him, I nodded, and he began to move.

Oh, my days, this was not going to take me long, and Will was lost, thrusting himself into me, watching me through glazed eyes. He looked almost meditative. We found a rhythm but not for long because I was beginning to build, and I needed my release, but just as I was almost there, Will stopped and slowly pulled away.

'Will, what are you doing? I was nearly there.'

But as if he wasn't listening to me, he just said, 'Turn over.'

I looked at him with uncertainty, and he repeated himself, 'Lucy, turn over.'

So, I did, and he immediately pulled my hips back towards him and entered me again.

'Ah,' I screamed into the mattress, it felt so much deeper this way, and he stilled.

Then his fingers started circling me, and it felt divine. He began to move again, and his hands travelled onto my hips so that he could pull me onto his every thrust. It was so deep, but it felt so good. His hands then moved up towards my tits which were half-pressed onto the bed, and he lifted me, drawing me back towards his chest so that I was essentially riding him, and he had full access to my breasts. He kneaded them while I moved up and down, toying with my nipples. It was so erotic.

He started kissing my neck, and I was building again. My head lolled back onto his shoulder, and I was nearly there, but then Will pushed me back down, and this time, I was on all fours, which meant I had some leverage against him. He was so hard, and I could feel him pulsating inside me, he was clinging to my hips, and his fingertips were digging into me, and then suddenly, he took one hand away and grabbed my hair, pulling my head back, increasing the tempo. He kind of growled and then let go of my hair, circling me again, but as soon as he touched me, I exploded, my legs trembling as his thrusts became more and more persistent until he came, somehow forcing himself in deeper still and I thought his fingernails were going to penetrate my skin. '

'Jesus!' he said before stilling for the final time.

He pulled away, and I all but collapsed and then turned onto my side. He sorted out the condom and then jokingly face-planted the bed before turning to face me.

'Christ, Lucy, you make me do things that I'm not sure I'm allowed to do without consent. Are you okay?'

'Yeah,' I said. 'I'm not sure about my hips, though.'

'You would tell me to stop if it was too much?' he asked.

'I did not want you to stop!'

I stretched out, trying to calm my legs. 'You are so responsive,' he said as he moved onto his side, 'I love it.'

Then he kissed me again, his eyes shining with satisfaction.

'Come on. Now I've made you whole, we need to get some sleep.'

Will took hold of the sheets, pulling them up over us before half-draping himself over me. The last thing I remember was the gentle caress of his fingers, covering every contour of my body.

Chapter 30

Oh my God, I was hot.

I opened my eyes, but Will wasn't there. I sat up, clawing at the cotton sheet to get it off me. It sounded busy outside. I could hear vehicles and people wandering about. I peeped out, the site was half empty, and there were quite a few people carrying equipment and tents. It was baking, and I could already see a mirage in the distance. I was delighted to discover that there was a loo and shower in the teepee and even more thrilled when I found the fully stocked minibar. I took a bottle of water, holding the bottle on my forehead in an attempt to cool myself down before drinking some. I looked up to see if there was any way of letting more air in, standing on the bed to get a better look, and suddenly someone opened the zip on the door.

'Shit.'

I quickly sat down and grabbed the sheet in a rubbish attempt to cover myself. It was Will holding two coffees in one hand, my case in the other, and a paper bag in his mouth. He looked at me and smiled, drinking me in before he stepped in. Dropping the bag out of his mouth onto the bed, he said, 'Good morning, beautiful. Or should I say afternoon?'

What time was it? The coffee smelt so good. He passed me one.

'Hi, thank you, are you okay?' I asked.

'Yeah, I'm good, really good actually. I slept well until the heat woke me up.'

I smiled, and he took a massive bite of one of the croissants.

'What's everyone up to? Have you seen the girls?'

'Mmm hmm,' he said, finishing his mouthful. 'Everyone is just packing up. The girls were sitting outside the teepee when I went by earlier. They asked after you. I said you were sleeping. How about you?'

'I think I'd still be asleep if it wasn't for the heat, but I slept well.'

I rummaged around in my bag until I found my phone to see the time, but it was dead.

'What is the time?'

He looked at his watch.

'Half-twelve,' he said with half a mouth full.

'Wow, I guess I'd better get ready to go,' I said, looking down at the floor, wondering how we were going to address the *going home* situation. I glanced up at Will, but he seemed unfazed, so I abruptly stood up and headed to the shower.

Will was lying on the bed, sipping his coffee when I got out, and he watched me as I dried myself, his expression placid. Despite showering, I was immediately covered in a sheen of sweat, and after drying my hair, I dabbed at my skin. I was getting agitated. We needed to talk. Why wasn't he talking?

I picked up my case and flung it on the bed, clawing through it to find a fresh pair of knickers. After dragging them up over my damp skin, I fished around in my sponge bag to find my hairbrush. Will was still watching me. It was distracting, and I wasn't getting ready in my usual order, flitting between my case and sponge bag, not really knowing what I was looking for. I swear I could detect a smirk on Will's face. The huge elephant in the room loomed over us.

'This coffee is so good,' he mused.

I glared at him, trying to get a hold of the anger that was bubbling up inside me.

At one point, I had to lean across him to retrieve my vest, and he took the opportunity to look down at my cleavage. I eventually finished getting ready and flung everything back into my case. I was so hot and bothered by the time I zipped my suitcase, I needed to get outside.

With a frustrated sigh, I stomped towards the door and bent down to open the zip. Will leapt off the bed and grabbed me, dragging me back to the bed and pulling me onto his lap.

'Where are you going?'

'I was... I was going to step out to cool off, um, and take my things back to the car... to go home, and you need to get ready to go home.'

The frustration turned into a sharp intake of breath as I started to well up.

'Lucy, take it easy,' he said, kissing me gently, wiping a stray tear from my cheek. 'I spoke to our agent this morning. The 'king Band has been nominated for a G.A.M. award which is in London this year, so we've been asked to stay.'

I looked up at him, a glimmer of hope washing over me.

'Normally, I'd be itching to get home, so I'd record a preliminary acceptance speech, but... I dunno, there's something,' he looked up, thinking, 'someone...'

'Will?' I pressed, smacking him on his chest, eager for him to finish his sentence.

'What?' he teased, looking back at me with a half-smile.

'So, you're staying in the UK?'

'Until Saturday, and then I *have* to...'

He didn't have the opportunity to finish his sentence because I grabbed his face and kissed him.

'What's a G.A.M. award anyway?' I asked, and he looked at me frowning.

'Global Arts & Music. Have you not heard of them?'

'Of course,' I said, lying, 'and what about Paul and Jake?'

'They've got some friends they wanna hook up with, so we're gonna meet up with them at the award ceremony.'

'We?'

'Yeah... *we*! You'll come with me, right?'

Will closed my mouth by lifting my chin with his index finger and smiled at me.

'Where are you going to stay in the meantime?' I asked, and Will's smile faltered.

'Err,' he hesitated, looking at me for a sign, and I tried so hard to keep the smile from my face, but the second he saw me crack, he tickled me, and I shrieked with laughter.

'I dunno, know anyone with a B&B?'

'Hmmm, I'll have to check my bookings,' I said, grinning, and he kissed me, but I pushed him back.

'You do realise that I have work,' I thought out loud, suddenly thinking on a practical level.

'That's cool, I can get on with some writing,' he suggested and kissed me again, but I pushed him away.

'But what happens when you need to go home, and we've invested more time in our relationship? Surely it will delay the inevitable and make things so much harder.'

'I don't know. I can't see into the future, but I do know that I wanna be with you, and if that means me spending more time in the UK... we'll work it out.'

'Really? You'd actually consider that?'

'The only thing keeping me in the States was Ben, I felt duty-bound to look out for him, but I won't do it anymore. He needs to go into rehab and get himself sorted out. I can't do that for him. I realise that now.'

'I'm sure your brother will be fine with the right support.'

'And that is one of the things I love about you. After all he's done, you can still see the positives.'

He went to kiss me, and then hesitated, 'Can I kiss you now?'

I smiled, nodding, and we sat there lazily kissing until we couldn't delay our departure.

⸺◉⸺

It was a bit difficult to figure out how we should exit as the site had been dismantled, so we drove down to the cabin with the girls in Steph's car behind mine. All the logs had been piled up onto a pickup truck, and Jimmy was standing in the cabin's doorway. I pulled up beside him, yanked the hand brake up, and jumped out to say goodbye.

'Hiya, Queen.'

I gave him a great big hug.

'Thank you for everything,' I said earnestly.

'All in a day's work,' he replied, wrapping me up for the biggest squeeze.

'Hey, she's spoken for,' Will called over.

'I'm glad to hear it,' he said, laughing heartily.

'Is Han Solo around?' I asked.

'He's in there, but you do not want to see him!'

'Is that Lucy?' Someone mumbled from inside the cabin, sounding significantly worse for wear.

'It's Leia, actually,' I called, owning my Star Wars character.

I really wanted to keep in touch with him. He was such a lovely guy.

'I have your number... we all have your number. I'll be in touch. You just need to remember to take your phone with you.'

Ah.

Then I heard someone heave, and I looked at Jimmy pitifully.

'All in a day's work,' Jimmy repeated.

Hugging him once more, I got back in the car, and as I did so, I spotted Terry had pulled up behind us. Everyone waved at Jimmy as he directed us out of the site. It was so sad to be leaving the small village we had been living in for the last couple of nights. Our little temporary community being dismantled all around us. It had been nice to socialise with Will and not worry about fans or journalists. I had made some wonderful friends and a boyfriend, it would seem. I glanced over at Will.

'You okay, Daniels?'

He leaned over and wiped an escapee from my cheek. I sniffed loudly and nodded.

As we waited in line to leave the site, I plugged my phone in to charge. I had a lot of missed calls from lots of different people and unrecognised numbers from Saturday. I grimaced, thinking again about how much trouble I had caused. I also had a voicemail from Mike. Oh God, something must have happened to one of the boys, I immediately thought. I rang my voicemail.

'Lucy, where are you? I've just had a call from Matt Thomas estate agents saying they want to do the filming at the house, but you aren't in. Can you call me?'

'Shit,' I said aloud, looking at my watch.

'Everything okay?' Will asked, concern all over his face.

'That was Mike. I had organised for one of the agents to come over and do some filming this afternoon and completely forgot.'

Mike would be so cross with me, especially as I was with Will.

'So, you arrange it for another day?' Will said, shrugging, not understanding how this would ultimately affect his relationship with my ex-husband. I'd have to call him back as soon as we arrived home.

A couple of hours later, we rolled onto the driveway. I switched the engine off, jumped out, and stretched as Will gathered our things and quickly chatted with Terry before releasing him from duty.

'Mum!' Paddy said. 'Look!'

He showed me his phone with a picture of me on stage with Will as he kissed me.

'I've had so many texts from my mates asking me if it's you.'

I used my hands to smooth the hair out of my face trying to rid myself of the memory.

'I told you not to search up that stuff,' I said, switching it off. 'Have you had a good weekend, Paddy? And where's Frankie and the dogs?'

'Frankie and Emily took the dogs out for a walk. She stayed here on Saturday night, and I told Frankie I'd tell.'

'It's fine, she's allowed to stay here if she wants. Frankie already checked.'

'They were kissing on the sofa. It sounded disgusting.'

Will was trying not to laugh, so he took his guitar and bag up to his room. I hugged Paddy and ruffled his hair.

'I'm glad you're okay,' I said, squeezing him before he could get away.

'You smell sweaty.'

And he wandered off to respond to another text message.

I shouldn't put it off any longer, so I took myself off to my treatment room to make the call I'd been dreading during our journey home.

'Lucy! The amazing disappearing Lucy Daniels,' he answered sarcastically but not with too much malice, thankfully. 'I see you've made the papers again.'

Oh shit, there was no getting out of this one.

'I'm sorry, Mike, I forgot they were coming. It's completely my fault, and I'll try to get them booked back in as soon as possible.'

There was a pause, and I was about to grovel some more when he said, 'It's fine. In fact, you can call and tell them we won't need their services,' he said with a smile in his voice.

'What? Why?' I asked.

'I got the job!'

'Oh my God, but I thought they'd given it to Tom?'

'They had, but he decided he didn't want the extra responsibility, so he's turned it down.'

'You have no idea how relieved I am... and happy for you, obviously.'

'Well, it would have been a shame to break up the boys.'

'So, when do you start?'

'Not officially for a few weeks, but they've already increased my salary as a sweetener for being a runner-up.'

'That's amazing, Mike, and I guess now you can use the redundancy money on something else.'

'Yeah, I might take the boys on an elaborate holiday in celebration,' he mused, and I smiled.

'Well, I had better get the dinner on but well done.'

'Thanks, speak soon.'

He hung up.

Well, that went a lot smoother than I thought it would. I sighed a tremendous sigh of relief before walking out into the kitchen. Frankie had just arrived home with two very warn out dogs, and a very timid looking Emily. Introductions were made, the poor girl nearly died when Will came back down and introduced himself, as if he needed to. I checked the fridge and freezer for inspiration only to discover that Frankie and Paddy had eaten us out of house and home.

'Pizza?' I called to a resoundingly positive response.

Once the dogs had settled, Frankie and Emily headed upstairs, and Will followed me into the lounge, putting his arms around me.

'How did it go with Mike?'

'Better than expected, actually,' I said, sitting down on the sofa and pulling on his hand to sit down with me. 'We don't have to put the house on the market anymore. He got the job!'

'Oh wow, good for him. I guess that takes the pressure off you too.'

'Yeah, I hadn't realised how stressed I was about it until he called. It has made me realise I need to sort the house out and think about making my financial situation a little more secure. I might look into buying him out, seeing if I can afford it... and getting a divorce.'

'You're still married?' he asked, shocked. Oh crap, I hadn't thought to mention it before.

'Err, yeah, umm, we just never... got around to...' leaning over, he took both of my hands and rolled back onto the sofa, pulling me on top of him.

'You mean I'm screwing a married woman?' he whispered with a wicked look in his eye, and I laughed.

'Well, right now, you're not.'

Suddenly, we switched positions and were precariously close to the edge of the sofa. Will's eyes were darkening, but I was more than aware that we could be interrupted at any moment. I forced a swallow, silently praying that Will would understand that I did not feel comfortable being intimate in front of the boys despite our status. The slightest of curls lifted at the edge of his lips before grazing them over mine, and then he pushed himself back up.

'So, what's your favourite pizza?' he asked.

Chapter 31

Over the next few days, we slipped into a new routine. While I was working, Will would write, and the moment I finished, he would appear in the doorway of my treatment room. We would either go for a walk, sit in the garden with a beer, have dinner together as a family, and while the evenings away by playing cards and talking. Talking about our pasts, places we'd visited, favourite foods, dreams, and funny recollections.

However, we slept in separate rooms, which Will surprisingly accepted, but in the mornings, once the kids had gone to school, he would find me and promise to take the dogs out so that he could have his wicked way with me. And wicked way he had. We had pretty much done it in every room, apart from the boys' bedrooms, and although he gently coaxed me into trying new things, I couldn't help but get the feeling he was holding back.

Despite becoming more and more comfortable around each other, as the days ticked by, I fought back the blanket of doom. The sadness that I would bear once he had gone home, in an attempt to enjoy every last moment with him. I just couldn't see a future for us past the awards night. It was as if we were going round in circles.

We had purposefully avoided pubs and restaurants in the hope we didn't end up with the paparazzi on my doorstep again. But tonight, his last night in Clevedon, we decided to stop at a bar while we were out for an evening stroll.

It was reasonably quiet, being early evening, and we got a table outside. The sun was low in the sky, and it felt muggy. It wouldn't be long before a summer storm. I sipped on my half-pint of lager, ignoring the stares and the odd person talking behind their hand. How did he put up with it all the time?

Will leaned in.

'They'll get bored after a while. It's always worse when there's been something in the press.'

'Do you not worry that people are trying to listen in all the time?' I half-whispered.

'Not really. It's no different to anyone else's conversation, and don't tell me that you don't listen to them,' he said, raising an eyebrow. 'Plus, I've become pretty good a spotting paps over the years.'

'Does it ever put you off going out?' I asked.

'Sometimes... when it's bad, but that only really happens now when it's publicised as to where we're gonna be, and in those scenarios, the fans are managed by security.' He took a long sip of his beer. 'Day to day, it's just the odd selfie or autograph, and that's cool cos it's kinda my job,' he said, shrugging.

How did I manage to find him, my boyfriend, when I wasn't even looking? Considering his fame, he was pretty grounded.

'What?' Will asked, snapping me out of my reverie.

'Nothing,' I said, biting my lip to stop myself from smiling. I checked my watch. I didn't want another late night. I was finding myself yawning at work because we had stayed up until the early hours talking and kissing and generally acting like a pair of teenagers. Plus, Will had to be in London by noon for some interviews a day prior to the award ceremony.

'Sorry, do you mind if we get going? I really need an early night.'

He necked the rest of his beer and stood up. On the way out, he squeezed my bum, and I couldn't help but think that he'd done it to cause a stir amongst the gawkers. We headed home, hand in hand, neither of us said much, and I wondered if Will was feeling the blanket of doom too.

'Terry is picking me up at eight in the morning,' Will announced as we arrived back home.

'Okay,' I replied, trying desperately not to voice any feelings of sorrow in that one word. I quickly pushed the side door open to escape the claws of sadness taking hold, but Will suddenly whipped me around, crushing me against the back of the door and bruising my lips with his. I whimpered at the sudden display of lust, but he drew back, pressing his forehead to mine, his forearms on either side of my head.

'We're going to be fine,' he said, looking deep into my eyes as if he was trying to reassure me with his soul. 'And besides, nowadays, we don't just have to rely on phone sex,' he added with a wide grin, and I laughed.

His expression tempered, and I watched as his eyes went from emerald green to racing green.

'Sleep with me,' he said in a low sexy voice, and my breath hitched.

'Please,' he begged, and I looked down at the floor, preparing my excuses. 'I just want to hold you,' he added.

I looked back up, and suddenly I could see the doom his eyes reflected in mine. He was chasing the sadness away too. How could I resist?

After getting ready for bed in my room, I quietly padded across the landing. I prayed that the boys were asleep, skipping the last few steps in a flurry to get into Will's room without being caught. He grabbed me the second I entered and kissed away the yelp that escaped me.

'I thought you just wanted to hold me.' I murmured.

'I lied.'

Terry was waiting outside. I was stood by the front door, wrapped in my dressing gown, watching Will gather the last of his things.

'So, you're going out with the girls tonight, right?'

'Yes, it's quiz night.'

'And I'll see you tomorrow,' he confirmed, slinging his backpack over his shoulder.

A flutter of nerves taking flight in my belly.

'Terry will pick you up.'

I nodded as he cupped my cheek with his hand before kissing me.

'I can't wait...' he faltered, and I frowned, 'to have you on my arm.'

I gave him a shy smile. It would be the first time I would be out in public with him at an event. He gave me one last kiss and left.

That afternoon, I started to panic about what I was going to wear to the awards night. I had never been to anything like

it before. I kept thinking about the pictures I had looked at
of Will when I searched up *Will Reynolds* a few weeks ago.
Women wore gowns. Sparkly, shiny, and sexy. I didn't own
a gown. I wasn't one of *those* women. I had nothing in my
wardrobe that would be suitable.

Girls, I need your help!

I messaged them as a group in desperation, and within
minutes we had a plan. We binned the quiz night off, and by
seven, they had all turned up to mine with a suitcase and a
bottle of wine.

'Right! Let's get started.' Steph clapped. 'Strip!' She ordered me.

There were dresses, shoes, two pieces, scarves, jump suits,
bags, a faux fur shoulder wrap, statement jewellery, and lots
of wine. Within a couple of hours, we had agreed on an outfit. It was a dark green, wide-leg jumpsuit in a soft chiffon
material. The top half was fitted with spaghetti straps, and
thanks to the cowl neckline, my boobs were just about covered. There was a light dusting of black sparkles, which
matched the kitten heel sandals and the necklace Will had
given me.

'Thanks, guys. I don't look half bad,' I said, turning to my
side in the mirror.

Crap, from that angle, my tits looked huge, but they
were covered. That was the main thing.

After packing everything away, we sat in the lounge, wine
flowing and having a much-needed catch-up.

'Oh no, I'm not going to see him again. He lives in
Brighton,' Zara said after telling us about her night of passion at the festival.

'Erm, Sister, we have living proof that distance is not a barrier,' Claire said, pushing my arm.

'So come on, Lu, what's the latest? Oh, hold on,' she said, holding her hand up to stop me from saying anything. 'You're having his baby?' Everyone laughed, and I rolled my eyes.

'No, I'm not having his baby,' I said simply.

'But you're in love with the guy, right?' Steph asked, and I blushed.

'He admitted that he was falling for me,' I said, and my flush spread all the way down to my neck as the girls all 'ahh'd'.

'On the subject of babies, though... has he got kids?' Steph asked.

'I don't think so, he hasn't mentioned any, and I'm guessing he would have said something by now,' I replied.

'So, you haven't had the baby conversation yet then?' Zara asked.

'Does there need to be a baby conversation?' I asked, frowning.

'Of course, there does,' Claire confirmed. 'He might want kids. Do you want any more kids?'

'No,' I said without hesitation.

'So, there you go, you need to have the conversation, babe.'

Really?

I guess it would be the sensible thing to do. Surely, if it were on his agenda, he would have mentioned it by now? Oh crap, we were going to have to have another difficult conversation, and I thought we were done with those for the time being.

The conversation moved on, and despite the weird feeling in my tummy, a mixture of nerves, excitement, and aching dejection, it was so nice to have the girls over to talk it out.

'What's happening with Ben?' Claire asked out of the blue.

'Well, because it was Ben's first offence in the UK, he's likely only to receive a fine rather than a custodial sentence.'

'So, is he still in the UK?' Steph asked.

'I don't know.'

'And so, he's free to do it again?' Zara asked.

Well, these questions were not ones I wanted to dwell on. I nodded in response.

'Girls, do you know what? I think I'm gonna head to bed.'

'Oh babe, don't be like that,' Claire said.

'I'm not being like anything, it's ten forty-five, and I have a big day tomorrow.'

'You're right,' Steph said, sensing my anxiety. 'I can't believe you're going to the G.A.M. awards. You're going to see sooo many famous people.'

She gave me a big squeeze as I let out a low rumble of dread.

'You'll be fine.'

Chapter 32

I'd had a fretful night, what with drifting off with thoughts of Ben, wondering how I was going to approach the baby conversation, the nerves which had fully taken hold, and the fact that this would be our last night together for a while. My inner voices were warring with each other. One was saying, smile, you'll have an amazing night. The other reminded me over and over that he was going home tomorrow.

Home.

An eight-hour flight home.

I was due at Will's hotel at three. Having learnt from my previous lesson, I was not wearing jeans. I had a floral summer button-through dress on and my sandals. I even remembered the sunglasses in case we were in a situation where they would be required.

As we got closer, my thoughts began to consume me. I was desperate to have a fun night with Will, but at the same time, I had questions that needed answering. I didn't want to waste our time with a heavy conversation, but they were not *over the phone* subjects. And despite being perfectly happy with my outfit last night, would it really be good enough? Would I be good enough? I wasn't one of them.

Oh God.

'Terry, could you pull over?' I blurted out suddenly.

'Yes, ma'am.'

Ma'am? What?

As soon as he had found an appropriate place, I jumped out, took a huge gulp of air, and slumped back against the car. The heat was oppressive, and it wasn't doing anything to clear my head. What was I doing? Alysa and Ben's comments came floating back into the forefront of my mind. I wasn't one of them.

'Is everything okay, Lucy?'

I jumped as Terry leant against the car next to me.

'Yes!' I said automatically.

I couldn't tell Terry. He'd think I was a psycho.

'Just needed a moment.'

I smiled brightly and turned back to the car, and Terry opened the door for me.

'Thank you,' I murmured.

I watched as he slowly walked back around the car.

'You know, it's natural to be nervous,' he said, eyeing me in the rear-view mirror as he sat down, but I didn't reply, and he didn't speak again until we arrived.

I chuckled to myself when we pulled up, 'The Exhibitionist' was the name of the hotel, and as Terry guided me through, I could see why Will had chosen it. It was quirky, colourful, and bright. The sides of the reception desk were made up of books resting on their sides, and the corridors were lit with neon lighting. As we ascended in the lift, Terry was messaging someone. Upon reaching the room, he knocked on the door on my behalf.

Will answered, stuffing his phone into his back pocket.

'Hey, beautiful,' he said, taking my hand and pulling me into the room.

'Thanks, Terry,' he added without looking at him as Terry popped my case inside the door and promptly left.

I laughed as we moved into the suite. The enormous bed had a huge headboard, which looked like it had been made up of smooth square bricks. A great big black heart with a cupid's arrow had been graffitied over the top. Fitting. There was a huge brass cow standing in the seating area, and I spotted a dining chair with 'Love Hurts' painted on the backrest.

'You like?' Will asked as he fed his arms around my waist.

'It's very you,' I smiled.

'I missed you,' he said without preamble, kissing me. 'Did you have fun last night?'

'Ah ha.' I replied between kisses, not wanting to be reminded of the conversations I'd had with the girls. Our kisses became needy as we reconnected, and his hand lowered to the hem of my dress. I tensed. I didn't want to be intimate with him before knowing where we stood.

'I just need to go and freshen up.'

He pulled away and looked at me. His brow furrowing momentarily.

'Okay,' he said simply, raking his hand through his hair as he released me.

As soon as I got into the bathroom, I grasped onto the edges of the basin and stared at myself in the heavily framed mirror. How was I going to broach this?

Ben.

Babies.

Our future.

Not being one of them.

It occurred to me then that none of it actually mattered if there wasn't a future for us. I turned away from the basin and almost choked when I saw the word 'Imperfection' sprayed across the wall. I closed my eyes and shook my head. Okay, so maybe the fact that I didn't fit in needed addressing too.

'Lucy, can I come in?' Will asked, startling me as he opened the door without waiting for a response, stalking across the room.

'Is everything okay?' he asked, lifting my chin, but before I could answer, he added, 'Terry said you were... nervous.'

I looked up at him, and he was looking straight back.

'What's wrong?'

I sighed. Where did I start?

'Why do I feel like I have to prise information out of you every time we talk?'

'Because...' I swallowed, 'I'm rubbish at putting my feelings into words, and you're so good at it.'

He smiled and took my hand, pulling me back into the suite and ushering me onto the bed. He shrugged his jacket off and settled himself beside me, lying on his side and propping his head in his hand so he could look at me.

'I put stuff into words for a living. So just say it, whatever it is.'

'I'm not like you,' I stated, and he frowned. 'I'm not... one of those women that you've been to these things before with,' I said in a rush, glanced at him, and then looked away.

There was a pause. I could feel him looking at me. Time seemed to stretch.

'No, you're not,' he agreed eventually, and I looked up into his eyes.

'You're my *girlfriend*, Lucy, and I want everyone to know you're mine.'

I gasped.

'And you're way more beautiful than *those women that I've been to these things before with*.' He leant over and kissed me.

'Don't ever compare yourself to them,' he added, kissing me again. 'I won't hear of it... but it's not just that, is it?'

I turned to face him and went to say something but stopped, and patted the side of my hand on my thigh in an attempt to tap the words out of me. Will took a breath in to say something but suddenly the words came.

'There's going to be three thousand miles between us, and I have the boys and a business to run. It's not as if I can just *pop* over. I've never done the long-distance thing. How are we supposed to build a relationship from here?'

Although the daylight from the window was streaming in behind me, I hoped that the shadow that covered my face was dark enough because I could feel the threat of tears brewing, and this conversation that we'd both been putting off needed to happen without unruly emotion taking over.

'I've been thinking about that, and I figured that each time we say goodbye, we have to know when we're gonna see each other next. Have a date in the diary that we can look forward to. Something to work towards.'

'Like, next year sometime, when I've saved every spare penny I've earned and sold my soul to the devil to pay for a flight?'

I had humour in my voice, and Will laughed, flopping down onto his back beside me, but I don't think he quite understood how close to reality that was.

'Nooo, I was thinking more August twelfth, are you free?'

That was only a few weeks away.

'But I thought you'd finished all of your UK tour dates.'

'We have,' he said.

I looked over at him, and he had mischief dancing in his eyes.

'Are you free, Lucy?'

'Um, I guess so. The date doesn't ring a bell,' I replied, automatically turning to look for my phone which I'd absent-mindedly put down somewhere.

'Cool, it's Paul and Hannah's wedding. I'll tell Paul you're coming.'

I shot my head back round to look at him.

'Paul and Hannah as in your Paul, the Paul in the band?' I asked, unable to mask the excitement in my voice.

'I don't think I know any other Pauls,' he said, looking up to the ceiling, putting an arm behind his head as if he was lying on a sandy beach.

'What! You want me to come to New York?'

My excitement bubbling over.

'Well, to The Hamptons, actually, but I'm sure we can squeeze in a visit to New York somewhere along the way.'

I jumped on him, straddling him, and he laughed, but then my senses prevailed.

'Will,' I began, closing my eyes and swallowing hard, but Will sat up suddenly.

'Lucy,' he reprimanded me, propping himself up with one arm and using the other to shunt my hips towards him, his eyes morphing into that racing green again, as I felt him hardening beneath me. 'I want you at that wedding,' he demanded, kissing me, while deftly undoing the first button of my dress with one hand.

'I'll pay for your flight,' he said, undoing a couple more, my pulse beginning to race.

'And you can stay for as long as you like,' he added, kissing my collarbone and opening another as my breathing began to stammer.

'And in the meantime,' unfastening the last button, 'I'll phone you every day.'

Kiss.

'And send you dirty text messages.'

Nip.

'And when the boys are out,' he said, pushing the dress off my shoulders, 'I'll FaceTime you.'

Kiss.

'So, I can watch the expression on your face when you come using your fingers.'

I gasped as he pushed his hand up into my hair and kissed me, pulling me down on top of him before rolling us both over and kissing me hard until we were both breathless and my nipples were tingling.

'Because Lucy... I can't get enough of you.'

His hand travelled down from my neck, grazing his knuckles over my nipple, causing by breath to catch. Smoothing his hand over the skin of my waist and hips, he pushed his fingers seamlessly under the waistband of my knickers and moved them down and off as he carried on smoothing his hand toward my knee. As his hand back tracked languidly, brushing his fingers from my toes to my knee, he suddenly lifted my leg up, causing me to gasp again.

'I can't get enough of touching you,' he breathed.

He was demonstrating exactly that by pushing my knee out to the side and trailing his fingers from there to the apex of my thighs. His thumb slid along the seam, coating it with the wetness he discovered there and circling my clit with pressure so perfect that it was satisfying yet tantalising.

'I can't get enough of the noises you make,' he whispered.

As he pushed his fingers inside me, I moaned on cue. His words and his actions caused those pleasurable licks of heat that seared through my body far sooner than I would like. I moved my hand down to the hem of his t-shirt and lifted it up and off him, training my thoughts toward pleasing him rather than focusing on what he was doing to me.

I bumped my fingers back down over his pecs and ribs, I undid his fly, but before I even reached my goal, he captured my hand and shoved it back into the mattress with such force it shocked me. He delicately kissed my lips, the shock immediately abating with his tenderness.

'I can't get enough of watching you come undone beneath me,' he murmured.

Kneeling up suddenly, pushing his jeans and boxers down, he tore a condom open, rolling it down himself. He edged forward, spreading his knees and using both hands to tug my hips into place above his. He watched me as he moved the tip of his dick up and down, coating himself and

then positioning himself at my cleft. I quivered with anticipation.

He rose slightly, my hips rising with his, and the heavy
weight of my aching tits jolted with the movement. And
then he leaned forward, the pressure nearly penetrating me
as he placed a hand behind each of my hips. I looked down at
the point of near connection, panting, and as I lifted my gaze
to meet his eyes, he yanked my hips towards him, simultaneously thrusting himself into me. The sweet cry that escaped
me drowned out the groan that he made, and I only detected
it, due to the vibrations it created through our bodies.

'And God damn it, Lucy, I can't get enough of fucking
you.'

I was lost.

Sensation overload.

The sounds of our bodies crashing together mixed with
tiny yelps, deep grunts, and erratic breathing. The fizz of
nerves stimulated every time Will drove into me, followed
by the delicious flutter that emanated from my clit with
every grind. If only I could bottle this feeling, press pause,
and hold on to this devoted passion between us.

It was affectionate, tender, and caring, yet lustful, crazed,
and hasty.

It was euphoric.

Our bodies synchronised in the only way two people
could as we chased our climaxes, but Will slowed. Our bodies were covered in a sheen of sweat, my panting hard and
fast, and I could hear myself cry out a garbled plea. Will
brought his forehead to mine, our eyes locking as I accepted
his teasing pace. I detected the mischievous glint in his eyes

as I was sure he could see my needy desperation, and he smiled. The pace he held, not allowing my orgasm to ebb away or take hold.

'Are you good?' he asked breathlessly, his eyes searching mine, and he bit down on his lower lip as he suppressed a laugh.

'Will!' I bit out, frustrated tears pooling in my eyes from the torture, 'please.'

'Will you come on the twelfth?' he asked suddenly.

'What?' I asked, incredulous that he was asking questions at this moment in time.

'The twelfth. The wedding. I want you at the wedding.'

'Fuck! Yes! I'll come to the bloody wedding.'

He smiled a great big grin that took over his mouth and eyes. It was infectious. He lifted my arms above my head, my body arching in need, and my nipples brushing against his chest. He looked down at them, kissing the swell of each one in turn, and finally, he began to pick up his pace. The impact of each thrust jostled my tits as Will switched between watching them and looking into my eyes.

I couldn't contain the words and noises that passed my lips as Will finally allowed my orgasm to consume me. The delay caused the sensation to rip through me, the intimate contractions setting Will off, milking him while elongating every blissful wave of mine.

⸺⬥⸺

When I switched the shower off, I could hear voices, and my stomach churned. The last time that happened, the media team had arrived and blown my mind, but before I could tune in to their conversation, Will came into the bathroom.

'Perfect timing,' he said, dragging his eyes over my body as I grabbed a towel. Will unhooked one of the bathrobes and handed it to me. 'Put this on.'

'Has something happened?' I asked, slipping into the robe.

'Relax,' Will assured me and took my hand, leading me out into the suite.

I stopped in my tracks as I absorbed the sight in front of me. Two women stood on either side of a chair in front of a mirror. A pull-along trolly on one side, laden with hair products and a blow dryer, and a concertinaed case on the other with all the make-up you could ever imagine. I looked at Will, and he had a massive grin on his face.

'Hi, Lucy, I'm Emma, and this is Olivia. Please, take a seat.'

I must have looked like a goldfish because Will was more than amused, and as he guided me to sit down, he crouched down beside me.

'I'm just popping next door to see Paul and Jake. Back in a bit.'

He kissed me and left.

Forty-five minutes later, I couldn't believe I was looking at the same person. My make-up was natural, but Emma somehow managed to cover every blemish and dark circle without making me look like I had a thick layer of foundation. My eyes were awake, and my lips were tinted with a rosy hue. My hair looked glossy, partly up and partly down, with soft curls here and there. Olivia smiled as I gently prodded one of the curls.

'I hope you have the best time tonight,' Emma said.

'I can't thank you enough,' I replied in a daze.

Before I could snap back into reality, they had packed up and left, and I headed back into the bathroom to get dressed. Nerves were taking hold. As I was fiddling with the clasp of my necklace, I could hear Will arrive back with Paul and Jake, followed by the patio doors that led out to the balcony being slid open.

Taking a deep breath and one last check in the mirror, I picked up my clutch and headed out into the bedroom. As I crossed the room, I was surprised to see the three men standing on the patio in black-tie dinner suits. I don't know why. It was the most obvious thing for them to wear, but I hadn't ever envisaged Will wearing one. Will had his back to me, and I slowed, taking in the sight of him.

'Don't you think it's gonna be a bit of a shock when she comes over?'

I heard Paul ask Will.

What were they talking about?

'She'll be cool,' he replied, and Jake frowned at him before looking over his shoulder and spotting me. He took a double take before dropping his jaw.

'Woah!' He nodded in my direction, and Will turned.

God, he looked hot.

So different from his normal attire but rocking it all the same.

He wore his bow tie and top button undone and the bottom of his shirt wasn't tucked in fully, as if he'd just arrived home from a night out rather than setting out on one. He wore a large, chunky silver ring on his index finger with a big black cross framed with tiny white sparkly stones. And his hair. Just fucked hair.

Will's face lit up as he slowly took every inch of me in, from kitten heel to hips, to boobs, to lips, and as he captured his lower lip in his teeth, he grinned salaciously as our eyes finally met. I stood there awkwardly, looking back, becoming more and more self-conscious.

'Would you get the girl a drink, man,' Paul said, shoving Will's shoulder, but he was completely unfazed, not taking his eyes off me once as he stepped towards me. Slipping his arm around my waist, he suddenly tugged me into him.

'Fuck,' he said, with delight. 'You look incredible,' and then he kissed my neck, just below my ear, and whispered, 'instantly hard.'

I laughed in shock as he pulled back, as Jake was handing me a glass of bubbles.

'Stunning, Lucy,' he said with a wink, 'we're so lucky to have you as our date.'

'Fuck you. I'm not sharing her,' Will said, taking the glass of bubbles to hand it to me himself.

Paul and Jake laughed.

'You're about to share her with the world,' Paul announced, and my stomach convulsed.

Chapter 33

The four of us sat in the car, waiting in line for the red carpet, and despite their best efforts to ease my nerves, telling me it would be over within seconds and just to keep smiling, I was very thankful for the arctic air conditioning.

'We're up next,' I heard the driver say.

Terry was in the passenger seat, and it did not make my nerves abate at all, knowing that he was taking the role of bodyguard this evening. He had already explained that Paul and Jake would get out first, Will next, and me. I was to stand on Will's right, Jake and Paul on my right, and Terry would follow. I was fully aware that this meant I was sandwiched between them all.

'Ready?' Will asked, and I just looked at him.

I couldn't speak.

'You'll be fine,' he said as the car door opened.

A whoosh of hot air engulfed us as Paul and Jake got out.

Someone shouted, 'The 'king Band!' and I was momentarily blinded by the flash of lights. There was so much shouting that you couldn't decipher what anyone was saying. Will was next to climb out, the screaming intensified, and he did his best to shield me with his body in the doorframe until I was ready, but he had to pull me out in the end as my legs were not moving on their own accord.

If I thought the sound was deafening before, I was very much mistaken because the moment Will shifted his body, the paparazzi went wild, and it was as if I had stepped into another dimension. The flashes morphed into one bright light like someone had switched the sun back on, and the noise was making my ears ring.

Will guided me into position, placing his hand on the small of my back and whispering something in my ear, but I couldn't hear him. As the flashes and noise subsided slightly, we began to move along the red carpet towards the building, and I managed to tune in to what some of the crowd were shouting.

'Will! Are you moving to the UK?'

'Jake, over here!'

'Will, is Lucy your girlfriend?'

'Paul, when's the big day?'

'Lucy, have you recovered after the assault?'

What. The. Fuck.

How did they... oh, God. The boys.

I could feel Will pulling me in closer.

'Just ignore them. Keep smiling, baby,' I heard Will coax amongst the mayhem.

We had reached the huge bank of doors to the venue, and I was vaguely aware that Jake had taken my arm but acutely aware that Will had left my side. We headed up the marble steps, the space opened out into a huge marble foyer, and although the atmosphere was somewhat calmer, the noise of chatter echoing around the grand space was dizzying.

I turned to witness a kerfuffle just outside. As the door closed, I could see Will through the windowpane. His face centimetres away from some guy on the other side of the barrier. Will's expression was livid, and he was pointing aggressively at the man's face, but the guy just stood there looking at Will with a satisfied smirk. Paul and Terry managed to pull Will away just as it looked like he was about to headbutt the guy.

'Ahhh, just as I thought it was going to get spicy,' Jake said, giving me a sideways glance, a sparkle of excitement in his eye, as Terry pushed Will through the door. Will's eyes were wild. He strode up the remaining steps, two at a time, and pulled me into him out of Jakes' hold.

'You okay?' he asked, gently moving a curl away from my face.

I hadn't even had a moment to gather my thoughts. I was astounded that the paparazzi knew about the assault and asked me about it on the red carpet! The boys were probably watching... live. Had Will just had a go at the guy that asked?

'I. I... should contact the b...' I stammered, but before I could finish my sentence, we were interrupted.

'Well, if it isn't the bad boy of rock and roll himself,' the man behind Will said. The man... that was in those films. My brain went blank. It was... HIM. What was his name? Daniel? Craig? David?

Oh, my actual God.

Will was staring at me, concern morphing into amusement before he turned to greet him.

'Craig,' Will said in greeting, 'what are you doing here?'

He shook his hand. HIS hand.

'This isn't your scene,' Will added as he turned me to face him, squeezing my hip until I could feel his fingertips digging in as I realised I was just staring, and I snapped my mouth shut.

'I'm presenting an award,' he replied and then turned his attention to me, 'and who might we have here?' he asked, smiling kindly.

'Lucy, Craig. Craig, this is my girlfriend, Lucy,' Will said as he gestured between us, and HE offered me his hand.

'Lucy,' he said warmly, 'first time on the red carpet?'

I stared a beat longer before finding my voice and shaking his hand. Soft. Firm.

'Is it that obvious?' I asked with a nervous laugh.

'Your breathtaking flush betrays you,' he replied.

Will rolled his eyes dramatically.

'It's a pleasure to meet you.'

Before I could reply, someone tapped him on his shoulder.

'Apologies, you'll have to excuse me. Laters, Reynolds,' he said before turning.

Will moved into my line of sight, a huge grin on his face as I released a breath.

'Are you okay?' Will asked for the second time as I tried to get my head around what just happened, simultaneously becoming hyper-aware that pretty much everyone around us was famous.

'I... do you happen to know where the ladies are?'

'What? So, you can go and freak out on your own?' he guessed, raising his eyebrows as he put a hand on my waist and pulled me in close so that he could speak into my ear.

'Lucy, you're doing fine. You look absolutely stunning. Let's get a drink. You can text the boys while we wait.'

He drew back slightly and kissed me on the corner of my mouth, not wanting to ruin my make-up.

I was thankful that he was making decisions for me because it would appear I was incapable. Will took my hand, leading me through the crowd at a steady pace, nodding to various people as we went. Some I recognised, others not, but I did notice that as we moved, people would look up, sensing Will's aura approaching, and after trying to catch his eye, they would stare at me with peculiar looks. I imagined they were all thinking, what on earth is this unbelievably ordinary woman doing here?

We reached the bar, it was busy, but service was quick as there was no money exchanging hands.

'Curious,' Will whispered.

'About what?' I asked, confused.

'About you,' he nodded back towards the crowd, 'they're intrigued. They'll be trying to figure out who you are.'

'Well, they'll be bitterly disappointed when they do,' I said, digging my phone out of my clutch, but before I knew it, Will had me in a vice-like grip, crushing his lips against mine. I was so taken aback that I nearly dropped my purse. When I tried to pull away, Will held me tighter, slipping his tongue into my mouth, and for a moment, I forgot where we were. Just as I relaxed into his hold, he slowly retreated, looking into my eyes like I was the only person in the room.

'You will never be a disappointment, Lucy. Don't ever think that.'

He looked at me with a challenge in his eyes, not to be crossed, and I swallowed before slowly looking around us.

'What can I get you?' the barman asked, and Will turned to place our order while I quickly tapped out a text.

'Marking his territory already, I see.'

I looked up to see Paul grinning at me, my cheeks pinching again. Will turned back with our drinks, and Jake joined us just as an announcement was made.

'Ladies and Gentlemen, welcome to the G.A.M. awards. May I kindly ask that you make your way through to the grand hall to find your table and take your seats?'

Everyone began to filter past the bar, and the four of us joined the stream. Jake leaned into Will.

'Yeah, so, about the table...' but before he had finished his sentence, as we rounded the corner, we came face to face with Alysa and another woman I didn't recognise. We all stopped, forcing people to file around us. Will transferred his glass from one hand to the other and placed his free hand on the small of my back.

'Alysa. Katia,' Will said through gritted teeth.

'Oh, hi, Will. Paul. Jake,' Alysa said sweetly before simply looking me up and down without addressing me. 'We're just on our way to the restrooms to freshen up, but don't worry, we won't be long.'

With that, the two women brushed past us, forcing Will to move his hand away from me.

Will shook his head in disbelief, jaw slack.

'What the fuck is she doing here?' Will asked no one in particular.

'Apparently, her flights got changed along with ours, and she was automatically sent an invitation,' Jake confirmed.

'So, what, she's sitting on our fucking table?' Will asked, 'and what the fuck is Katia doing here?'

Jake just shrugged before one of the stewards ushered us along.

Well, this was awkward.

As we weaved around the tables in the vast room, I looked around in awe. I wasn't sure I'd ever been in a room so big. The huge chandeliers twinkled above us, the round tables dressed in simple white tablecloths, the chair coverings blood red with a gold sash tied in bows behind them. The stage was ahead with two podiums, one on each side of the stage, matching the red and gold of the chairs. Everything about the room was opulent, no expense spared.

We arrived at our table, and I don't know why but I was surprised to see my name at one of the place settings. Lucy Daniels. I hovered by the chair, staring at it. Not a plus one, not a 'guest of', or blank even, but my actual name. Just like Will Reynolds or Craig thingamajig. I was snapped out of my reverie when Paul suddenly picked up my place setting and switched it.

'You're sitting over there,' Paul instructed.

I was sat between Will and Jake, Paul on Will's other side, and although that meant that Alysa and Katia were opposite us, it also meant that they weren't sat next to Will or me, and they also had their backs to the stage. Will placed his arm over the backrest of my chair and leaned in.

'We could always go,' Will suggested.

'You're not fucking leaving us with them,' Paul interjected.

'It's fine. I'm a big girl.' I assured him.

Will glanced down at my cleavage and looked back up with a filthy smile.

'I know,' he mouthed, and I shook my head, smiling back.

Alysa and Katia arrived at the table, Alysa's face showing her annoyance at the table arrangement just as another announcement came over the tannoy.

'Ladies and Gentlemen, it gives me great pleasure to introduce your host for the evening, playwright, comedian, actor, and loyal supporter of the G.A.M. awards, Howard Coggins.'

Applause ricocheted through the audience. I couldn't believe it. Howard Coggins. I'd always wanted to meet him.

As Howard took us through the order of the evening and the categories for the awards, a large screen was revealed on the stage, showing snippets of the artists nominated. I spotted the film crew by the stage, and as my eyes roamed around the room, I noticed there were cameramen and camerawomen randomly punctuated throughout the crowd.

Wine flowed, excitement mounted, rapturous applause was given, and everyone had smiles on their faces. Everyone, apart from Alysa. We all knew that she was here purely to make Will's evening difficult. There was no other reason for her presence. After several trips to the ladies, which I initially thought she was doing to give herself a break from the constant attention Will was giving me, it was clear from the smudges of make-up, untidy hair, and glazed look in her eyes that she was on something.

I had to admit, I was pretty tipsy myself, and Will's sometimes risqué advances were beginning to take effect.

As the nominees for the next award were being announced, Will nuzzled into the side of my neck, dusting kisses up to my ear.

'It's a crying shame that you're wearing an all-in-one,' he said, dancing his fingers up my inner thigh before drawing back to look into my eyes with desire.

'Why? What exactly would you have done had I been wearing a skirt?' I asked, enjoying the game, and encouraging him.

'I'm not sure you'd be able to stay seated if I told you, these chair coverings are not very forgiving.'

I pulled away to look him in the eye, unsure if I'd heard him correctly or what he meant exactly. His face serious, eyes darkening.

'You wouldn't wanna make them wet.'

Just then, the presenter announced the winner, and everyone rose automatically to congratulate them, apart from Will, who pulled me back down onto his lap and kissed me as if no one was there. I wriggled to get out of his grip before everyone sat back down and saw us, but he anchored me in place, wrapping an arm across my hips, pulling me back against his chest, and holding on to the hair at the nape of my neck in a fist.

The presenter informed the audience that we would be having a break, and everyone around us began chatting, scraping chairs, and using the opportunity to get drinks or use the facilities, but Will just held me there.

'If you had been wearing a skirt, Lucy, I would have had my fingers inside you before they had announced the first winner.'

A small gasp escaped me as he kissed me just below my ear.

'I would have coated them in your arousal and teased your clit until you couldn't hold on any longer.'

I closed my eyes, worried that if someone looked at me, they would see the exact same image that Will was depicting in my eyes.

'I would drag you to that door over there,' he said, angling my head in the direction of the door as I opened my eyes briefly to see it.

'Sucking your sweet cream off my fingers as we went, and I would pull you into the closest vacant dressing room and fuck you until you were screaming out my name.'

I mewled and realised he wasn't gripping my hair any longer but rather supporting my head as I had succumbed to the dirty assault on my ears. Will shifted in his seat as everyone settled back down for the next round of awards, and it was only then that I realised that I wasn't the only one aroused by his words.

'The winner, for *Best Festival Performance* goes to...' I heard the presenter say somewhere in the distance.

'And don't even think about wriggling again, Lucy, otherwise you'll undo...'

'The 'king Band!' the presenter shouted.

'Shit,' Will said as the room erupted, and all eyes, screens, and lenses were suddenly focused on us.

Everything from that point forward went in slow motion. Will pulled my knees around so that I sat sideways on his lap. He tilted me over his knee and kissed me, and as the cameras flashed, the crowd cheered and clapped, seemingly happy to witness our celebratory kiss.

He adjusted himself before pulling me to stand. Meanwhile, Paul and Jake had been jumping up and down in each other's embrace, patting the other on the back in a manly fashion.

'Congratulations,' I said, pulling away, laughing and clapping as I let Will have his moment.

Will just looked at me, biting his lip, grinning as Paul slapped him on the back and Jake grabbed me, lifting me up into the air. Paul turned me around as Jake set me back down to kiss me on the cheek while Jake and Will shook hands and did some silly wiggly thing with their fingers. The steward was waiting patiently to usher the band onto the stage to collect their award, and it wasn't until then that I even remembered that Alysa and Katia were also at our table. The pair of them looked really pissed off.

'I'll be back in a moment,' Will said, pulling me in so I could hear him over the crowd, 'and then I'm going to take you back to the hotel.'

'Not the dressing room then?'

He laughed before turning to follow Paul, and Jake and I sat back down, glancing across to Alysa and Katia, but Alysa wasn't there. Katia gave me a sly smile, and when I looked back to watch the band as they approached the stage, I noticed that Alysa had joined them.

'Unbelievable,' I muttered to myself.

I guess she had been part of the team, so she probably had a right to be up there, but as I watched them gather themselves around the mic next to the podium, I couldn't help but notice that Alysa had positioned herself next to Will and slipped an arm around his waist. I sighed with frustration, particularly because Will didn't do anything about it. As they accepted the award and Will thanked those that needed thanking, I was aware that someone was behind me.

'They look good together, don't they?'

I didn't need to look back, I knew it was Katia, but I wasn't going to let her rile me.

'You will never replace her. They've known each other since they were kids, and everyone knows that they'll marry, eventually.'

I stayed seated, determined not to let her words anger me.

'Will's just going out with you to get back at her for upsetting him.'

I took a deep, cleansing breath in. Katia was becoming *cattier* by the minute.

'Did he tell you he was falling for you after making you come more than once?'

My breath hitched. How would she know that?

'He's a good fuck, isn't he?'

What? Had they had sex?

'Aww, did you think you were the special one?'

Suddenly I pushed my seat out as she cackled in my ear, actually cackled, and I stood up to face her just as the crowd began to clap, following Will's speech.

'How dare you?' I said, 'you know nothing about me or what Will and I have, and I can assure you, he has never mentioned you.'

I pushed past her, and despite my words, the seed had well and truly been planted, and the sting of tears threatened as I rushed toward the back of the room.

Chapter 34

'Lucy!' I heard Will call from behind me, but I kept on walking. I just needed to be on my own for a moment to gather my thoughts.

'Lucy,' he called again, closer this time, but I was nearly at the door, and as I lifted my hands to push it, Terry suddenly appeared in front of me.

'Is everything okay, Ma'am?' Terry asked as Will caught up with me.

'Lucy, where are you going?' Will asked breathlessly.

I turned to face him, and genuine concern clouded his face when he saw my eyes brimming.

'Look, I didn't know she was going to join us on the stage,' he said, jumping to conclusions.

I shook my head and then looked around, aware that we were attracting attention. Will took hold of my arm and pulled me through the door I had tried to reach moments before. Walking me around the perimeter corridor until he found a quiet alcove.

'Lucy, talk to me. Why are you upset?' he asked, trying to get a hold of my waist, but I stepped back. I needed the distance.

'Katia,' I said simply, and I could see Will push his bottom jaw out as he closed his eyes, 'you could have told me.'

He took a step towards me, but I took another step back, my back now up against the wall, his face twisting in anger.

'She was nothing to me,' he said through a clenched jaw. 'I didn't know she was going to be here. What did you want me to do? Introduce you? Katia, this is my girlfriend, Lucy. Lucy, this is Katia, who I fucked one time?'

My jaw dropped. Was he really going to turn this on me?

'No, Will, I don't expect you to do that, but when you tell your girlfriend that you're falling for her, I don't expect to hear that you've said those very same words to someone you *fucked one time*.'

The tears tracked down my face as Will tried to contain his anger. He quickly glanced around and then stepped forward, placing a hand on the wall above me and using the other to wipe the tears from my face.

'I can explain.'

'You're not denying it then?'

There was a pause.

'No. I *did* say that.'

I shook my head and closed my eyes.

'But it meant nothing. She meant nothing. They meant nothing.'

'They?' I asked incredulously.

Will looked up at the ceiling as if he was calling upon a greater being to help him out.

'There was a period of my life...' he said on an out breath, raking his hand through his hair, 'that I regret. I didn't even like myself, let alone the people I was with.'

Someone walked by, and Will paused, sighing heavily.

'I did things, said things, things I didn't mean, hurtful things.'

He brushed a curl from my face, cupping my cheek, and I was vaguely aware that there was a commotion going on in the great hall.

'What I'm trying to say is... that's not me. That's not us.'

A security guard suddenly dashed by.

'I *am* falling for you, Lucy,' he scrubbed his face with his hand, 'fuck it, I am in...'

'Wilba!' Jake shouted, and Will scrunched his eyes shut.

'Fuck,' he gritted out, thumping his hand on the wall behind me, making me jump, 'this better be fucking good, Jake,' he said, pushing himself back into the line of sight along the corridor.

'There you are,' Jake said, jogging over to us, 'it's Alysa. She's fucking OD'd! Katia is losing her shit down there. Paul's doing CPR.'

Just then, a paramedic crew charged through the doors, and Will closed his eyes for a second. Upon opening them, he turned to me, looking straight into my eyes. I could see regret, concern, and sorrow all in that one look. I could also see he was torn. Katia was right. Alysa and Will go way back, and nothing was ever going to change that.

'Go,' I said, wiping another tear away.

The night had been ruined, anyway. Jake gave me a rueful smile.

'I'll see you back at the hotel, okay?' Will said gruffly, grabbing my hand and pulling me in for a kiss, but he didn't wait for a reply. He just nodded at Terry, who had suddenly appeared, and ran off with Jake.

Had Terry been there that entire time? Had he heard our exchange in the alcove?

'Ma'am,' Terry nodded, 'can I escort you to the car?'

'Lucy, please,' I said irritably, and he nodded again, putting his arm out for me to take.

It was the sweetest gesture, the sort of thing my Dad would have done.

As we passed back through the bar and the vast reception hall, which was practically deserted, I remembered the paparazzi and abruptly halted.

'I need to go and get the car. Wait here,' Terry said, gesturing toward a bench at the side.

I obediently did as I was told as he headed off, and I sat for a moment gathering my thoughts. A glamorous couple walked by, looked at me, and whispered to each other. My make-up was probably smeared all over my face. I glanced over at the bar, and even the staff were looking on and talking behind their hands. I felt so out of place. So self-conscious.

Suddenly the paramedics came rushing back through, Alysa being pushed along on a stretcher, Will running beside the bed, Jake, and then Paul with his arm around Katia trailing behind. Will didn't even notice me, anguish and distress written on his face. The difference between his life and mine expanded until they were out of sight.

I wanted to go home, not stay in that hotel room that teased me of imperfections and feelings of love. I needed the comfort of familiar surroundings. When Terry arrived back, I let him drop me at the hotel, and as soon as he was gone, I packed up my things, booked a cab to the train station, and managed to board the last train back to Bristol.

I was racked with guilt about leaving before talking to Will, but there was no guarantee that he would even get back to the hotel before his flight, and it wasn't as if I could call him. And what was I supposed to do, hang around while he tended to his ex? His ex that everyone thought he was going to marry? Or should that be exes? An ex that he fucked one time. And what had he meant by *they*? Together they, or was there more than one they? The list of questions was mounting.

As I travelled back, too wired to sleep, I checked my phone. Steph had text to say she'd seen pictures of me on the red carpet, and I looked like a celebrity. Claire had sent me a link, I clicked on it, and it took me through to a report. A picture of Will kissing me at the table when the award was announced. *Will Reynolds celebrates with a kiss for his new girlfriend, Lucy Daniels.* I stared at the picture for a long while. I looked at all the people in the background clapping with smiles, expensive gowns, and suits, glittering jewellery, shiny bowties, and then I looked back at myself. I didn't even look like me. It was as if I was acting... me.

I was trying to be someone else to be with him.

This was never going to work.

By the time I got myself into bed, it was two thirty in the morning. I worked out that if I texted Will now, he wouldn't have time to come back here before his flight.

I can't do this, I'm sorry x

I quickly switched my phone off in case he tried to call, and eventually, eventually, I fell asleep.

The next morning, I woke up late. The boys must have taken the dogs out, assuming I wasn't there as the house was empty. I went downstairs to make myself a coffee, and as I walked past the dining table, I saw Paddy's tablet. They'd obviously been looking at the gossip sites while having breakfast.

I hesitated. I knew I shouldn't look, but curiosity got the better of me, and I picked it up. It was the pictures that I saw first. Will, with his arms wrapped around Katia, taken in the midst of the mayhem in the great hall as she sobbed into his chest. Will looking at me apologetically with Terry standing in the background, my eyes brimming, looking back at him just after he'd collected the award. The third one was of Will sitting on a chair beside Alysa's hospital bed, clutching her hand with his head bowed. He looked tired, sad, but above all, heartbroken. The woman he was going to marry was fighting for her life.

It wasn't until I read the headline and subheadings that my lip began to tremble.

We Will Rock You

New York's bad boy of rock is breaking hearts left, right, and centre, but he knows where his heart lies.

The article went on to discuss the pros and cons of each woman.

Personally, I would have chosen Katia, the model-come-party-girl who wasn't suffering from drug addiction or a pathetic mother of two from a seaside village. It was the pity from the paper's avid supporters that got to me the most. They felt sorry for me because I stupidly thought I was worthy enough. And why would Will date a woman who turns up to the G.A.M. awards wearing a jumpsuit from a high street store?

My tears rained down as I practically dropped the tablet back on the table. The assumptions, pity, lies, and humiliation were all getting the better of me. I dragged my pathetic self back upstairs, eying my high street jumpsuit in a crumpled mess on the floor. I switched my phone on to call Steph. I needed to see a friendly face. There was a ridiculous amount of missed calls from Will and one text.

Please pick up, Lucy. I love you x

THE END... FOR NOW

To find out what happens next in Lucy & Will's story you can pre-order book two in The Hearsay Series, My Girl Next Door by clicking on the link below:

https://www.amazon.co.uk/Everything-Else-Hearsay-Rock-Romance-ebook/dp/B0BTFJJTCG/ref=sr_1_1?crid=3RLZQR6HUDC5O&key-words=every-thing+else+is+hearsay&qid=1676550806&s=digital-text&sprefix=%2Cdigital-text%2C76&sr=1-1

Sign up to my mailing list for updates and be notified of launch dates, free bonus scenes and new titles.

www.rblackwrites.com[1]

Follow Rebecca Black on social media

https://www.facebook.com/pro-file.php?id=100082847830078

Please take a moment to leave a review on Amazon or goodreads, as an independent author it would mean the world to me.

Acknowledgments

F irst and foremost, thank you to my husband and kids, for putting up with my mood swings and time spent writing this book. To the doggos, for making me leave my iPad, take you for walks to clear my head, and give me some fresh air in between writing.

To Rachael, Elise, Justy, and Jackie for reading the book in record time and for your thorough feedback. I hope I've ticked all the boxes.

To Howard, I know you'll be remembered for many things, but I couldn't pass up the opportunity to honour you in this way. 'Always tell your friends you love them because we don't say it enough.' I love you.

Thank you to the internet, 'a little bit of everything, all of the time' - Bo Burnham, Inside being the soundtrack on repeat as I zoned out of Lucy and Will's world for moments of sanity and realism.

A huge thank you to Caroline Ridding for your wealth of knowledge, help, and general advice to get me to the point of self-publishing. Apologies for not removing all the 'fucks'. There are at least fifty less than the original draft!

Ashley Santoro for the cover design. It took so long but was so worth it.

Victoria Straw, how did I manage to find you in the final hour? Your encouragement, advice, and support has been boundless, and I thank you with all my heart.

And to all of you out there who have contributed to my life's experiences - thanks for the ride.

About the Author

My love for romance books began during my recovery from chemotherapy in 2020. I love everything from romcom to dark romance and everything in-between. I had never thought about writing a book, but for Christmas 2021 my husband bought me a keyboard for my iPad, and I wanted to write something to try it out. Once I'd finished the obligatory 'thank you' letters, I started writing a story.

There was no plan, no light bulb moment, I just started writing and two weeks later I had the first draft of my very own spicy romance novel. Since then, I haven't been able to stop! Characters have taken up residence in my head and I think about them daily, conjuring up scenarios for them to act out.

As with any independent author, getting my first book to the point of publication has been a very long but educational journey. Thanks to the fantastic support from friends, family and people I have met in the industry, I have stuck with it, and I hope to go on to write many more.

Printed in Great Britain
by Amazon